PRAISE FOR THE
STEEL BROTHERS SAGA

*"Hold onto the reins:
this red-hot Steel story is one wild ride."*
~ A Love So True

"A spellbinding read from a
New York Times *bestselling author!"*
~ BookBub

*"I'm in complete awe of this author. She has gone and
delivered an epic, all-consuming, addicting, insanely
intense story that's had me holding my breath, my
heart pounding and my mind reeling."*
~ The Sassy Nerd

"Absolutely UNPUTDOWNABLE!"
~ Bookalicious Babes

DESCENT

DESCENT

STEEL BROTHERS SAGA

BOOK FIFTEEN

HELEN HARDT

WATERHOUSE PRESS

For Our Heroes

PROLOGUE

Brad

Present day...

My son Jonah didn't leave. For a moment I thought he would, but he seemed to change his mind because he stayed seated.

"Has your mother said anything else?"

He shook his head. "Nothing that makes any sense. She asked about her puppy. I told her all the dogs were fine."

I lifted my eyebrows. "Her puppy?"

"Yeah. I assumed she meant Jewel and the pups, from the island. Juliet has Jewel, Talon's boys have two of the pups, and Ruby has the other."

"But she said puppy? Singular? Not dogs? Not puppies?"

"Yeah. Singular." He arched his eyebrows. "Does that mean something to you?"

I didn't answer right away. Daphne had an old stuffed puppy she'd brought to the ranch after Jonah was born. She called him Puppy, which was why the word stood out to me.

I hadn't seen the thing in years.

"You going to speak?" Jonah asked.

"I'm just thinking. Do you remember an old stuffed dog of your mother's?"

He shook his head. "No. Should I?"

1

"No reason you should, but the toy meant a lot to her. It was the only thing from her childhood she ever kept. She never would have thrown it away, but she's been gone from the main house so long. It can't possibly still be there."

"You're saying that's the puppy she's asking about?"

"It could be. Your mother's illness has her trapped in time when we were all much younger. She may well remember the stuffed dog."

"Should I try to find it for her?"

"I don't know. It was old and tattered back then."

"Did you get rid of it?"

"It meant too much to her. I never would have thrown it out."

"I don't remember seeing it, but we didn't throw anything out after you"—air quotes—"*died* the first time."

I cringed. Couldn't help it.

"It must still be in the main house somewhere," he said.

"Maybe you should look for it. If your mother is mentioning it, maybe it means something to her. It might give her comfort."

"I think it'll be like looking for a needle in a haystack, but I'll tell Tal and Jade to look for it. Maybe it's down in the basement crawl space with all your old files."

My brows shot up. Like a file in my mind, I saw myself packing Daphne's things after I sent her away and told the children she had died. That old tattered puppy. I couldn't bear to get rid of it because it had meant so much to her. How could I have forgotten?

"It is. That's where it is."

"What?"

"Crazy. The memory just spiked into my mind when you

said crawl space. I can't believe I forgot. Though it was thirty years ago now. There should be an old box marked Daphne in the crawl space. Look for it. You'll find the stuffed animal."

He sighed. "All right. If you think it will give her comfort, I will. Anything for my mother."

"Thank you, son."

He didn't reply. I figured he'd get up and leave, but he didn't.

What seemed like an hour passed.

Finally, he looked me straight in the eye. "Level with me."

"About what?" I asked.

"About Mom. Talon, Marj, and I have been talking."

"Not Ryan?"

"You know how Ryan feels. She's not his mother."

"She loved him as much as she loved the rest of you."

"I believe she did. That's the kind of woman she was. Capable of so much love. What broke her?"

I shook my head. "I don't know."

Such a fucking lie. It tasted like sour milk on my tongue.

But no. Just no. Never would I reveal Daphne's secrets to her firstborn son. She'd overcome so much because of him. *For* him.

He needed to remember his mother the way she was. Strong and determined.

But *did* he remember her that way?

If any of them could, Jonah could. He was nearly fifteen when I orchestrated her "death." I hadn't called it a suicide, but my firstborn had figured it out. He'd come to me, demanding the truth.

I couldn't tell him the real truth—that she was alive and shuffled away to a place where she could live in her own world—so I'd invented the suicide myth.

The reality? Daphne never would have ended her life. She was devoted to her children.

We both were, though my children most likely no longer believed that of me.

Everything I'd done had been for them and for their mother.

I didn't expect forgiveness. I didn't even hope for it.

It was enough to see my son through the glass, hear his voice through the phone. My firstborn, for whom I'd created my legacy.

He met my gaze, his dark eyes burning through the bulletproof glass. "What is the secret, Dad? What is she holding on to?"

"I don't know, son."

I honestly didn't. Daphne never found out what had happened to her before her junior year of high school—how she and her friend Sage had been beaten and raped by three men, which led Sage to end her life. How Daphne had lost a year of her life to other personalities and medication.

For a while, I'd attempted to find the three men who'd violated her so harshly, but they'd covered their tracks well. So I left it alone, buried in the past where it wouldn't harm the woman I loved most in the world.

Daphne didn't know. I'd protected her from the truth, and though her therapist at the time had predicted she might dissociate again, it hadn't happened.

She'd stayed whole.

Until...

Until...

I closed my eyes.

Jonah already knew the rest of the story—how I'd succumbed to Wendy and impregnated her with Ryan.

Again, to protect Daphne and my children.

Again...

And again... I'd failed.

CHAPTER ONE

Brad

Forty years earlier...

I picked up the phone in my truck when it rang. I didn't give this number out to just anyone, so I knew the call would be important.

"Steel," I said.

"Mr. Steel, it's Dr. Pelletier."

"What's the word, Doc?"

"Given your father has held me at gunpoint, I don't think you should be calling me by a nickname."

"I'm paying you a shit ton of money, so I'll call you what I want. I hope you have good news for me. How much longer will Wendy be committed?"

"She won't be. That hasn't changed. She's been a model patient, and she's getting out sometime next month."

Fuck. I'd tried everything, and no dice. "What do you want, then?"

"I want to talk to you about your wife."

My heart softened. Daphne. "I'm sorry. Is she all right?"

"I told you after our first session that she had remembered some of the patients who were with her when she was hospitalized."

"Yeah."

"The facility finally got her old records to me. Apparently there was some turnover in the records department that caused the delay."

Damn. I'd paid that department a lot to get those records unsealed and to Dr. Pelletier. Delay my ass. Good thing I hadn't gone with my first instinct months ago and had them all destroyed.

"Some heads are going to roll. But at least you have them now. You can review them and help her even more."

"I *have* reviewed them, Mr. Steel. That's the issue."

"Okay..." My stomach churned. "I assume there's something in there I should know."

"There's a lot in there you should know," he said, "but the most alarming is that your wife was heavily medicated."

"I assumed so. That explains why she has such significant memory loss from that time."

He cleared his throat. "That could be a partial explanation, yes."

"What other explanation could there be?"

"Her diagnosis."

"I know what her diagnosis was. Anxiety and depression."

"Anxiety and depression were some of her symptoms, but her actual diagnosis was dissociative identity disorder."

"Dissocia— What?"

"It's also known as multiple personality disorder."

"What the hell is that?"

"Did you read the book *Sybil*? It came out a few years ago."

"I was in college for the last several years. I didn't have time to read for pleasure, and I doubt I'd read some girlie book. What the hell are you talking about?"

"Dissociative identity disorder is the new name for split personality."

"I'm still not following."

"Like I said, she was kept heavily medicated," he said. "And even when she wasn't medicated, she had limited interaction with other patients. I always thought it odd that she remembered the patients but not their actual names. Now I have an explanation."

My gut convulsed. "What's the explanation, then?"

"The patients are all *her*. Aspects of her. Different personalities."

The receiver dropped out of my hand and thudded onto my lap. I quickly picked it up and put it back to my ear.

"Mr. Steel? Are you there?"

"Yeah, yeah. I'm here."

"It's a classic case. She has memories of these so-called separate people. The memories are becoming more vivid."

Multiple personalities. My Daphne. My Daphne whose personality was the sweetest in the world. Why hadn't Jonathan told me?

Jonathan Wade isn't who you think he is, son. Be careful.

I swallowed. "What does this all mean?"

"It means"—he cleared his throat—"she's likely to dissociate again."

I gulped.

She's likely to dissociate again.

Into what? Or more accurately, who?

"Can you tell me about these personalities?"

"I wish I could. She hasn't signed a records release, and I'm already skating on thin ice telling you about her diagnosis. I haven't yet told her. I'm trying to figure out exactly how to tell a young mother such a diagnosis."

Daphne didn't know. Good. I didn't want her to know. I had to protect her. "Don't tell her."

"I have to tell her, Mr. Steel."

"Why? Just keep her from splitting off again, and she never has to know."

"She can't heal if she doesn't—"

"At the risk of repeating myself, Doctor, I'm paying you a shit ton of money."

He cleared his throat. "I'm aware of our circumstances, Mr. Steel. You haven't given me a lot of choice in the matter."

"Listen, I—"

"Please don't patronize me, Mr. Steel. I know exactly what our situation is."

"Have I threatened you in any way?"

"Just because you haven't held a gun to my head yet doesn't mean you haven't threatened me. You made it clear when I agreed to help your wife that I had no choice in the matter."

"Not once did I threaten your life."

"Perhaps not in those words. But what did you expect I'd think when you told me your father had left you all his money and all his guns?"

Yeah, not my finest moment, but I'd been desperate.

"I'm—"

"Please," he said. "Don't bother apologizing or trying to make excuses for your words. We both know it's bullshit."

"Hey, I—"

"Let me finish. I care about your wife, Mr. Steel. I believe I can help her, and I believe that's what you want from me. She's been through so much trauma that she had to split off from herself to deal with it. She needs therapy. Good therapy, and I can provide that."

"That's what I'm paying you for."

"I want to help her. I do. But if she dissociates, she may require hospitalization."

"Then you need to make sure she doesn't dissociate again. Our child needs her intact."

"I'm afraid I won't have any control over that. It's doubtful she'll dissociate in a session. If it happens, it will be because she either remembers something traumatic, or because something new and traumatic happens. You'll need to watch for the signs."

God help me. My sweet Daphne. I exhaled. "What signs?"

"Loss of memory, for one. She may not remember an interaction with you that you recall clearly."

My mind raced. Had that happened? No, it hadn't. At least not yet. Good.

"A loss of self-identity."

"What's that?"

"You know your wife. She's a devoted mother. If that changes, she may be dissociating."

"I can't imagine she'd turn her back on our child."

"She wouldn't. At least *Daphne* wouldn't. The other personalities may not have the emotional attachment to the baby, however."

I cleared my throat. A question hovered on my lips—a question I didn't want to ask but had to.

"Doctor, is my child safe with Daphne?"

CHAPTER TWO

Daphne

I ran into the library and uncrumpled the wad of paper in my hand.

Dear Brad Steel,

How important is it to you that your wife never finds out what happened to her? How much are you willing to pay?

I'll wait for your call.

A friend

I gulped.

His wife? *I* was Brad's wife. Something had happened to me? Something I didn't know about?

My heart dropped into my stomach.

My hands shook as I attempted to smooth out the crumpled paper. I couldn't put it back in the envelope now. Why had I even looked?

What could I do?

Nothing had happened to me. Except...there was still a lot I didn't remember. A phone number was written on the bottom of the paper.

There was one way to find out what this was about.

I'd call the number.

"Hello?"

"This is Daphne Steel. Brad Steel's wife."

A throat cleared. "Mrs. Steel. What can I do for you?"

"You can tell me where the hell you get off trying to extort money from my husband."

The words left my throat before I could think about them. I wasn't going to allow this to happen to my husband, to our family.

I became a lioness, fierce and protective.

I was no longer timid Daphne Wade, a colorless flower.

I was Daphne Steel, a full yellow bloom.

And I was angry.

Passionately angry.

"I beg your pardon?"

"I got your message. Let's come to terms *now*."

★ ★ ★

The deli owner's daughter listened intently to the voice on the other end of the phone.

She didn't blink. She didn't falter.

She'd always been able to separate logic from emotion, ever since she began working in her father's shop. There was something soothing about slicing deli meats. Thick, thin, or shaved. The rhythm of the industrial slicer.

Pull. Slice. Wrap. Hand to customer and smile. "What else can I get for you today?"

It was just meat. Not a dead animal. Meat. Sustenance. Her family's livelihood. She loved deli sandwiches, especially the Bronx Bomber. Pastrami and egg salad. The reuben was also great. Corned beef on rye with sauerkraut and swiss cheese.

Yum.

"I see," she said to the voice. "What proof do you have of any of this?"

The woman's voice rattled off one fact after another.

Sad. So sad. Daphne had a lot to live with. It was the deli owner's daughter's job to make sure she could.

"And you say you know who did this to her?"

"Yes," the voice said. She listed three names.

Hmm. Two of them sounded vaguely familiar. Maybe all three did. Perhaps they'd come into the shop a few times. The deli owner's daughter dealt with a lot of different people, and she prided herself on recalling the names of her customers.

"Why weren't they prosecuted?" she asked the woman on the other end of the phone.

"They weren't caught."

"You clearly know who they are. Why haven't you turned them in?"

"I'd rather use the information for my own gain."

Pull. Slice. Wrap. Hand to customer and smile. "What else can I get for you today?"

The rhythm that kept the deli owner's daughter in step. The rhythm she fell into when emotion threatened to overcome her.

"Is there anything else I can get for you?" she asked into the phone.

"What? I mean…yeah. You can pay me. I need some money. If you don't want this information made public… Why wouldn't you want it made public? This is about you, Mrs. Steel."

Mrs. Steel? Odd. She was the deli owner's daughter. She was here to protect Mrs. Steel. Mrs. Daphne Steel. People often mistook her for Daphne, but that was okay. She was here to protect Daphne.

"I think you have the wrong number," the deli owner's daughter said.

"I have the wrong number? You called me, remember?"

The deli owner's daughter wrinkled her forehead. "No, I didn't. I didn't call anyone. You must have called me. Our special this week is corned beef."

"For God's sake. I need to talk to Brad Steel. Could you get him for me, please?"

"Hold on. I'll see if he's here in the deli."

"The deli?"

"Yes, hold on a minute." I put my hand over the receiver. "Is there a Brad Steel here?"

No response. Maybe she should use the intercom. Where was the button? She looked around. Hmm. Not where it usually was. She put the phone back up to her ear.

"I'm sorry. He doesn't seem to be here."

"The hell with this. I don't know who you are, but you need to forget everything I just told you."

"Of course. Have a wonderful day." The deli owner's daughter hung up the phone.

But she wouldn't forget. She'd just keep the information from Daphne.

On the desk in front of her sat a crumpled note.

Dear Brad Steel,

How important is it to you that your wife never find out what happened to her? How much are you willing to pay?

I'll wait for your call.

A friend

Hmm. Brad Steel. Daphne's husband. Was the person who wrote this note the person who'd called? The deli owner's daughter recited the names in her mind. She needed a mnemonic device.

Nah. She'd remember. If she could remember the names of all the thirty-three different kinds of ham in the deli, she could remember three names.

She tore the note into pieces and threw it in the wastebasket next to the desk.

Pull. Slice. Wrap. Hand to customer and smile. "What else can I get for you today?"

Logic. Logic and a system. So much better than emotion.

Where was she, anyway? Her father must have sent her on an errand to someone's office.

Maybe—

She jerked at a baby's cry.

CHAPTER THREE

Brad

"From what I can tell, none of Daphne's personalities are violent to the point of harming another human being, though one does appear to be aggressive. It's also unlikely that any one of them would do anything that her main personality wouldn't do."

"Can you guarantee that?"

"A doctor can't guarantee anything, Mr. Steel."

"I can't take the baby away from her. It would devastate her. She's devoted to him."

"I don't believe she's capable of harming anyone, especially her child."

I heaved a sigh. "Thank God. I don't either."

"I would caution against her being left alone, though."

"Why?"

"I don't know enough about these personalities to say for sure that Daphne won't harm herself."

"Daphne would never leave me and the baby."

"No, *Daphne* wouldn't, but I'm not sure about her alternates."

"Then we need to make sure she doesn't dissociate."

"That's what I'm working on," he said. "But like I've already told you, I can't guarantee anything. In the meantime, is there anyone else in the house?"

"My mother, a housekeeper, and Daphne's bodyguard."

"Good. The less she's left alone, the better. At least until I have a handle on whether she'll dissociate again. I'd like to continue to see her twice a week for now. I've already worked it out with Maryann to use her Snow Creek office. It's important."

"Of course, and it goes without saying that you'll be well compensated."

"I'll settle for my normal rate and no more threats to my life."

I didn't reply.

I wanted to tell him yes. I wanted to tell him I'd pay him my entire fortune and never threaten him again as long as he helped my sweet Daphne.

But I didn't.

Something inside me stopped me.

The voice of my father? Intuition? My own voice?

I wasn't sure.

"I'll pay you what I feel is appropriate, Doctor. Nothing is more important to me than my wife and child. I want her whole. She deserves to live a wonderful life free from demons."

I ended the call.

Perhaps I could ensure that Daphne would eventually be free from her demons.

Unfortunately, I'd never be free from mine.

★ ★ ★

I pulled into the large parking lot at Piney Oaks Mental Health Hospital in Grand Junction. Wendy had not yet been released, but she would be any day now. If I was going to ensure Daphne's safety, I needed to talk to Wendy before she was free.

I'd been here once before—during the night to check to make sure she was here and not out wreaking havoc somewhere. I'd found her asleep in her bed, alone. I'd searched her room to make sure she wasn't hiding her drugs.

I'd found nothing.

Still, I had no doubt she'd been hiding something.

Today, I went by the book. No sneaking in and greasing greedy night employees' palms. I checked in at the front desk, signed in, and asked to see Wendy Madigan.

"Looks like she's unavailable at the moment," the receptionist said.

"Unavailable? Where the hell is she?"

"Please don't use that tone with me, sir."

"Sorry." I should have been sorrier than I was. "Can you tell me where she is?"

"I'm not at liberty to say."

"Why not?"

"Because medical records are private, sir."

I resisted an eye roll. Sure, they were private … until I came up with the right price. But I couldn't do that right now in broad daylight. Besides, I'd get the information from Pelletier later.

"Can you tell me when she'll be available?"

"In about thirty minutes. You may wait if you'd care to."

"Thank you. I will."

I took a seat in the lounge area and picked up a magazine. I leafed through it, not actually reading or even seeing any of it. A few moments later, I set it back down on the table. I rose and walked to the water cooler, filled one of those paper cups that was pointed on the end, and drank it down. I tossed the oddly shaped cup in the trash can by the cooler.

Then I paced.

And I paced some more.

I watched the clock on the wall, alternating between it and my watch.

Until finally—

"Sir?"

I walked to the reception desk. "Yes?"

"Ms. Madigan is available for a visit now, and she's accepted your request. A nurse will be out to take you to the patients' visitation lounge."

"Great. Thanks."

This was it.

I'd interact with Wendy for the first time since I'd witnessed her get committed against her will.

My nerves jittered under my skin.

I could handle Wendy. Indeed, I was the only one who could.

But could I *still*?

What would greet me in this visitation lounge?

I didn't know.

I wasn't sure I *wanted* to know.

But I had no choice. I had to see her. See for myself what was being released into society in a few days and also let her know that I expected her to stay the hell out of my wife's life, my child's life, and my life.

I steeled my countenance.

Wendy Madigan no longer had any hold on me. She hadn't since I'd met Daphne.

Today she'd learn the truth of that.

CHAPTER FOUR

Daphne

What was I doing in Brad's office? Had I lost time again?

I shrugged. I forced the issue from my mind. It didn't matter. Nothing mattered except Jonah's cry. My baby needed me.

"I'm coming, little dove," I said.

My breasts tingled as they let down their milk. Just hearing my child's cry made my milk release. I was used to it.

I walked out of the office and down the hallway to the kitchen. Mazie held Jonah and attempted to comfort him.

"There's your mama," she said. "I think he's hungry. It's a hungry cry."

I nodded. Definitely a hungry cry. I'd learned to distinguish his cries. Mazie was pretty good at it, but no one knew my baby like I did.

"Hey, little dove," I said, taking him. "My goodness you're getting heavy."

"He's a Steel, all right." Mazie smiled. "Big stock. He'll be big and broad just like his daddy."

"Yes, he will be." Not a doubt in my mind. Jonah would be the spitting image of the man I adored.

Brad Steel.

How I loved him.

I sighed as I walked down to the family room, sat down, and opened my blouse and bra. Jonah latched on eagerly.

If only Brad were around more often.

I was determined to be an understanding wife, not a needy one. The man I married was responsible for a multimillion-dollar ranch. A multimillion-dollar business. With the premature death of his father, the business took most of Brad's time.

Mazie followed me down and took a seat on the leather couch. "Did I hear the doorbell ring earlier?"

I cocked my head. Sounded vaguely familiar. "Maybe. I don't recall."

"Didn't you answer it?"

Had I? No. "No. Check with Belinda."

"She's at the grocery store."

"Oh. Well, whoever it was must have gone away. If it was important, they'll be back."

"Sure enough. I'm just a little jittery about the door lately, ever since..."

Ever since we'd gotten a typewritten message in a Western Union envelope threatening the baby's life. I was more than a little jittery myself.

Two threats had come in when he was no more than a week old, but since then, nothing.

No more threats.

It seemed to be over, thank God.

I had enough to worry about. My good friend Patty had left months ago to join the Peace Corps out of the blue, and her boyfriend, Ennis, had returned to his hometown of London to deal with his heartbreak. They were the only two friends I'd made during my short tenure at college, except for Brad's friend Sean Murphy, who'd died at our wedding.

What a start to married life.

When I looked down at Jonah's cherubic face, though, I knew my life was good. Yes, I'd suffered losses. So had Brad. But we had each other and our child.

We'd be okay.

★ ★ ★

Brad didn't make it home for dinner. Belinda had prepared beef stew, one of his favorites. For a man who'd grown up with every privilege in life, Brad loved the simple things. Beef stew. A ride across the ranch on his horse. An afternoon rain shower. Picking a bouquet of wildflowers for me.

He hadn't done the latter in a while. He hadn't been home to do it.

It doesn't matter, I told myself. *Mazie's greenhouse keeps us full of fresh blooms all the time.*

But the wildflowers weren't what mattered to me. The fact that Brad picked them for me was.

No reason to be unhappy, though. Not when I was nursing the most beautiful baby in the world.

Little Joe was three months old now and thriving. He was off the charts in height and weight. He was a Steel, all right.

Big and strong like his daddy.

I loved the feeling of nursing him. My nipples had long since healed from the chapped pain nursing had caused at the beginning. Now, as he tugged, I felt only the pure joy a mother can feel when she's providing for her child.

Pure joy.

I strived to find the joy in every day—a promise I'd made

to myself after my junior year of high school when I'd been hospitalized for anxiety and depression. I loved the sun, Mazie's yellow tulips, animals of all kinds . . . but mostly I loved my baby. It was a new kind of love—something beautiful I'd never imagined before he was born.

I felt the most joy, of course, when Brad was here with me. Still, even though he was gone a lot of the time, I forced myself to find the joy in everything.

Every single thing.

Even the ominous note I'd gotten earlier.

Ominous note? What ominous note?

"Daphne?"

"Yeah?" I said to Mazie.

"Are you okay? You got kind of pale all of a sudden."

"Yeah. Yeah, I'm fine."

Had I lost time again? Why had I been in Brad's office?

No.

No, no, no.

I would not allow myself to lose time again. It had happened a few times at college, a few times since then, but recently, since Joe's birth, I could account for every second.

Until now.

Why had I been in Brad's office?

He hadn't said it was off limits, but I'd never gone in there before unless he was there. I must have had some reason—some reason that escaped me now.

Jonah finished eating and nodded off to sleep. I put him down in the nursery and retraced my steps to Brad's office.

I'd been standing by his desk when I heard Jonah's cry. That was when I realized where I was. But why had I been there in the first place?

Mazie said the doorbell rang. Sounded sort of familiar. Had I been in the office when it rang?

Think, Daphne, think!

Why did I come in here?

I scanned his desk. Nothing of interest to me. Then I looked around the office. Same as it always was. Well-kept, with a few file folders scattered around. Had I come in to look at one of the files?

I perused them quickly. They all pertained to the ranch. That was Brad's domain. I had no idea how to run a ranch, so I wouldn't have been looking for any of that information.

I sighed.

If Brad were here, he'd hold me, kiss the top of my head, and tell me everything was fine. That he'd take care of us and there was no reason to worry.

I worried anyway.

Thank goodness I had a session with Dr. Pelletier tomorrow. Perhaps he could help me get to the bottom of this.

CHAPTER FIVE

Brad

"Hello, Brad."

"Hello, Wendy."

"It's nice to see you."

You too. The words didn't come out, though. I couldn't make them. Hell, I didn't even try, to be honest. It wasn't nice to see her. Not at all.

She looked good, though. She'd cut her medium-brown hair into a short style a la Dorothy Hamill. She wasn't wearing any makeup, and her blue eyes sparkled.

No medication today. Pelletier had warned me of that. She was off her meds and ready to be released into the world.

I just wasn't sure the world was ready for her.

She was wearing street clothes, which surprised me. Jeans and a navy T-shirt. I'd expected a hospital gown or sweats or something.

"How are you?" I asked.

"I'm good, Brad. I'm really good."

Her tone seemed sincere, but I knew better than to take anything about Wendy at face value. "I'm glad to hear that."

"I want you to know that I don't hold a grudge against you. You know, for what you did."

"What I did?"

"Yeah. You know, having me committed."

"Your parents had you committed, Wendy. You pulled a gun on a guy. You're lucky you weren't arrested."

"My parents." She raised an eyebrow. "That's what the papers say, but I know you were behind it."

"I wasn't."

"Then why were you there the day they took me in?"

To make sure you went. To make sure you were out of commission so I could marry Daphne.

"I was coming to see you. That's all."

"I'm not stupid, Brad."

No, she was far from stupid. She had a genius IQ. I'd come here to get her cooperation, so why was I lying to her? I was the only—the *only* one—she might actually listen to.

"I'm sorry," I said. "You're right. I was there because I wanted to make sure you got the help you needed."

Not a lie. Just not the whole truth.

"You put my parents up to it."

"What if I did? You threatened a man at gunpoint. You were either going to prison or to a mental facility. Which would you have preferred?"

She lowered her eyelids. I almost thought she was feeling remorse. Was she? Or was she acting? You just never knew with Wendy.

"I'm sorry for that. I truly am." Then she met my gaze. "How is Sean, anyway?"

How is Sean? Did she really just ask me that?

"He's dead, Wendy."

She gasped, turning pale. Was she truly surprised? Or was it an act?

Wendy never put on an act around me. Never. She always

said exactly what she felt. So either she had changed and was acting, or she was actually surprised.

One or the other. I just wasn't sure which.

"What happened?"

"He was drugged and poisoned."

"Who would do such a thing?"

I couldn't help myself. "Maybe someone who had threatened him with a deadly weapon in the past?"

"But... I've been here. When did this happen?"

"At my wedding, Wendy. It happened at my wedding."

"He actually died at your wedding?"

"He passed out. He died several hours later at the ER."

"Oh my God." Her hands trembled as she rubbed her chin. "I was never going to hurt him, Brad. You have to believe me."

"You know how to use a gun, Wendy. I taught you myself."

"But I'm not a killer. I'm not. I swear to you. Did they find out who did this to Sean?"

"Did *they*? You mean the police? No, they haven't, and neither have I."

She nodded. "Of course. You and your father got PIs involved. That's what you'd do."

"That's what we did. But now my father's dead as well." Might as well stick to the story.

She dropped her mouth open. "George? But he's so young."

"Young, but he smoked for years and struggled with emphysema. It was a heart attack that got him in the end."

"Why didn't anyone tell me?"

"Who would have told you? You were hospitalized."

"But my parents... They came to see me every week. Why didn't they— Oh."

"What?"

"My parents and my doctors kept telling me I had to get over you. That you'd moved on and that I had to if I was going to have any kind of life. So of course they wouldn't tell me what was going on in your life."

Also it was none of your business. But I didn't say that.

I cleared my throat. "So have you?"

"Have I what?"

"Gotten over me?"

She was still visibly shuddering from my news. If I didn't know her better, I'd swear this was the first she'd heard any of it.

Problem was, I *did* know her better.

And I wasn't buying what she was selling.

"I'm working on it, Brad. I know your future is with someone else. I always thought we'd be together, but I'm dealing with it. I'll be okay."

"Just so you know, I have restraining orders in place. You're not to come anywhere near my wife or my son."

"Son?"

"Yes. My son. Jonah. He's three months old."

She hiccupped, and moisture welled in the bottoms of her eyes. No tears fell, though. She sniffled them away. "Congratulations."

"Thank you. We're very happy."

She sniffed again. "Then I'm happy for you."

"Are you?"

She nodded. "I'm trying, Brad. I am. The feelings I had for you were partly obsession. I get that now. But they were partly love as well."

I nodded. I actually understood, in a way. I'd loved her

once too, as a teenage boy loves his first serious girlfriend. As a teenage boy loves the woman who takes his virginity and vice versa.

"The love part is normal, Wendy. Relationships don't always work out, but that doesn't mean there wasn't love."

"I know. My therapists have been very helpful."

"What next, then? Are you going home to Snow Creek?"

Please say no. Please say no.

She shook her head, thank God.

"I'm going back to school. If I load up, I can complete my degree in a year."

"Good. That's good. You're finishing in investigative journalism?"

"Yeah. I think I can be really good at it, Brad."

I didn't doubt it. Wendy was so smart. If she applied herself, she could be a success at anything. As long as she didn't go mental again.

"Who's picking you up? Your parents?"

"Yes. In two days. They're taking me straight back to Denver. I've enrolled in a few summer classes."

Good. Very good. She wasn't going to stay in Snow Creek at all. Halle-fucking-lujah.

"May I ask you a question, Brad?"

"Sure. Go ahead."

"Are you happy?"

A loaded question if ever there was one. She meant with Daphne, and yes, I was. But so much else had taken over my life. First and foremost, Dr. Pelletier's revelations about Daphne's original diagnosis and the fact that she might be headed for another breakdown. My father's untimely "death" and the responsibilities he'd left me with. Murph's and Patty's murders, which we were no closer to solving. And Theo, Tom, and Larry . . . which reminded me.

"Why did Theo visit you here?" I asked.

She widened her eyes. "Aren't you going to answer my question?"

"Yes, I'm happy. Now you answer mine."

"I don't remember Theo visiting me."

"At night."

She wrinkled her forehead. "No one visited me at night, Brad. I was asleep. They gave me medication to help me drift off. I doubt anyone could have woken me up."

"Do you remember me being here at night?"

"No . . . Did you come to see me?" Her face brightened— just a bit, but I noticed.

She was still holding a torch for me. Well, Rome wasn't built in a day.

"Only once. At night."

"How did you get in at night?" Pause. Then, "Money, of course."

"I was concerned," I said. "I wanted to see for myself that you were here."

"Why?"

"You know why, Wendy."

"You thought I might be responsible for Sean's death."

And Patty's, but I kept that to myself.

"And where was I when you visited?" she asked.

"In bed. Asleep."

"Exactly. Did you really think I could escape this place? Believe me, I tried at first. Several times. I was mad as hell at you and at my parents for doing this to me. I planned several escapes, but none of them worked. I only ended up being strapped down for a few days, which was more than enough punishment. Trust me."

I suppressed a chuckle. I'd tied Wendy up many times. Apparently she was no longer a fan. At least not when orgasms weren't involved.

"How many times did you try to get out?"

"Three. The third time I almost made it too."

"Oh?"

"Yeah. I made it out of the building, but the police got here before I could get off the grounds. They tasered me. Do yourself a favor, Brad. Don't ever get tasered."

"Wasn't planning on it. What made you stop trying to get out?"

"A change in mindset eventually. The therapists here are good. They helped me."

"I'm truly glad to hear that." Truth. Even though I didn't believe what she was saying.

"I see now that I wasn't fair to you. You moved on, and I didn't. That in itself wasn't the problem, though. It was how I dealt with it. Sometimes relationships end for one person but not the other."

"I'd say that's pretty common," I said.

"Of course it is. The problem was how I reacted."

"I'm sure I didn't help either. I always let you come back."

"You did. Until Daphne. I've worked through a lot of that. I see now that my reaction wasn't fair to you or to me."

"You can't fix what's already broken, Wendy."

"I know. I see that now. For a while I didn't, because to me, it was never broken."

I didn't know what to say. Wasn't broken? How many times had she yelled at me to get the fuck away from her and never come back? Granted, I'd done the same. It had been broken for a long, long time. How had she not seen it?

"I think part of our relationship was always broken, Wendy," I said truthfully. "It wasn't ever normal."

"No, it wasn't. I see that now." She sighed. "We never really had a chance, did we?"

"No, we didn't."

"I can't say I'm not sad about it. A part of me will always love you, but it's time to move on."

"Yes, it is."

"I want you to know that I'm no threat to you or anyone you love, Brad. I mean that with all my heart."

Did she? Did she really? I didn't believe her, but I had to make her think I did. "Thank you," I said. "I appreciate that. I wish you only the best. You'll be a great journalist."

I stood.

And I left.

For good. If I had it my way, I'd never see Wendy Madigan again.

CHAPTER SIX

Daphne

I ran into Brad's arms when he came through the door at eleven p.m. I'd just finished feeding the baby, and he was down for the night. He usually slept for six hours after his night feeding.

"Hey. Easy, baby." Brad kissed the top of my head. "I'm glad to see you too. Everything okay?"

"It is now," I said into his chest.

He pulled away slightly and met my gaze. "I know. I've missed you too. And Jonah. I don't like being away so much."

"I know you don't, and I understand all your responsibilities. I'm trying to be a grown-up about it."

"I know you are." He kissed my lips softly.

"It's not that I have too much to do. Mazie is here, and Belinda during the day. I just miss you terribly."

"I miss you too, baby." He took my hand. "Right now, though, I need some sleep."

I nodded. I'd been hoping we'd make love, but I didn't say anything. I didn't want to be some needy wife after he'd been out until eleven doing his work. I walked with him to the bedroom. He stopped at the nursery and peeked in at Jonah. He was sleeping peacefully, his baby breaths coming in sweet puffs.

"He's so beautiful," Brad said.

"Of course he is. He looks just like you."

"There's a lot of you in him too." Brad smiled.

We left the nursery quietly and walked to the bedroom. Brad raked his fingers through his hair and sat down on one of the wingback chairs. Should I ask about his day? I wasn't sure. He looked so fatigued. I didn't want to make him relive the day when all he seemed to want at the moment was to be free of it.

"Let me help you." I knelt beside him and pulled off one of his cowboy boots and then the other.

"Thanks, my love." He leaned back into the chair and closed his eyes.

I smiled and pulled off his socks. Then I reached to unbuckle his belt and unsnap and unzip his pants. Brad in a suit was still a new thing for me. His blue jeans days were gone now. He was a businessman, always off to make a new deal. Sad, because I knew what he loved most was getting outdoors and doing hands-on work in the orchard or on the ranch.

"I need to hire a winemaker," he said absently. "I took oenology at school, but the vineyards are going to have their first harvest this fall. I need someone who knows what he's doing."

"So hire a winemaker," I said, sliding his slacks over his hips.

"I put an ad out, but I haven't had time to do any interviewing. Too much else going on."

"What else?"

He didn't respond right away. Then, "Just business stuff. The usual."

"Hiring a winemaker is also business stuff."

"True."

"You have a huge office staff. Let one of them hire the vintner."

"Maybe . . . " He sighed. "I'm so fucking tired, Daphne. So much inside my head. So much I need to do. The responsibility never ends."

"I know," I said. "If only your father hadn't died so suddenly."

He jerked his eyes open. "What?"

"Your father. His death has thrown you into the business much sooner than you anticipated."

"Yeah. Right." He closed his eyes once more.

Hmm. Strange reaction, but I wasn't going to dwell on it. Brad still wore his underwear. I placed my fingers under the waistband, and his dick sprang to life.

He chuckled softly. "I'm so tired I could sleep for days, but just your touch arouses me."

Maybe we'd make love after all. I slid his undies off him and then grabbed his cock. Within a few seconds, it had hardened into velvet-covered steel. A drop of clear fluid emerged at the tip. I licked it off. Salty. Salty and wonderful.

"Daph . . . " he said.

"Shh. Let me take care of you. Please."

I needed this. I needed it—*him*—so badly. Even if we didn't end up making love, at least I could give him something. Show him I was here for him. Because I was. Always.

He still wore his shirt and tie but was naked from the waist down.

"Stay where you are," I said.

Then I swirled my tongue around the tip of his cock.

"Fuck, Daphne. You drive me insane."

I smiled against his shaft. Good. Exactly what I was after.

I needed to escape this day. I might have lost time, and I'd talk to Dr. Pelletier tomorrow and figure it out, but tonight? I wanted to hide everything negative in the back of my mind and concentrate on the man I loved.

I sucked softly on the head of his cock and took him as far as I could. I was still a novice at oral sex, but I wanted so much to please Brad. Men loved blowjobs, and I wanted to give Brad a good one.

But he stopped me. "Daph, I can't."

I let his cock drop out of my mouth. "Please. Let me."

"Not tonight."

"Please, Brad. I want to."

He softened then, and he drew me into his arms until I was sitting in his lap. He pulled my head down and our lips met.

It was a soft kiss at first, but as we both opened our mouths and our lips slid together, it become more demanding.

I grabbed his tie and loosened it, our mouths still fused together. Then I unbuttoned his shirt and parted the two sides of fabric, running my fingertips over his warm, hard chest.

He groaned into my mouth.

I broke the kiss swiftly and climbed off his lap. I pulled my T-shirt over my head and removed my bra. Brad sucked in a breath.

I dropped my gaze to his cock. Still hard. Big and hard and ready for me. I needed him so badly, and yes, he was tired, said he couldn't do this right now, but I was making this decision.

I was going to fuck him. Right here in this chair. And yeah, it would be a fuck, because that was what he needed right now. Later, maybe we'd make slow, sweet love.

For now?

I'd fuck the daylights out of him.

I peeled my sweatpants and panties from my body and stalked back to him, sitting back down on him and centering myself over his cock.

"Do it," he said. "Take it."

I sank onto him, moaning.

He filled me so completely. I was tight but wet, wet and ready, and the burn of him inside me, stretching me, completed me.

I stayed there, relishing the fullness, until I couldn't wait any longer. I rose and sank back down.

"God, baby. God." Brad gritted his teeth.

"You feel so wonderful inside me, Brad." I brushed my lips against his.

He let me take the lead, find the rhythm. And oh, it was perfect. Like the notes of a flawless melody.

I slid against his chest as I pistoned my hips, and my clit rubbed against his pubic bone, creating a luscious friction. I leaned in farther and clamped my mouth onto his.

I wanted to kiss him. I wanted our bodies melded together in all ways possible when my climax came.

And it was coming. It was coming quickly.

With each plunge upon him, I came closer to the peak in the distance. The peak of the highest mountain in the Rockies.

I moaned into his mouth, our kiss deepening, and then—

I shattered. Shattered into a million pieces that broke apart and then found their way back together in Brad. I was part of him and he was part of me.

He broke the kiss, grunting. "Come, baby. That's it. Come with me."

I knew the exact second he released. He pushed down on my hips and held me there, my orgasm still rolling through me.

I closed my eyes and held the moment. Held it in my heart and in my soul.

One perfect moment in a lifetime.

One perfect moment...

When the climax finally subsided, we were both breathing heavily, sweat coating our bodies. Brad nipped at my neck, slid his tongue over my flesh.

"Can't ever get enough of you," he said, panting. "Never enough."

I knew the feeling well.

I was glad he still did.

CHAPTER SEVEN

Brad

I hadn't meant to give in. Hadn't meant to make love to her tonight. So much I had to tell her.

She'd hear it from me. Not Dr. Pelletier or anyone else.

Her diagnosis.

Dissociative identity disorder.

The words sounded so ominous as they echoed inside my head.

And Wendy was free. Released. Yes, she'd promised we'd never hear from her again, but I didn't believe her.

I hoped she was sincere, but I had no intention of holding my breath.

Daphne had to know Wendy was out there.

I couldn't keep any of this from her.

"Hey," I said against her soft neck. "Let's go to bed."

We'd talk in the morning.

★ ★ ★

I woke at six o'clock. Five was normal for me, but I allowed myself an extra hour. I turned in bed to touch my beautiful wife, but she was gone.

I smiled.

Probably feeding the baby. She was such a good mother.

So devoted.

Is my child safe with her?

The question I'd asked Dr. Pelletier. He couldn't guarantee anything, but he wasn't concerned.

Now I wondered why I'd even asked the question. There wasn't a more devoted mother on the planet than my Daphne.

I rose and pulled on some pajama pants and a T-shirt. Then I padded out of the bedroom and peeked into the nursery. Yes, there she was in her rocking chair, feeding our son.

"That's a beautiful sight," I said.

She smiled. "My favorite part of the day. Beginning a new day with my precious son. We'll go watch the sunrise together in a few minutes."

"I'll join you. I'll get some coffee on."

"Your mother already started a pot."

"Great. I'll pour us both a cup and wait for you on the deck."

She nodded. "I won't be long."

I walked to the kitchen. "Hey, Mom."

My mother looked up from the paper. "Hi, sweetie. Coffee's ready."

"Thanks." I poured two cups. "Daphne and I are going to watch the sunrise. Want to join us?"

"Sounds like I might be a third wheel. You go ahead."

I nodded and walked out onto the deck. Ebony and Brandy bounded up to greet me. I scratched behind their ears. "I've missed you, girls," I said.

Daphne arrived and sat in an Adirondack rocker, holding baby Joe. The sun was just beginning to peek over the Rocky Mountains. Daphne's eyes were glued to the east, a beautiful smile gracing her face. The royal purple of the peaks was iridescent as the orange rays of the rising sun cascaded over them. Above the mountainous horizon, a few fluffy clouds were tinted the light orange of a Creamsicle, and above them, an orangey pink.

It wouldn't last long. Once the sun ascended all the way past the horizon, the clouds would become their normal white, and the mountains their normal greenish purple in the distance.

But for a few scant moments, the sunrise painted its own tapestry of beauty. Even more beautiful than the image in the east was the serene look of contemplation on Daphne's face.

My Daphne was more beautiful than any Rocky Mountain sunrise.

And in her arms she held something else that was more beautiful than the sunrise. My son. Jonah Bradford Steel. My heir, legacy to everything I was building here.

Jonah would have a different life than mine. He wouldn't grow up knowing how to use a gun, having the temptation. He would learn integrity. The value of a good day's work. He would understand his privilege and would not let it weaken him. He would be honest in his dealings and never resort to threats.

If it was the last thing I did, I'd make sure of that.

And he wouldn't grow up alone. I'd promised my father I'd fill this house with children he and my mother couldn't have.

Should I? Could Daphne handle more children? She was devoted to Jonah, but according to Dr. Pelletier, she was not mentally stable.

We'd made love last night, and I hadn't even given a thought to birth control. She was nursing, so pregnancy was unlikely but not impossible. She had no experience with birth control. The only time she'd tried to get oral contraception, she found out she was pregnant with Jonah.

Oral contraception was a must now. Until Daphne was mentally stable, we shouldn't have any more children. But how could I bring this up to her? Already, I had to tell her that Wendy had been released from Piney Oaks and that she—Daphne—had a diagnosis she wasn't aware of.

Why didn't Jonathan—or Lucy—tell me?

Jonathan Wade isn't who you think he is, son. Be careful.

My father had said those words for a reason, and I would take them seriously.

I just bought myself some time.

Before I told Daphne about her diagnosis, I needed to speak to her father. Jonathan was the one who'd told me Daphne's history. He'd wanted to make sure I wouldn't turn tail and run. I hadn't, of course, and I wouldn't. I loved Daphne, and she'd been carrying my child. But did he tell me everything?

Jonathan had mentioned a journal that Daphne had kept during her time at the hospital. He said he'd never been able to bring himself to read it.

Had he been lying? Did he know about Daphne's other personalities? And if so, why had he kept that information from me?

I was going to find out.

I cleared my throat, ready to tell Daphne I had to make a phone call, when I changed my mind.

This was too important for a phone call. Too damned important.

I was driving to Denver today.

"Hey, baby," I said.

Daphne tore her gaze away from the rising sun and met mine. "Yes?"

"I have to go take my shower. I'm going to Denver today."

"Another trip?"

"Part of the business. You know that."

"Can't little Joe and I go with you? Especially if you're spending the night. I could spend some time with my mother."

I considered her words. It wasn't a terrible idea. She and the baby could visit with Lucy, and I could take Jonathan to his favorite little Irish pub.

And then interrogate him.

"All right."

If we left within an hour, we'd make it to Denver before noon. I could drop Daphne off at her parents' home, and then I could pay a visit to Jonathan at his office. To do my "business."

I truly hated lying to Daphne. Unfortunately, I was getting used to it. I had been lying by omission to her since I met her parents.

I vowed when I first fell in love with her that I would protect her. If I had to lie to accomplish that goal, it was a no-brainer. Protecting Daphne was of the utmost importance. No matter what I had to do to achieve that goal.

CHAPTER EIGHT

Daphne

We arrived at my home in Westminster before noon. I'd called my mom, and she had a lunch prepared for us.

"I wish I could stay, Lucy," Brad said, "but I'm here on business."

"You can't take an hour for lunch?" I asked.

"Lunch is part of business, I'm afraid." Brad smiled and then gave me a kiss on my forehead. Then he kissed Jonah's sweet-smelling head.

The baby giggled and smiled.

"He's smiling so much now," Mom said.

"See you later, partner," Brad said. Then he kissed me again, this time on the lips. "I should be back here by dinnertime."

"I hope so," Mom said. "Jonathan will be thrilled to see you. What would you like for dinner, Daphne? Anything you want."

"Everything you make is good, Mom. Just make sure—"

"—the meat is humanely raised," she finished for me and smiled.

Brad left, taking part of my heart with him as he always did. But today would be a good day. I had my baby, and I was with my mother, who was doing very well. Her suicide attempt seemed very far in the past. According to my father, therapy was going great, and she was on a new medication that was working wonders.

I believed it. She looked younger than she had in years, and the smile on her face seemed genuine. Not pasted on, as it had seemed so many times since I returned from my hospitalization junior year.

"Let me see that big boy!" She took Jonah out of my arms and snuggled him against her.

He let out a wail.

"Little dove, you remember your grandma." I stroked his hair.

He gulped back a sob at my touch.

"He'll get used to you in a few minutes, Mom."

"I'm not worried. You were the same way. Only Mommy and Daddy for you." She handed Joe back to me.

"Are you hungry?"

"Do you even have to ask?" I was constantly famished. A side effect of nursing, and a fringe benefit, to be frank. I could eat everything in the world and not gain an ounce. I was feeding two. "Let me just set up his portable playpen, and then we can eat."

"I'll get it on the table while you do that." Mom headed back to the kitchen, whistling.

Whatever medication she was on was a wonder drug. I put the playpen together in the dining area and set Jonah inside with a rattle and a set of teething keys. He wasn't teething yet, but he liked to suck on them.

Mom had made bacon, lettuce, and tomato sandwiches—my favorites, but bacon always reminded me of Patty. She had introduced me to humanely raised cured bacon. I missed her so much. Why had she left so suddenly? Serving the Peace Corps was a noble calling, to be sure, but she and Ennis had just fallen in love. She had only completed one year of college.

So much of it didn't make sense.

Having a friend had been nice. I still had Ennis, of course, but he was back in England now. I wasn't sure I'd ever see him again. Brad had promised me I could go visit Ennis anytime, but leaving Brad and the baby didn't feel right.

Plus, why hadn't Patty written? I'd written three letters to the address Brad got for me, but she hadn't answered any of them. I didn't know much about the Peace Corps, but I did know that most of the volunteers wrote to their friends at home. Maybe I could call her parents and see if they'd heard from her. Surely she was writing to them.

It all reminded me of Sage Peterson from high school— my best friend who had moved away before junior year. I'd written her several times, but she never wrote me back.

I was still sad about her. And now the same thing was happening with Patty. If I left a friend, I'd want to keep in touch.

Mazie's pale-green tulips popped into my mind. Whenever I got sad, I thought of the pale-green blooms that were her favorite. To me, they lacked color and vibrancy. I much preferred the sunny yellow blooms. Sadness made me colorless, so I forced a smile on my face.

My baby gurgled in his crib. He was happiness rolled into a sweet little cherub. Then there was Brad. My amazing husband who, though I missed him terribly when he was gone so often, was the heart and soul of me. And my pretty mother, who was assembling a BLT just the way I liked it, with extra tomatoes and a touch of mustard with the mayonnaise. She looked happy—happier than she'd been in quite a while.

Life was good. I was the yellow tulip again.

★ ★ ★

After lunch, I nursed Jonah and was ready to put him down for a nap in his portable crib when my mother took him from me.

"May I hold him while he sleeps?"

"Of course."

She sat down in my father's La-Z-Boy and cradled him as he dozed. "He looks a lot like you, sweetheart."

"Really? Most people say he looks like a clone of Brad."

"You and Brad have roughly the same coloring, the same fine features. I see a lot of you *and* him."

I smiled. The thought warmed me. No doubt, little Joe favored his father, but when I looked closely, I saw that my mother was right. His eyes, which had just turned brown, were dark, dark brown like mine. Brad's were slightly lighter. And the shape of his ears—small with attached lobes. Like mini replicas of mine.

"He's a beautiful child, Daphne," my mother said.

"He's everything to me."

My mother met my gaze and smiled. "You don't understand that feeling until you become a mother."

My mother's eyes glistened. Just a touch, but I noticed. She wasn't going to cry, but emotion was getting to her. And something in me understood her, perhaps for the first time. She felt about me the way I felt about Jonah. My troubled junior year must have nearly killed her.

If Jonah ever . . .

No. Can't go there. Can't even let the thought creep into my head.

Never, little dove. Never will you be unhappy or hurt. Not as long as I am your mother.

I couldn't bear the thought.

Whatever Jonah needed, I would provide.

Whatever he needed.

★ ★ ★

The deli owner's daughter left the pretty woman holding the baby and walked up a short flight of stairs to a cluster of three bedrooms. She knew which one to enter. On the top shelf of the closet sat a sewing kit. She didn't question why it was there. She simply grabbed it and brought it over to the bed.

Then she went to the desk. To the right of the green blotter sat a cube of light-blue notepaper. She removed the top piece, pulled a pen from the tin can covered in contact paper, and swiftly wrote down the three names given to her by the woman she'd talked to on the phone recently. She folded the paper in half and then in half again before she returned to the bed where the sewing kit sat next to a very old and well-loved stuffed dog.

The deli owner's daughter picked up the dog. She'd seen the toy before, many times. On the underside of its belly was a seam. She grabbed the seam ripper from the sewing box and carefully opened the seam, as methodically as if she were using a scalpel to perform surgery. She parted the two sides of fabric and shoved the piece of paper inside with the others. Then she threaded a needle with light-brown thread to match the stuffed dog's fur. Again, methodically, she sewed the two sides of fabric back together with short, even stitches. After knotting the thread, she admired her work.

Perfect. No one could tell the seam had been opened.

This is where she hid her innermost thoughts—things only she knew. Things she protected Daphne from. If she didn't protect Daphne, both of their lives would be over.

The deli owner's daughter had a friend. He was called the scary guy. He was tattooed and fearless, and he seemed to appear whenever he perceived a threat. The deli owner's daughter was the logic, and the scary guy was the muscle. There were others, but they didn't come around nearly as often. The deli owner's daughter was capable of handling most things, sometimes with the scary guy's help.

Pull. Slice. Wrap. Hand to customer and smile. "What else can I get for you today?"

Mission accomplished.

CHAPTER NINE

Brad

"I'm here to see Jonathan Wade."

"This is his lunch hour, sir." The receptionist smiled flirtatiously.

I returned her smile. I wasn't above using my good looks to get what I wanted. It certainly wasn't the first time. "I'll wait then. Do you know when he'll be back?"

"He's actually here now. He brought his lunch today, and he's eating in his office."

"Perfect. Just direct me to his office, and I'll be out of your way."

"I can't let you disturb him during lunch."

"I'm sorry. Did I mention who I was?"

"No."

"I'm Brad Steel." I forced my grin wider. "His son-in-law."

"Oh." Her smile faded. "I'm sure it's okay, then. Down that hallway, second door on the right."

"Thank you, Liz," I said, eyeing the nameplate on her desk.

I followed Liz's directions until I was standing in front of Jonathan's closed door. I raised my hand to knock but then thought better of it and simply turned the doorknob and barged in.

For a second, I wondered what I might walk in on.

Jonathan Wade isn't who you think he is, son. Be careful.

I could be walking in on anything.

So I was mildly surprised when I saw him sitting at his desk eating lunch, just as Liz had said.

He stopped chewing, his eyes wide.

"Good afternoon, Jonathan."

He swallowed with an audible gulp. "Brad. What are you doing here?"

"I'm here on business." Not a lie. Daphne *was* my business.

"I see. It was nice to stop by to say hello. I'd ask you to join me, but Lucy only packed enough for one, and I'm almost done."

"Good. Then I'm not interrupting your lunch."

"I don't want to keep you from your meetings."

"I came to town to talk to *you*, Jonathan."

"You said business."

"I did. It's *personal* business."

Jonathan took a drink from his bottle of soda. "Okay. Are Daphne and the baby all right?"

"Jonah is fine. He's the picture of health, off the charts for both height and weight."

He cleared his throat. "And Daphne?"

"She's in therapy, Jonathan."

He nodded. "I think that's good for her."

"I agree. But I found out some things that are concerning."

He wrinkled his forehead. If my old man were here, he'd know right away whether Jonathan was feigning concern or whether he truly was worried. I hadn't quite mastered reading people yet. It was something I needed to perfect.

"What things?" he asked.

"Her therapist requested her records from her hospitalization."

"He did? She was a minor. Those records should be sealed."

"Even to the patient? That hardly makes sense."

"We arranged for—" He stopped midsentence.

His use of the pronoun "we" aroused my suspicion. He could be talking about himself and Lucy, but I had the distinct impression he wasn't.

"Everything is available for the right price, Jonathan."

He stiffened slightly. I was getting better at reading people. He said nothing.

"Why did you lie to me?"

He stood, rubbing his jawline. "I need your discretion with this, Brad. Lucy doesn't know."

"About Daphne's diagnosis? Or about other stuff as well?"

"You've seen that Lucy's emotional state is far from stable. I kept the actual diagnosis from her to protect her. For good reason, it turned out. I knew she was vulnerable, but I didn't realize how vulnerable until she attempted suicide."

"She can't help her daughter without knowing the truth," I said.

"Daphne got better. I made sure of it. Dr. Payne and I worked together to make her whole again."

"Are you sure she was cured?"

"Of course. She got through her senior year of high school with no issues."

"She says she had no friends that year. Does that seem normal to you for someone as bright and beautiful as Daphne?"

"The other students were just jealous. Especially the girls."

"That excuse makes no sense. Daphne has always been bright and beautiful, but she had no trouble making friends before the incident, did she?"

"She's always been shy. Always preferred the company of a few good friends to a big crowd. Plus...the crime. People were afraid to approach her."

"I've done my research, Jonathan. The crime was never made public."

"Daphne and Sage were both minors. That was for their protection."

"I understand that. My point is that if no one knew what happened to Daphne, why would the other students be wary of her?"

Jonathan rubbed his temples. Beads of sweat emerged on his upper lip.

He was lying.

"Sit down, Jonathan," I said.

He plunked back down in his chair.

I sat across from him. "Time's up. I need the truth. Daphne is my wife and the mother of my child. I can't help her if I don't know everything I'm dealing with."

Jonathan let out a long sigh.

"Who paid for Daphne's treatment, Jonathan?"

"I did, of course."

"Where did you get that kind of money?"

"I have health insurance, Brad."

"You have an indemnity policy. You were responsible for twenty percent of Daphne's bills, which amounted to over a hundred thousand dollars."

"Yes, I paid it."

"With what?"

"With savings."

"Nice try."

"What's that supposed to mean?"

I scooted my chair closer to Jonathan's desk, so that only about four feet separated us. "It means I know you didn't have that kind of money sitting around."

"Exactly how would you know that?"

"Didn't I already tell you?" I looked him straight in the eye. "Everything is available for the right price."

"I'll have you arrested. Bank records are—"

"You'll have to arrest a dead man. It was my father who found this information. I found it in his files after he died."

"Why would your father care who paid for Daphne's treatment?"

"Why *wouldn't* he? Daphne was his daughter-in-law."

"For God's sake, Brad. What does it matter who paid for it as long as it got paid for? As long as she got the treatment she needed?"

"In the abstract, I agree with you. But you kept information from me, Jonathan. Important information about the woman I was going to marry."

"Would you have declined to marry Daphne if you'd known?"

"Of course not. I love her. And I love our baby. You trusted me when you told me about the crime that sent her into this tailspin. Why didn't you trust me with the rest?"

"Because," he said, looking down at his desk, "Daphne isn't the only person I have to protect."

CHAPTER TEN

Daphne

I picked up Puppy and snuggled him against my cheek. I hadn't brought him along to college, and subsequently, when I moved in with Brad at the ranch, I still hadn't brought him. I was a wife and mother now, and having a stuffed animal seemed grossly immature. Kind of like a security blanket.

But what was wrong with a security blanket? I smiled. Puppy was coming home with me. I could give him to Jonah, but even as I thought the words, I knew I wouldn't. Puppy was mine. Jonah would have something of his own that was special to him. He already had about fifty stuffed animals in his nursery, and he was too young yet to favor any of them.

I secured Puppy in the duffel bag I brought from the ranch. He was going home with me.

Funny. The ranch was home for me now. Brad's home was now my home. This house, where I'd grown up, was now only a place to visit.

Brad had given me so much. I was eternally grateful. If only I could do something as amazing for him.

Then I laughed out loud. I'd given him a beautiful baby. I longed to give him another and another still. I wanted to fill that huge house with grandchildren for George and Mazie. George was gone, hadn't lived to see the grandchild he'd wanted so badly. He was gruff for sure, but he would've had a sweet spot for Jonah.

Yes, I'd already given Brad the most special gift, but he'd also given it to me.

I was the vibrant yellow tulip when Brad was with me. I needed to be the vibrant yellow tulip even when he was gone. For my son.

And I would be.

I walked back downstairs. Jonah was still napping on my mother's lap. She rocked slowly in the recliner.

"You look good with him, Mom."

She put a finger to her lips, urging me to speak softly. "He almost woke up a few minutes ago."

I nodded.

"He's so amazing, Daphne. I'd nearly forgotten what it felt like to love a child."

Her words shocked me, and I widened my eyes.

"Oh, honey, I didn't mean it like that. All I meant was that when a baby is small, like this, and completely dependent on you for everything, it's a feeling like no other. Your baby has complete trust in you to see to his needs. It feels good to be needed, doesn't it?"

"It does. And I still need you, Mom."

"No, you don't. You're making an amazing life for yourself, and I couldn't be happier."

But I did need my mother. Her words scared me a little. She'd attempted suicide when she thought I was taken care of. She was doing well now and seemed so happy, but I couldn't let her think I didn't need her.

"That's not true. I'll always need you, and so will Jonah."

She smiled. My mother was so pretty when she was happy.

"I'm glad you feel that way, because I'm not going anywhere."
She stood and placed Jonah in his travel crib. "Come out back
with me. I want to show you something."

I followed her out onto the porch.

"Your father is going to build me a greenhouse," she said.

"He is?"

"Yes. We're converting half of the patio." She gestured.
"This half will be enclosed in glass. I was so happy when I spent
time with Mazie in her greenhouse. This won't be anything
like hers, of course. It will be about a tenth of the size, but I
want to have flowers all year round, Daphne."

I smiled, warming inside as if my heart were the sun itself,
casting rays throughout my body. This would be good for my
mom. Good for me too, for that matter. I loved spending time
in Mazie's greenhouse at home, and having one here would
be wonderful for when I visited. I wanted Jonah to grow up
around all kinds of beautiful things. Flowers year-round were
definitely a beautiful thing.

Our ranch was also beautiful. My son would grow up in
the most beautiful place imaginable, learning skills from his
father and learning love and beauty from me.

"This will be great for you, Mom. I'm so glad you're
progressing so well."

"I won't lie to you, Daphne. It hasn't been easy."

"Mom, if anyone knows that to be true, I do."

"I know you do. Your father has been great. I try not to be
too needy, but whatever I need, he gives me. The greenhouse
was my idea. I was worried that we wouldn't be able to afford
such a remodel, but he told me not to worry about it. He'd find
the money."

"Mom, you know you never have to worry about money.

I'm happy to—"

"No, Daphne. We would never ask you for money."

"But I'm happy to help. You and Dad have done so much for me. I know I didn't make your life easy that year. I want to help in any way I can. I want to make it up to you."

"Honey, your dad and I would go to hell and back for you. You know that because you would go to hell and back for that sleeping baby inside."

She wasn't wrong. Still, I had the resources to make my parents lives' easier. "Brad and I couldn't spend our money in five lifetimes. What good is it if I can't help the people I love?"

"Just take care of that baby. That's all you need to do for your dad and me."

"But—"

"Stop it." My mother touched my cheek. "You're a good girl to suggest it and to want to do it. But parents take care of their children, not the other way around."

I didn't agree. Children often took care of elderly parents. Of course, my parents were far from elderly, but I wouldn't push the issue. My mom knew that if she ever needed anything, she could come to me.

"I decided to take Puppy home to the ranch."

My mother smiled. "To be frank, I was surprised you didn't take him to college."

"I guess I wanted to pretend I was more grown up than I actually was."

"Oh, honey, there's no harm in having a sacred relic from your childhood to give you comfort. Why do you think I keep Nana's old ratty afghan around?"

Nana was my great-grandmother, Mom's grandmother. The afghan—crocheted in browns and greens that resembled vomit—had been the only thing my mother wanted when my great-grandmother died.

"Whenever I was sick and had to stay at my grandmother's home while my parents went to work," Mom said, "she wrapped me in that afghan, fed me chicken soup, and told me stories."

"How did I not know this?"

"I guess I never told you. Since no one else wanted that old afghan, I didn't have to give any reason why I wanted it. Not many kids had parents who both worked back then. Luckily, my grandmother was around to take care of me when my parents couldn't."

That old puke-colored afghan suddenly became beautiful in my mind. Almost as beautiful as my tattered old stuffed puppy. "Mom, someday I think I'd like to have that afghan."

"You'll get everything, Daphne. You're my only child."

I was. This conversation became uncomfortable quickly. I'd come way too close to losing my mother recently, and I didn't want to contemplate the day when she would be gone. Best to change the subject.

"So . . . when will the greenhouse be finished?"

"I was hoping by the holidays, but that probably won't happen."

"Has Dad hired a contractor?"

"No. He thinks he's going to do it himself on weekends."

"Then you might be waiting awhile." I couldn't help laughing. My father wasn't exactly a handyman.

"He's determined," she said.

I forced myself not to grin. I had just come up with the best Christmas present for my mom.

CHAPTER ELEVEN

Brad

"I know," I said. "You made it very clear that Lucy is your priority now. I get that."

He cleared his throat. "Yes, Lucy."

Something in his tone made me pause. I believed he loved his wife and wanted to take care of her, but I got the distinct impression his comment had meant more than that.

"Anyone else, Jonathan? Anyone else you need to protect?"

He cleared his throat again, longer this time. Sounded like he had a glob of phlegm caught in there.

"There's Larry."

Of course. Larry was his son, but he was a grown man in law school and engaged to be married. Why did Larry need protection?

"Is Larry in some kind of trouble?" I asked.

"Why would you think that?"

"Because Larry is my age. He's in law school and will make a good living." He was already making a damned good living, but I didn't say that. Did Jonathan even know his son was a millionaire?

"He's still my child."

"He is, but so is Daphne, and you made it quite clear to me

that Daphne was *my* responsibility now."

"It's a different situation altogether," he said. "You have unlimited resources to care for Daphne. All her needs will be met. All your son's needs will be met. Larry doesn't have those kinds of resources."

Maybe not the kind I had, but Larry had resources. Clearly, his father didn't know about Larry's Future Lawmakers dealings.

"What needs does Larry have, then?"

"Larry is . . . Let's just say he's been in therapy."

"I believe Daphne mentioned that, but only in passing."

"Daphne doesn't know Larry very well."

"Why is that, Jonathan? I've always wondered."

"A lot of reasons. The biggest one is that things did not end well between Larry's mother and me."

"Did you pay for his prep school and his college?"

"I paid my regular child support while he was in high school. Once he turned eighteen, I no longer had any obligation to support him, but I continued with my monthly amount until he graduated."

"What about college?"

"Lisa paid for that. At least I assume she did. Neither one of them asked me for anything."

Easy enough for me to deduce how he paid for it. His Future Lawmakers earnings. Same for law school.

"It doesn't seem like Larry needs your financial support," I said.

"He's still my son."

"You seem to be forgetting that I *know* Larry. He and I were friends all through high school. He came to my wedding more for me than for the half sister he barely knows."

"I'm aware you were friends in high school."

"Are you aware that he and I were in business together at one time?"

"He may have mentioned something about some kind of high school business, yes."

"Have you met his fiancée, Greta?"

"I haven't. I'd like to have a better relationship with Larry, but because things are so strained between Lisa and me, it's not always easy."

"Larry has been a legal adult for four years now. What does it matter whether the relationship between you and his mother is strained?"

Jonathan shifted in his chair. "Brad, is there a point to this interrogation? I understand you and Larry were friends. Maybe you still are. You should care what happens to him."

"I do care about Larry. I just don't quite understand what you feel your obligation is to him. With all due respect, Jonathan, you basically pawned your daughter off on me."

Jonathan opened his mouth to respond, but I gestured him to stay quiet.

"Don't take that the wrong way," I said. "I am happy beyond measure with Daphne and our life together, and I will see to all her needs as long as I live. My point is only that you seemed happy and relieved to have me take over. Yet you sit here and tell me you still need to take care of Larry, your son, who is older than your daughter, is putting himself through law school, and is engaged to be married."

"I told you. He's had some mental issues of his own."

"Anything like Daphne's mental issues?"

Jonathan shook his head. "No." But he didn't meet my gaze.

"It's time to level with me," I said. "Larry and I are friends. Tell me what's going on."

"I've told you all I can. If you want to know more, you'll have to ask Larry himself."

"All right. I'll do that. Besides Larry, is there anyone else you're protecting?"

He looked down again. His classic tell. He was about to lie to me.

"No," he said.

I was about to give up on this conversation when I remembered something.

"You once told me that Daphne kept a journal during her hospitalization."

He didn't respond. Had that been another lie?

"You also told me you hadn't read the journal, that you hadn't been able to bring yourself to read it. I accepted that at the time, but now, I have to tell you it disturbs me. If you truly wanted to protect Daphne, why didn't you read the journal?"

"Journals are private."

"True. I won't argue the point. But here's what I think, Jonathan. I think one of two things happened. Either you *did* read the journal, and you don't want to tell me what was in it, or there is no journal at all."

He sighed—a heavy, exhausted sigh. Then he slowly opened a desk drawer and pulled something out.

"Here." He pushed a spiral notebook across the desk to me. "Daphne's journal."

I didn't take the notebook. Not at first. I simply stared at it. The vibrant pink cover was worn, and someone—presumably Daphne—had doodled ink drawings all over it. Mostly flowers.

"I was telling the truth when I said I didn't read it,"

Jonathan said. "I just . . . I just didn't want to know."

"Sometimes knowledge is our best defense, Jonathan." I picked up the journal.

"And sometimes, Brad," he said, his voice serious, "ignorance is bliss."

Something clicked then—a fundamental difference between Jonathan and me. He would avoid where I would attack.

He loved his daughter. Of that, I had no doubt. I also had no doubt that he loved Larry, his son.

He was also hiding something about Larry. Something that had taken its toll on him as a father, so much so that when his daughter went down a similar path, he had a hard time going back to that place.

What had happened to Larry? What was Jonathan hiding?

I didn't open the journal, but I took it with me when I left Jonathan's office. He had told me all he was willing to, and unless I pulled a George Steel and held a gun to his head, he wasn't about to divulge anything more.

I was armed. I could've pulled out my piece, but threatening my father-in-law with a firearm would be crossing the line.

I wasn't ready to go there.

I suspected, though, I wouldn't have a choice in the future.

Jonathan Wade isn't who you think he is, son. Be careful.

My father was right.

I had Daphne's journal now. I hadn't decided yet whether I would read it. Perhaps I would give it to Dr. Pelletier. Right now it was burning a hole in my briefcase.

Did Daphne even remember keeping a journal? One way to find out.

CHAPTER TWELVE

Daphne

Something wasn't right.

My mother cooked a delicious dinner—one of my favorite meals of pork chops and mashed potatoes—but it all tasted like sawdust on my tongue.

Because something wasn't right.

Oh, everyone was polite enough, but tension in the air was palpable.

Not with me or Mom.

With Brad and my father.

They conversed as jovially as ever. Call it intuition, but something was off between them. I couldn't put my finger on it, but it was there. Definitely there. My husband and my father were the two most important men in my life, and something was definitely up.

My mother didn't seem to notice, and I was glad. I didn't want anything to mess with her newfound mental health.

I didn't want anything to mess with mine, either. My sessions with Dr. Pelletier were doing me a world of good. I always felt stronger after I left a session—strong and able to take on the world and be the best wife and mother ever. Strong and full of light, like my favorite yellow tulips in Mazie's greenhouse.

Jonah was my priority, of course. I loved Brad with all my heart, but he could take care of himself. Jonah needed me, and he needed me whole. I was determined to stay that way.

Dessert went slowly. Mom had made rice pudding, another favorite of mine, and I sprinkled cinnamon and nutmeg on my portion and ate it quickly, hoping to end the meal and get Brad alone so I could ask him what was wrong.

The others seemed to eat in slow motion. Maybe it was just in my head, but would this meal ever end? I'd so been looking forward to seeing my family, and now I couldn't wait to be done with them.

Coffee on the deck after dinner, of course.

"I think I'll pass," I said. "Brad, could I talk to you?"

"Let him have his coffee, honey," Mom said.

"I won't be long." Brad smiled.

Yeah, something was definitely off. Brad would never make me wait if I had to talk to him. He and my father were acting *too* normal.

I nodded and went to check on Jonah. He was gurgling in his portable crib. "Are you hungry, little dove?" I picked him up, carried him to the recliner, and began to nurse him.

"Something's bothering your daddy, little dove," I said softly. "They're all out on the deck, drinking coffee and acting normal, but I know something's not right. I'll find out tonight. It's nothing for you to worry about. I'll take care of you no matter what, little dove. Always."

He tugged urgently at my nipple. He was definitely hungry. After he was done eating, I snapped my bra back in place and held him on my lap, talking to him and watching him smile.

This was happiness.

This was the yellow tulip.

My son made everything all right—even when I knew something wasn't.

★ ★ ★

"Brad," I said, once we'd brought Jonah's crib up to my room and we were getting ready for bed, "what's going on between you and my father?"

He wrinkled his forehead. "What do you mean? Nothing's going on."

"I know you both better than that. There was tension between you two at dinner."

He kissed my lips. "I think you're imagining things."

"I'm not imagining anything."

"You are, baby. Everything's fine. But I do have a question for you."

I sighed. "Fine. What is it?"

"Did you ever keep a journal?"

I wrinkled my forehead this time. A journal? Had I? It sounded vaguely familiar. "I think I might have ... while I was ... "

"In the hospital?"

"Yeah. I think I did. Man, I haven't thought of that in forever."

"Do you remember what you wrote in it?"

"I'm not even sure I kept one. I sure as heck don't remember what I might have written in it."

"Okay." He brushed my hair out of my face. "You look beautiful."

"Sleep in here with me. Please."

He smiled. "Baby, we've been over this. I'm a big guy. We

can't both sleep in this twin bed. We'll be more comfortable with me in the guest room."

He was right, of course. My tiny bed couldn't accommodate us both. Plus, this was a strange place for Jonah. He'd probably be up several times during the night, and I didn't want to wake Brad up by rustling around in that tiny bed.

"Good night, then." I kissed his lips.

He walked to the crib and patted a sleeping Jonah. "Night, partner." Then he left and closed the door behind him.

I sighed. I'd already put Puppy away in my bag, but I rooted him out and cuddled him close.

This was the first time in a while I'd needed him. My security blanket.

I wasn't sure why.

CHAPTER THIRTEEN

Brad

After washing up and donning my lounge pants and a T-shirt, I lay down in the twin bed in the guest room. I'd first slept here the night we told Daphne's parents about our pregnancy and impending marriage.

Also the night Lucy had attempted suicide.

Now, a year later, I sat on the same bed holding Daphne's journal. I hadn't opened it yet.

I wasn't sure I wanted to.

Maybe I should just give it to Dr. Pelletier and let him deal with it.

No.

If I was going to protect Daphne, I needed all the information. I opened it. On the first page, in Daphne's handwriting, was only one short paragraph. I squinted for a moment, making the words blurry. Then I inhaled and began to read.

I'm supposed to keep a journal. Write something down every day. I don't know what to write though. I want to go home. I miss Mom and Dad. I miss Sage. The only thing I have from home is Puppy. I sleep with him every night, but it's not enough. I just want to go home.

The next day:

Last night I woke up screaming. I can't remember why, but the night nurse came in and gave me some medicine. I went to sleep after that. This morning I'm woozy. I didn't eat my breakfast. I can't write anymore.

Meds, of course. Were the nightmares the reason they started giving Daphne meds?

I'd ask Dr. Pelletier about that. In fact, I'd ask to see all of Daphne's records. He'd give me some foolishness about her not signing a records release, but I knew ways to get around that. And Dr. Pelletier knew I knew.

Next entry:

I feel like there's something in my brain that I can't get to. It's the strangest feeling, like I'm swimming in rough waters trying to get to an island. It's in sight, but no matter how hard I kick and thrash against the current, I just can't get there. It's frustrating. I told my therapist about it today, and she said I should try meditating. She guided me through some relaxation exercises, but they didn't work for me. She says I'm trying too hard. That's the dumbest thing I ever heard. I've tried hard my whole life. I try. I was taught always to try my best at everything I do. How can I not try?

That was my Daphne, all right. She had such strength and determination. So far, these entries were nothing to be concerned over.

I was tired after dealing with Jonathan. Should I call it a night?

No. I kept reading.
Next entry:

Sometimes I feel like I'm the only one here. I don't have a roommate, and the other people I see around are only blurs to me. No one talks to anyone else. My therapist says I'll have group therapy eventually, but not yet. Today I asked her why I was here. She told me I needed help dealing with some stuff. What stuff? I asked. She said I'd been through an ordeal. What ordeal? If I'd been through an ordeal, wouldn't I know what she's talking about? She changed the subject and asked me some questions about school and about Sage. I wonder where Sage is. When Mom and Dad come to visit this weekend, I'll ask them.

Next entry:

8:00 a.m. Thursday

I'm going to start writing the day and time down because I swear I just wrote in this journal a minute ago. But it must have been yesterday, because the journal was in my drawer, and I just ate my breakfast. Still, it seems like I just put the journal away. What else happened yesterday? Usually I see my therapist, but I can't remember seeing her. I can't remember what I had for lunch or dinner. Maybe I should start writing that down too.

Next entry:

8:21 a.m. Friday

Yesterday I met another patient. She was so sad. She didn't

speak, just sat in a chair in the patient lounge looking sad. I
tried to talk to her, but she didn't seem to know I was there. I
asked a nurse about her, but she didn't reply. I guess I'm not
allowed to know about the other patients. The nurse told me
to go back to my room because I was talking nonsense. How
is talking about another patient nonsense? This place is the
worst. I want to go home so badly. I have no friends here. It's
just me, all alone.

I closed my eyes for a moment. Talking nonsense.
What nurse would say that to a patient? Unless the patient
was another manifestation of Daphne herself. Was this the
beginning of her break with reality? Of splitting into alternate
versions of herself?

I continued reading.

8:15 a.m. ~~Saturday~~ Sunday

I was almost sure today was Saturday, but when the nurse
came in to bring breakfast, she corrected me. Except I wrote
in the journal yesterday morning, and it clearly states above
that it was Friday. My parents were supposed to come
on Saturday, but they never came. Or if they did, I don't
remember. This is scaring me. Why don't I remember a
whole day?

I closed the journal. I could feel the anxiety in Daphne as
I read the entry. It almost jumped off the page. She must have
been so scared. My poor baby. I opened the notebook once
more.

8:00 a.m. Monday

Some guy left a newspaper outside my door this morning. It was from a few weeks ago. I remember seeing him folding up newspapers in the lounge yesterday. I didn't see the sad girl. I never see more than one person at a time in the lounge. Everyone else is blurry. That seems strange. Maybe I should get my eyes checked. My mom wears contact lenses. Maybe my vision is deteriorating. I'll ask one of the nurses.

I closed the notebook.

It was all right there in black and white. The beginning of Daphne's descent into different identities. Had Jonathan truly never read this? I was almost scared to go on. Not to mention the fact that this was a serious violation of Daphne's privacy.

But I had to. Privacy or not, I had to know everything if I was going to help her. This was for Daphne. For Jonah. I had to know what I was potentially going to have to deal with if Dr. Pelletier was right and she might dissociate again.

I reopened the journal.

10:30 a.m. Tuesday

Hmm. Most of her entries were timed around eight a.m. Why was this one so much later?

Sage came to see me yesterday. At least I think it was Sage. She was blurry. Why is everything so blurry? I keep forgetting to ask one of the nurses to get my eyes checked.

Sage? None of Daphne's entries had an actual date, just the time and the day of the week. When had Sage died?

Sometime after she got out of the hospital for her injuries from the attack. She was most likely already gone when this entry was written, as Daphne had been in the main hospital after the attack as well. I'd look into that. I could easily find Sage's obituary.

I glanced back down to finish reading the entry—

When I jerked. The doorknob was turning slowly.

I slammed the notebook shut as Daphne opened the door to the guest room. I quickly shoved the journal under the covers.

"Brad?"

"What is it, baby?"

"I can't sleep."

"I'm sorry. What's the matter?"

She walked to the bed and sat down next to me. "I'm worried."

"About what?"

"My father." She hedged. "And . . . you."

"Oh?"

"Something was off between the two of you at dinner. I could sense it."

"Everything's fine, baby." God, I hated lying. More than that, I hated that lying to Daphne was becoming easier and easier for me. "You're imagining things."

"Don't say that to me."

"I only meant that—"

"I try very hard to live each moment. To make up for the time I lost during my junior year. I don't ever want to be in that position again."

"I understand."

"Do you? Because part of living each moment is being

observant. And what I observed tonight at dinner wasn't normal, Brad. Not at all."

She was right. Things *had* been tense between her father and me because of my visit to his office during his lunch hour. I didn't give my smart wife enough credit sometimes. She noticed all the little things. She'd trained herself to.

"Maybe your dad had a tough day at work."

"Maybe. I'll buy that. But that doesn't explain the tension coming from *you*."

Fuck. How to get out of this? If I told her she was imagining it again, I'd be patronizing her. She'd see through that in a minute. My Daphne was so smart and so observant.

I rose and locked the door to the bedroom. I wasn't keen on making love to my wife in this tiny bed—or in the house where her parents slept only twenty feet away—but it was the only way I could think of to get her mind off the subject at hand.

Plus, it was certainly no hardship on my part. I was erect just looking at her. She was so beautiful.

I sat back down on the bed and pulled Daphne into my lap.

"I am a little tense," I admitted.

CHAPTER FOURTEEN

Daphne

"Then let me help you." I moved closer to him.

"Daphne..."

"Please, let me do this for you. I want to help ease your tension."

As much as I wanted to figure out the issue between Brad and my father, helping my husband was more important right now.

He needed me. I would always be there for him when he needed me. Especially since I needed him too. So much.

I melted into his arms as our lips met and parted.

The kiss began slowly, a soft dance of lips and tongues. I savored his flavor, the velvet of his tongue against mine. My nipples hardened against my pajama top, and my breasts tingled as my milk let down.

I broke the kiss. "Brad..."

"Hmm?" He trailed his lips over my cheek to my earlobe, where he nipped at it, making me shiver.

"My... milk. It's going to make a mess."

"No worries." He hastily unbuttoned my top and kissed the top of my chest. Then he took a nipple into his mouth and sucked, covering the other with his hand.

My milk. He was drinking my milk. He'd gotten traces of

it before, but at the moment, he was suckling, taking it.

Taking milk from my baby.

I was both horrified and turned on.

"Brad..."

He let the nipple drop, and milk dribbled down over my areola. "Hmm?"

"Is it... Will there...?"

"So sweet."

My body warmed, and electricity surged between my legs.

I wanted him then. I always wanted him, but the ache inside me intensified.

He gently laid me on my back and tugged off my pajama bottoms. Then he stood and undressed himself.

I sucked in a breath. Every time. Every single time, his majestic beauty mesmerized me. Brad Steel had to be the most magnificent man alive.

And he was mine. All mine.

His dick was hard and ready, and I needed him inside me so badly.

He had other ideas, though. He slid down my body and seconds later glided his tongue through the folds of my pussy.

My breasts surged again, and milk drizzled over them. I didn't care. All I knew was Brad's mouth on me, tugging at my clit and eating me. I undulated my hips, moving myself against his lips and creating an intoxicating rhythm.

How long had it been since he'd gone down on me? Too long, and I was going to enjoy this for all it was worth.

It had been so. Damned. Long.

"God, I've missed you," I breathed, reaching down and threading my fingers through his soft hair. I anchored my feet on the bed, lifted my hips, and ground against Brad's face relentlessly.

I was taking. Taking for my own pleasure.

It went against my nature, but my God, it felt good. So good.

He didn't seem to mind. He ate me vigorously, sucking on my clit until I thought I'd burst but then moving down to my opening and tonguing me, making me itch for his fingers and cock.

"You taste so sweet, baby," he murmured against my flesh.

I moaned, my body on fire. "Please, Brad. Please."

"Please what, baby?"

"Please . . . I need . . . "

"What do you need, baby?"

"You. You inside me."

"Yeah. I need that too." He kept his voice soft and low. "But I'm going to make you come first. I'm going to make you come and come, and then when your pussy is throbbing and you're in the middle of your umpteenth orgasm, I'm going to shove my cock in you and feel you throb around me."

God. My parents across the hall. My baby in the next room. Everything. Everything I should be thinking about instead of this.

But the thoughts were fleeting.

I was all in. All in for this lovemaking fest. I'd stay quiet. I had to, but—

"God!" I cried out when he forced two fingers inside me.

I clamped down, the climax whirling through me at light speed. My nipples were still dribbling, but I no longer cared. Sheets could be changed. Clothes could be washed.

But this orgasm. This orgasm was special. So special. For the first time since long before Jonah was born, Brad and I were truly making love like we meant it.

Savoring each other's bodies, enjoying each other, being playful and dirty, reveling in the moment.

"I told you," he said, his voice still low and soft. "I'm going to make you come and come and come."

My God, I couldn't take it. I couldn't stay quiet. I just couldn't. I—

"Brad! My God!"

I rose to the peak again, and my whole body shattered from my head to my toes, like rays shooting outward and then inward once more, landing right where Brad was still licking me.

Then a baby's cry.

My body froze. The orgasm fled, all traces gone.

I was in mother mode. My breasts let down again.

"Brad."

Still, he worked between my legs.

"Brad. The baby. Jonah."

He lifted his head, his chin wet with my juices. "What?"

"The baby's crying. Don't you hear him?"

He cocked his head. "Yeah. Yeah."

I scrambled up and back into my pajamas as quickly as I could. "My top is wet."

"I'm sorry."

"It's not your fault. I'll put a T-shirt on. I've got to get to him."

"He's all right, Daphne. He'll be okay for a minute while you pull yourself together."

I stopped listening, opened the door, and ran out of the room and into the other.

My mother stood in my room, the baby in her arms.

Embarrassment flooded through me. I hadn't exactly been quiet.

"Hey, Mom."

"He's okay. Just a little out of place. He probably woke up and didn't know where he was."

"He usually sleeps through the night. Well, at least six hours."

She kissed his forehead. "He'll be okay. I can rock him for a while if you'd like."

"No. I'll take care of him." I took Jonah from her and had a hard time meeting her gaze. "I was just . . . "

"No need to explain, honey."

"But I—"

"You were doing what married people do. Or what they're supposed to do, anyway."

My cheeks warmed. *What married people do.* Obviously. We had a baby to prove it. Still, I was in my parents' house. In their guest room, letting my husband go down on me—

Wait. *What they're supposed to do, anyway.*

What did my mother mean by that? Did she and my father not have sex?

Man. Something I'd never given a second thought. It wasn't something kids ever thought about their parents.

"Mom?" I said hesitantly.

"It's nothing."

"Is everything . . . okay between you and Dad?"

"Yes. Well, no. But yes."

I opened my shirt, and Jonah latched on to my nipple. Topping him off usually got him back to sleep when he woke up at night.

"I have no idea what that means," I said.

"Ever since . . . Well, you know. He thinks I'm too fragile or something."

Had I been transported to another planet? I wasn't really talking to my mom about her sex life. I couldn't be.

Brad walked in the room then, dressed in a T-shirt and jeans, his feet bare. "Everything okay?"

"He's fine," I said.

I was both ecstatic for the interruption and also disappointed. Talking about my parents' sex life was uncomfortable, to say the least, but if something was bothering my mother, I wanted to help.

"I guess I'll get back to bed," my mother said. "Good night."

"Good night, Lucy," Brad said. "I'm sorry the baby woke you."

"He didn't. I wasn't sleeping." She left the room, closing the door.

God. She hadn't been sleeping. Which meant she'd heard all the noises, every time I'd shouted Brad's name.

What the heck had I been thinking, having sex twenty feet from my parents' bedroom?

It's what married people do. Or what they're supposed to do, anyway.

As freaked as I was that my mother had heard our lovemaking, her comment bothered me more.

"You need to level with me," I said to Brad. "What's going on with my father?"

"It's the middle of the night, Daphne."

"So? We're both awake."

"We're driving home tomorrow. I need to get a good night's sleep."

I sighed. "Fine. But we have a lot to talk about on the road."

Jonah had fallen back to sleep, so I laid him back in his portable crib.

I understood that Brad didn't tell me everything. I had no idea what it took to run a ranch—though he employed hundreds of people. Why did he have to work so hard?

Still, I got it. This was his life. His legacy for his son. His testament to his father. It was important to him, and because it was important to him, it was also important to me.

Maybe I should be more involved.

Once Jonah was a little older, I'd learn about our livelihood. I'd be a true partner to Brad.

In the meantime, though, what was going on between Brad and my father?

And why was my mother not getting any?

None of my business, for sure, but she'd brought it up.

I might not live here anymore, but I knew when something wasn't adding up.

My father was a little off.

And I aimed to find out why.

CHAPTER FIFTEEN

Brad

Daphne's journal still lay where I'd buried it under the covers.
What to do?

Daphne wasn't sure she even remembered keeping a journal.

Again I felt the guilt of keeping this from her, of reading her innermost thoughts without her knowing.

I was being pulled in two directions. In the end, I laid the book aside and closed my eyes. I'd told Daphne I needed to get a good night's sleep.

At least that wasn't another lie.

★ ★ ★

"Spill it," Daphne said, once we were on the road.

"Spill what?" Though I knew exactly what. She wasn't going to let this thing with her father go. Not that I blamed her.

"You know what."

"There's nothing going on between me and your father."

"Don't lie to me, Brad."

"I'd never lie to you, baby." Which was in itself a lie. I'd lied to her so many times, I'd lost count. True, the lies had been omissions most of the time, but still . . .

"Then spill it. I know my dad. He wasn't himself at dinner

last night or at breakfast this morning."

Breakfast had been quiet, but for me, breakfast was always quiet. I got up early for ranch work. I was used to sitting at the table with my father and drinking coffee. No talking, except when my mother had said, "Have a great day!" cheerfully when we left the kitchen.

"Daphne, if I knew, I'd tell you. Why don't you ask him?"

"Because it isn't just him. You're off too, Brad. I love you, and I want to help."

"I'm not off, baby. I've just got a lot on my plate since my dad died so suddenly. You know all this."

God, another lie. My dad wasn't even dead. Of course, I was the only one who knew that.

"I do know, Brad, and I've done my best to be supportive."

"You've been great. I know it's difficult being home alone so often."

"I'm not alone. I have little Joe and your mom. Belinda. Cliff. All my needs are met. All but the most private."

Me. She wanted me at home. I couldn't blame her. I wanted to be at home with her and Jonah more than anything. But their protection was paramount.

My Daphne was so smart and observant. She couldn't possibly be on the verge of dissociation. Dr. Pelletier must be mistaken.

But he was one of the best in his field. My father didn't use just anyone for his purposes. He sought out the best people available—and then he bought them.

Or threatened them at gunpoint.

Whichever was necessary.

Man. The thought—which originally had been so abhorrent to me—was starting to seem normal.

What the fuck had happened to me?

I'd actually entertained the notion of holding a gun on my father-in-law yesterday. What if I had? What would I say to Daphne, then?

Another lie, of course.

Lies. They were like rabbits. They bred quickly, one after another, until soon there were so many you didn't know where they'd all started.

And it became easier each time.

A chill skittered up my spine to my neck.

It became easier each time.

"I'm sorry," I said.

"I know. I know you want to be around more. Last night was wonderful . . . except for the part about my mom hearing the whole thing."

"I didn't mean for it to happen." God, another fucking lie. I'd gone down on her to get her to stop asking me about her father.

"I know. Neither did I. But it was amazing."

I smiled. "It was. It's always amazing with you."

"Brad . . . "

"Yeah?"

"I don't think my parents are having sex."

I kept myself from jerking in my seat, keeping my eyes on the road. Where the hell had that come from?

"I don't think that's any of our business, Daph."

"Well, it kind of is, because my mother mentioned it."

"She said that? In actual words?"

"Well, not in exact words, but she implied it."

"Still none of our business."

"I know."

"Maybe that explains what you observed was 'off' about your dad."

"Nice try. The tension I saw was coming from my father and you, Brad."

"To be honest," I said, "I'm a little worried about him."

"I am too."

"He seems to take on the weight of the world." Another lie. He'd pretty much given Daphne over to me. She was no longer a weight on his shoulders.

"He's worried about Mom."

"And probably Larry."

That got her attention. "Larry? What's wrong with Larry? He's in law school, and he just got engaged."

"That's what I told your dad."

"What?"

Shit.

Shit, shit, shit.

My observant wife was all over that little blunder.

"When exactly did you tell him that? I don't remember it. Unless..." She paused a few seconds. "Unless...no. No. I can't be losing time again."

Fuck.

My wife had just given me the ammunition I needed to make her believe Jonathan and I had spoken about Larry, and she didn't remember it.

But I couldn't do that to her. Absolutely not.

"I don't think so, baby. You probably just tuned us out. It's easy to do. I bore myself all the time."

Brad Steel, you're a fucking prick.

"No." She shook her head adamantly. "Absolutely not. I listen very carefully, Brad. If I missed something in the conversation, that means I blanked out. Lost time."

"Now don't you worry. No one can be on all the time. You probably heard the baby gurgle or something."

I'm going to hell. I'm really going to hell.

She perked up at the last comment though.

"Maybe. I do try to keep an eye and an ear on Jonah at all times."

"See? That's all it is. You hardly missed anything vital. I told your dad that Larry's fine."

"Weird that he's even concerned. He was never really part of Larry's life. Not that I knew of, anyway. I don't even know him. You know my brother better than I do."

"Only because he and I happened to go to the same high school."

"A private high school. I went to public high school. I never really thought about it, but why do you suppose Larry got to go to private school and I didn't?"

"His mother probably paid for it."

"Maybe. Something doesn't sound right, though. I never even knew Larry went to private high school until I found out you and he went to the same one."

"You're not envious, are you?"

"Not really. I got a decent education. I got a scholarship." Her voice sounded wistful.

The scholarship. My smart wife should be in college right now. Not married with a baby.

"I know what you're thinking," she said.

"Do you?"

"I'm proud of my scholarship, but I wouldn't trade what I have now for anything. I love you and I love Jonah."

I smiled. "We both love you too, baby."

Sometimes Daphne read my mind much too easily. What would happen if she could truly read my mind? Truly find out everything I was keeping from her?

I had to get better at this.

This was my life now. Time to get used to it. Time to harden myself against the emotion that threatened to derail everything.

My life was lies and omissions. Secrets and mysteries. All born from a fierce devotion to protect my wife and child.

From anything and everything.

Even from her own father.

CHAPTER SIXTEEN

Daphne

"How have you been, Daphne?" Dr. Pelletier asked.

"Fine."

"Good to hear. How is the baby?"

"He's wonderful. Thriving. He's getting so big."

"And your husband?"

"He's ... good."

"You hesitated a minute. Is everything okay between you two?"

"Yes. He's wonderful. It's just ... I think I lost some time recently."

"What makes you think that?"

"Brad says it's nothing. I probably just tuned out the conversation."

"All right. Let's back up. Tell me."

I relayed the story.

"I see," he said.

"It makes sense, right? They weren't talking about anything vital. Still, it doesn't seem right. Both Brad and my dad seemed off."

"What do you mean by *off*?"

"That's just it. I don't know what I mean. I just know. I know my father and I know my husband, and something was off between them."

"So it wasn't so much that either of them were off. It was more that whatever relationship they have seemed off."

"Yes! Exactly. I don't know why I couldn't put it in those words."

"It's my business. Tell me, then. Why is it so difficult for you to believe you might have just tuned out part of the conversation?"

"Because I'm very careful. You know that. I lost so much time during my junior year that I'm overly observant. I take note of everything, and when I can't recall something, I get frightened."

"It's okay not to pay attention to something mundane."

"But there's nothing mundane about my husband and my father. They're the two most important men in my life. I pay attention to them."

"This was just basic dinner conversation."

"I know. And yes, I was keeping one ear on the baby in the other room."

"So it makes perfect sense that you—"

"That's just it, Doctor. It *doesn't* make perfect sense. I know myself. I make it a point to remember everything."

"No one can remember everything, Daphne."

"I know. But . . . "

"I don't think this is anything to worry about. You probably just zoned out a little. Everyone does."

"Even you?"

"Not during a session." He smiled. "But during everyday conversation, of course I do. Like I said, everyone does."

I sighed. No one seemed to understand. This bothered me. A lot.

"Let's get back to your husband and your father being off."

"All right. It was a feeling. I can't explain it any better than that. A feeling gleaned from observing how they acted."

"How they acted or how they *re*acted to one another?"

"Yes! The second one." Again, why couldn't I have found those words? Because I wasn't a psychiatrist, I guessed.

"I see. Have your husband and father been in contact? Alone?"

"Not that I know of. Brad would have told me."

"All right." Dr. Pelletier jotted down a few notes. "Has anything else occurred that makes you think you lost time?"

"Not really. I did end up in my room while I was home in Denver. I didn't remember walking up the stairs, but I remembered leaving the baby with my mother in the living room."

"You were on autopilot, probably."

"Maybe. For some reason that doesn't bother me as much as the lost conversation during dinner."

"Probably because it was just a walk up the stairs. You didn't miss anything."

"I remember being in my bedroom and deciding to take my favorite stuffed animal home to the ranch. So I tossed it in my bag."

"Why did you decide to take the stuffed animal?"

"I don't know. I was feeling a little needy, I guess."

"Nothing wrong with being a little needy."

"Really? Because I have everything, Doctor. A husband I love. A baby I cherish. A beautiful home on a gorgeous ranch. All the money in the world."

"And you feel a little guilty about being needy?"

"Yeah. Wouldn't you?"

He smiled. "Things are nice. They make life easier

sometimes, but they don't replace people."

"But I *have* people. My husband. My son. My mother-in-law. She's such a sweetheart and a great help. And I have hired help as well."

"Maybe I didn't put that exactly right," he said. "You need love."

"I have that. So why was I feeling so needy?"

"That," he said, "is what we need to figure out. Tell me. Do you remember anything else about the year you were hospitalized? I mean, you began to recall the other patients who were there with you. Have you been able to remember any of their names?"

I shook my head. "I wish I could."

"That's okay. Do you remember what they looked like?"

"Everything was blurry."

"Oh?"

"Yeah. I remember wondering if I needed glasses or something. It seemed like every time I was in a common area, all the other people there were blurry. I couldn't make out any of their faces."

"Did you ask for some glasses?"

"I always meant to, but I don't think I ever did."

"And your vision now?"

"It's perfect. Twenty-twenty, like it's always been."

"It's possible some of your medications affected your vision. I'll look into that." He jotted down more notes.

"Yeah, that might make sense. Whatever they gave me really affected my memory, so maybe it affected my vision."

"Maybe."

Though he didn't sound convinced. How did I know that? Because I was observant. I'd learned to observe everything visually and aurally. And his tone was definitely not convinced.

"Doctor?"

"Yes?"

"What aren't you telling me?"

CHAPTER SEVENTEEN

Brad

Wendy had been released while Daphne and I were in Denver visiting her parents. I found that out when I got back. With consternation, I decided to pay a visit to her parents, Warren and Marie Madigan. They lived in Snow Creek.

"Brad." Warren cleared his throat after opening the door. "I expected we'd see you sometime soon. Come in."

I entered.

"Marie's in the kitchen." He called for her, and she joined us.

"I suppose you're here to discuss Wendy."

"I am."

"She's doing great," Marie said happily. "She's back at school getting registered for the fall semester. She's a little late, but she'll catch up."

I had no doubt. Wendy was brilliant.

"She's excited about a career in journalism," Warren added.

All stuff I already knew.

"And you think she's okay living alone in Denver?" I asked.

"Her doctors seem to think so. She's so sorry about what happened with your friend. She really didn't mean to harm him."

"He's dead," I said abruptly.

"Yes, we know," Warren said. "We're very sorry for your loss. But Wendy had nothing to do with that."

"I never said she did."

Marie patted her husband's hand. "We know that. Right, Warren?"

He nodded gruffly. Then, "What do you want, Brad?"

"I want to make sure my family is safe."

"They are, of course," Marie said. "Wendy would never harm you. You'll always be special to her."

I nodded. They weren't quite getting it. I knew Wendy wouldn't harm *me*. I worried she'd harm others to get to me. I still wasn't convinced she hadn't been involved in Sean's and Patty's deaths. Yeah, she'd been locked up, but that woman had her ways. I'd learned never to take anything for granted where Wendy Madigan was concerned.

"What about my wife and child?" I asked.

"Wendy would never hurt a child!" Marie gasped.

"Wendy has never hurt another human being," Warren said. "She went a little far with your friend, it's true. But he wasn't harmed."

"Not physically," I said.

"That's my point," Warren said.

"Physical harm isn't the only kind of harm. I want to keep my wife from all harm. Let me be frank. Wendy is jealous. Jealous of Daphne because I chose her."

"What makes you think she still pines for you?" Warren said.

"I know her," I said.

"Better than we do?"

Yes. I didn't say it, though. There was so much Warren and

Marie didn't know about their daughter. She was a millionaire, for one. She was a stalker, for another. She apparently knew how to pick locks. And she liked to be tied up and beaten during sex. At least by me.

I shoved my hand into the pocket of my jeans and touched the gold ring I'd had sawn off my finger and then soldered back together. I no longer wore it, but I kept it on my person always. For one reason and one reason only.

To never forget what Wendy was capable of.

If I started to go soft... If I started to feel sorry for her... If I started to remember happier times we'd shared... I stuffed my hand in my pocket and felt the ring.

And my heart turned to stone.

It worried me a bit.

I seemed to reach for the ring more and more, and not just to remember the truth about Wendy. Whenever emotion got to me—when I was talking to Dr. Pelletier and had second thoughts about offering him money in exchange for his ethic—I reached for the ring.

When I stood outside Jonathan's office that day at lunch, ready to confront him about the journal, I reached for the ring.

I reached for it when I considered pulling out my gun and threatening him.

Luckily it didn't have the desired effect that time.

But it would. Eventually.

I knew I should get rid of it. Toss it down the toilet. Or sell it for junk gold.

But something inside me made me keep it.

Something inside me knew I'd need it.

Soon.

I made it a point to hide it in my dresser drawer every

night when I disrobed. Explaining it to Daphne would be a chore I didn't need.

Another lie I'd have to tell.

Another lie I was already telling by omission.

God, this was a fucked-up life I'd made for myself.

If only my father hadn't decided to bail out and go it alone. He could still be the bad guy. He could be the one who had to bury his emotions and integrity and do whatever was necessary to protect those he loved.

But it was up to me now.

And I didn't like it. Not one bit.

But each day I disliked it a little less.

And that was truly frightening.

I stood. "I hope Wendy is mentally well now."

"But you don't believe she is," Warren said. "What do you think you know that her doctors don't?"

I nodded to them. "Goodbye, Warren. Marie. I'll let myself out."

I pondered his question as I got into my truck and headed home.

What do you think you know that her doctors don't?

I know her, Warren. I know her.

CHAPTER EIGHTEEN

Daphne

"Nothing, Daphne." Dr. Pelletier smiled. "What makes you think I'm not telling you something?"

I sighed. "Because I'm not an idiot, Doctor. I've learned how to observe. How to read people."

"Reading people is part of my job," he said. "I'm not keeping anything from you."

I didn't believe him. Not for a minute.

And maybe that was my problem. Was my radar off? Maybe it was. Maybe I *hadn't* lost time as I suspected. Maybe I truly had just zoned out during the dinner conversation between my father and Brad.

I was projecting—a term I'd learned during my therapy with Dr. Payne. I wasn't doubting Dr. Pelletier.

For the first time in a while, I was doubting *myself.*

I didn't like the feeling.

I tried too hard to be observant, to recall everything, even the mundane. Maybe, by concentrating too much on each tiny detail, I was missing part of the big picture.

"Tell me what to do," I said.

"About what?"

"About this lost time. About trying so hard to recall everything. About ..."

"Listen," he said. "Just be yourself. Be a human being. Human beings don't have infallible memories, no matter how hard they may try. I've read case study after case study about the human memory. People misrecall all the time. It's completely normal."

"It may be, but can you honestly tell me it's normal that I lost nearly an entire year of my life?"

"No, Daphne, that's not what I'm saying. You know that. Those were different circumstances. You were mentally ill. You're no longer mentally ill, and your memory is functioning just like everyone else's. Don't be so hard on yourself."

He made a lot of sense, but I was hard on myself for a good reason. Never again would I lose so much of my life.

Never again.

"Our time's up for today," Dr. Pelletier said. "For next time, I want you to give yourself a break. Stop forcing yourself to remember every single detail of every single moment. I think you'll find you remember what's important."

"All right. I'll try." I stood. "Thanks, Doctor."

"You're very welcome. Have a good day, and I'll see you next time."

I left his office and walked toward my car.

"Daphne, love?"

I turned.

"Ennis!" I ran into his arms. "What are you doing here?"

"Just walking around town a bit. I had no idea you were here."

"Why didn't you tell me you were coming to town!"

"I didn't know I was until two days ago. It was a rash decision."

"Oh?" My heart did a flip-flop. "Is everything okay?"

"I had a nightmare about Patty, and I had to come."

"Patty? I figured she was still in Africa."

"She is, as far as I know. But I had this horrid dream about her. That something terrible had happened. Here. In Colorado."

My heart nearly stopped. I knew well the power of nightmares. Even ones you couldn't remember, which were the kind I routinely had.

"I'm so sorry. But why would that make you want to come all the way out here? Not that I'm sorry. It's wonderful to see you. You should stay with us on the ranch."

"That's kind of you, but I've already booked a room at the hotel. The same room Patty and I stayed in when . . . "

"Oh. That's an eerie coincidence."

"Actually, I requested it."

A chill raced up my neck. "Why would you do that?"

"I don't know. I just did. I said the words before I thought about them."

"Are you still in love with her, Ennis?"

"It's only been a little over three months. I've tried getting over her. Tried telling myself that she left me. That leaving her home was more important than I was. I can't fault her. The Peace Corps is amazing. But she never once mentioned the thought to me. I've always thought it strange that she just left without saying anything to anyone. Especially not to me or to you. So when I had the dream, I couldn't help but be freaked out by it."

"It was just a dream, Ennis." Easy for me to say. I didn't buy the words for a minute.

"I know that, love. But haven't you ever had a dream that spoke to you? That felt so damned real you could almost feel it?"

I nodded. "Yeah. I have, actually."

"Then you know what I mean."

Unfortunately, I did. "What do you plan to do while you're here?"

"I'm not sure. I haven't thought it out yet. I just knew, after that dream, that I had to come."

"I'm on my way back to the ranch now. You won't believe how big Jonah is. You should come and stay for dinner."

"I was going to call you this afternoon," he said. "Running into you is so much better. I was hoping . . . "

"Hoping what?"

"That Brad might be able to help. I want to hire a private investigator. I'm just not sure Patty's actually in Africa."

"Ennis, you know I adore you, and I know you adored Patty, but her parents corroborated the story, remember?"

He nodded. "Of course I remember. I just have this eerie feeling. I swear, if a PI tells me she's definitely in Africa, I'll call it all off."

Poor Ennis. He was still dealing with heartbreak. "Come for dinner at six, okay? Or you can come home with me now."

"I'll be there at six," he said. "I've rented a car, so I have my own transport."

"All right. See you then. Belinda's making jambon farci tonight. It's delicious."

"Jambon? Isn't that ham?"

"Yup."

"You blokes actually eat something other than beef?" He smiled. It was clearly forced, but at least it was a smile.

"When it's humanely raised, yes, we do. See you tonight." I waved and walked toward the car.

I was feeling better already. Ennis was here. I had a friend again.

CHAPTER NINETEEN

Brad

After calling my best investigation firm to put a twenty-four-hour tail on Wendy, I drove to the outer edge of the Steel land.

My father waited for me in the old barn where I'd seen Patty's body. The corpse had long since been moved and cremated and the barn cleaned and sanitized.

This was where my father and I routinely met when necessary. And necessary was on his terms, not mine.

This was only the second time I'd met him here since I came out to find Patty's body.

I didn't know where my father was holed up. He wouldn't tell me. He wouldn't give me a number to reach him either. He said the less I knew the better. Though he was no doubt right, it still irked me that I had to wait for him to contact me.

He'd done so this morning, with instructions to meet him here.

Either I was early or he was late. I looked at my watch. I was early. I glanced around the barn, long since abandoned.

Cleaners had been here. Not just run-of-the-mill cleaning service, but true cleaners. People specially equipped to remove any possible evidence that a crime had been committed. According to my father, Patty had not been killed here, but traces of her blood might have been recoverable.

Hence, the cleaners.

That my father knew of such things still made my blood run cold.

I'd learned more about George Steel since his run-in with Dr. Pelletier than I ever imagined possible.

Cleaners. God.

The door creaked open, and I turned.

My father's silhouette was dark against the sun shining in through the doorway. "Hello, son."

"Dad."

He closed the door. "Did anyone see you come in here?"

"Who could have possibly seen me? We're in the middle of nowhere."

"Always keep your eyes open," he said.

"I do. Believe me. And I've seen more this past year than I ever wanted to see."

"It's not always pleasant," he said, "but being aware keeps you cautious. Keeps you safe. There's safety in knowledge."

I held back a scoff. Watching my father hold a gun to another human being kept me safe? In what world did that make any sense at all?

Except that it did.

I'd learned a lot that day. A lot about my father. A lot about how the world worked. A lot about the power of having another's life in your hands.

It was power I never wanted. Power I might have to wield in the future.

Or now.

Dad was here to discuss Wendy.

"I couldn't get him to lock her up any longer," I said.

"You could have. You and I both know you could have."

"Yeah, maybe. I decided not to go your route." Not yet, anyway.

"You can't go soft, son."

"I'm not soft. I've never been soft, Dad, and you know it." How could I have been, being raised as his son? This was the man who'd made me watch two beloved calves get slaughtered. Forced me to keep my eyes open.

No, I was anything but soft.

But I still had my soul. I wasn't quite ready to sell it off yet.

"I talked to Wendy. She claims she's changed. That she's sorry for everything."

"Talk is cheap."

"I know that. I didn't say I believed her. Her parents do, though. I just came from their place. They're convinced she's a changed woman."

"Where is she now?"

"She's back in Denver. She's returning to college to get her degree in journalism."

"Still a little too close for comfort," Dad said.

"Agreed."

"I can get her to transfer to someplace on the east coast," he said. "Arrange for an offer she can't refuse."

"She'd see right through that."

"So? If I can get her into a program at Harvard or Yale free of charge, why wouldn't she take it? It'd be a huge boon to her."

"You can try. My bet is she'll turn it down."

"How do you know?"

"Because I know her, Dad. I know her better than anyone does. She won't leave her parents." *And she won't leave me.*

Oh, she swore we were all safe from her, but I didn't believe a word of it.

"Besides," I continued. "Keep your friends close, and keep your enemies closer."

"That's good advice."

"It is. You said that to me a long time ago."

"I wish I'd come up with it. But it's true, no matter what. Good call, son. We'll leave her right where she is."

"I've got twenty-four-hour surveillance on her," I said.

"Another good call."

"It won't take long before she's onto them, though. Wendy figures everything out."

"A cunning mind inside that one."

"You're telling me." I cocked my head. "I'm wondering, Dad . . . "

"What?"

"Why? Why didn't you tell me about her long ago?"

"A man has to make his own mistakes."

I shook my head. "I don't get it. You're obviously not squeamish about pulling guns on people, so—"

"Wait a minute. What makes you say that?"

"Because I saw you do it. You were icy. Not one bit of a quiver."

"Doesn't mean I like doing it. I might be good at it—I've learned to be—but I hate doing it. I do what I have to do to protect those I love."

"If that's the case, why didn't you take care of Wendy long ago?"

"I've told you before. I'm not a killer. Never was."

"But if you wanted to protect me—"

He sighed. "Don't think I didn't consider it. I've considered some pretty abhorrent things."

"Why, then? You could have sent her away, gotten her away from me."

"I could have."

"So why—"

"As I said, a man has to learn from his mistakes. Besides, by the time I realized what Wendy Madigan was truly capable of, it was too late."

I stared at my father, at his sad eyes. He wasn't lying. No one—even me, at first—could comprehend everything inside Wendy's head.

He cleared his throat, then. "I'm going away for a while."

I raised my eyebrows. "What for? And where?"

"I need to go on the down low. Someone nearly recognized me yesterday in Pueblo."

"Who?"

"One of our old hands. Don't worry. I took care of him."

My skin chilled. "I don't like the sound of that."

"What kind of man do you think I am, Brad?"

"I don't fucking know, Dad. I saw you point a gun at a guy, remember?"

"I don't kill people. When I say I took care of him, I mean I got out of there quickly and made sure he was well compensated to keep everything to himself."

"Why do you have to leave, then?"

"Because it's the smart thing to do. Besides, I want to check out some property you own down in the Caribbean."

"I own prop—" Then I remembered. I'd seen the deeds in my father's files, but I hadn't paid much attention. Other stuff on my mind. "Those islands. Yeah. I saw the deeds in your files. When did you purchase them?"

"A couple years ago. I had this idea of building a huge resort, but then...other things got in the way. Anyway, my sources tell me an offer is coming in on one of them."

"I haven't heard anything. If I'm the owner now, wouldn't I have heard before you?"

"Not necessarily. I've got eyes and ears everywhere. You should hear in the next few days. In the meantime, I want to go down and check things out. See if it's worth selling."

"Shouldn't I be doing that? Or I can send someone. You shouldn't be out in the open."

"Who the hell is going to recognize me on a private island? Besides, it's perfect timing. I need to lie low. I can go down there, check the place out, and get a tan. God knows I could use a vacation."

"Being dead isn't a vacation in itself?" I couldn't help asking.

"Are you kidding me? It's been more work than I realized. Do yourself a favor, son." He looked me straight in the eye. "Never fake your own death. It's not worth it."

CHAPTER TWENTY

Daphne

Brad was late for dinner, as usual.

I tried not to let it get to me so I could enjoy Ennis's company. Unfortunately, he wasn't his jovial self. The dream he'd had about Patty still had him rattled.

He and I sat in the family room, talking alone, after I told Belinda to hold dinner for a half hour in case Brad arrived.

"Have you thought about talking to anyone about the dream?" I asked Ennis.

"I just had the dream a couple nights ago. I haven't been able to think about anything other than getting here and investigating."

"I just meant . . . " I cleared my throat. "I work with a psychiatrist. Dr. Pelletier. He's been a big help to me."

"I'm sorry, love. What are you struggling with?"

I wished I could jump back in time thirty seconds and erase what I'd just said. I'd never told Ennis or Patty the truth about my junior year of high school, and I didn't want to get into it now. They did know about my mother's suicide attempt though, and that was still part of what I was dealing with.

"He's helping me deal with what happened to my mother. I've had some anxiety and depression, and I don't want it to affect the baby."

"Of course. And he's helping you?"

I nodded. "He is."

"Honestly, this is the first time I've had a dream that seemed so real. I don't think I need counseling. I just needed to come here and make sure it wasn't true."

"I understand." More than he knew.

Brad walked into the kitchen then and opened the French doors. Ebony and Brandy ran in.

I stood. "Looks like it's time for dinner."

Ennis followed me into the kitchen. Belinda had set the table on the deck out back.

"Hey," I said. "We have company for dinner."

Brad looked up from the dogs. "Oh? Hey, Ennis."

"Hope you don't mind me barging in."

"Not at all. When did you get back in the States?"

"Just this morning, actually."

"Good to see you. I'm going to wash up. You two go ahead and start. Mom's already out there. Thanks for waiting dinner for me." He leaned down and brushed his lips across mine.

"No problem."

Ennis and I joined Mazie on the deck. We made some small talk until Brad arrived.

Belinda's dinner was delicious, but the conversation was mundane. Brad was quiet, and so was Ennis.

I heeded Dr. Pelletier's advice and tried to relax and not attempt to follow every word. It was easy. No one was talking about anything important.

Until Mazie finished and excused herself.

Then, Brad, to my astonishment, turned to Ennis. "What are you *really* doing here?"

Ennis's eyes widened.

"No offense, man," Brad continued, "but no one packs up and heads over the Atlantic without letting their friends know they're coming. Unless they left quickly."

"Brad . . . " I said.

"It's okay, Daph." Ennis forced out a chuckle. "We both know he's right." He quickly explained his troubling dream.

I watched Brad. His facial muscles didn't move as Ennis told his story. Completely immobile. Oddly immobile. As if he were forcing his expression to remain the same.

You're probably imagining it.

I actually heard the thought in Dr. Pelletier's voice.

But I knew my husband. He was off again, just like he'd been during dinner with my parents.

"I understand why you'd be upset by the nightmare," Brad said. "But Patty's parents are the ones who told us she'd decided to join the Peace Corps."

"I know that. But isn't it strange that she just left? Didn't bother telling any of us? We'd just declared our love for each other, for God's sake."

"It does seem strange," I said. "But she's not the first friend to leave me and never communicate with me again. It happened to me in high school." I relayed the story of Sage Peterson's move and failure to answer any of my letters.

"And that doesn't strike you as odd that it's happened twice?" Ennis said.

"If it's happened twice," I said, "maybe it's normal. I don't know."

Ennis wrinkled his forehead.

"I'll tell you what," Brad said. "Since you came all the way here, I'll make some phone calls. I have contacts just about everywhere. Someone must know someone at the Peace Corps.

I'll try to get confirmation that Patty's working with them."

Ennis nodded eagerly. "That would be great, Brad. Thank you."

"No problem. Always happy to help out a friend." Brad stood. "Either of you care for an after-dinner drink?"

"Not while I'm nursing." Though he already knew that.

"Sure. Anything's fine with me," Ennis said.

Brad left and returned a few minutes later with what looked like two bourbons. "I don't have any decent wine in the house. I'm looking to hire a vintner. Our vineyards bloomed in spring, and we're expecting a hell of a harvest. My father had a top-scale wine-producing facility built on the east quadrant a year and a half ago. If I don't find someone soon, I'll have to arrange to sell our grapes to another winery."

"I know a little about wine," Ennis said.

"You do?" Brad lifted his eyebrows.

"Sounds strange, huh? A Brit who knows about wine?" Ennis chuckled. "I have an uncle who married a Frenchwoman. They live in the Bordeaux region of France, where her father's a winemaker. I've visited there since I was a kid, and my aunt has taught me a lot."

"The job's yours, then."

Ennis laughed. "I said I know a *little*. I can't take the job, of course, but I could help you talk to candidates while I'm here."

"Really?" Brad lifted his drink in a toast. "That would be great. Thanks, man."

"Happy to help. Especially since you're looking into the Patty situation for me."

"I've got a folder full of résumés," Brad said. "I'd love it if you went through them and picked out the ones I should interview. Then, if you can stay awhile, you can sit in on the interviews with me."

"Sure."

"What about your work, Ennis?" I asked.

"I'm between jobs right now. Not an issue."

Odd. Ennis had chosen to leave college and he'd begun working at a marketing firm when he returned to London after Patty left. That was only three months ago. Had he lost his job?

I didn't feel comfortable asking.

Besides, I loved the idea of having Ennis around for a while. It was nice to have a friend again. One that wouldn't pick up and leave and then never communicate with me again.

"If you're going to be around for a while," I said, "you should stay here instead of the hotel. We have plenty of room. Right, Brad?"

Brad's facial muscles tensed, but only for a split second. "Yeah, sure. Love to have you."

"All right," Ennis said. "I appreciate it. I'll pack up in the morning and head back over here."

I left Brad and Ennis enjoying their drinks on the deck and went into the nursery to check on Jonah. He was sleeping soundly, but he'd be up in an hour or so for his evening feeding. I stood over his crib, just staring at his chubby little face, his perfect beauty.

"All for you, little dove. Everything Daddy and I do is for you."

CHAPTER TWENTY-ONE

Brad

Ennis was a good guy, but having him snooping around about Patty wasn't a good thing. Then Daphne invited him to stay with us, which normally wouldn't be an issue. I was still trying to figure out who'd been behind the threats against little Joe and the deaths of Murph and Patty. I couldn't do that with Patty's "jilted lover" hanging around.

The wine thing was a godsend. I'd sent him back to the hotel with a file folder full of résumés to review. I could keep him busy helping me find a vintner while I gathered a fake PI report that Patty was indeed in Africa working for the Peace Corps.

I was disgusted that my father's high-priced PIs hadn't uncovered the culprits behind all these messes. If I didn't know better, I'd have thought someone was paying them off *not* to find anything.

But who had that kind of money? Seriously, who had more money than I did and also wanted to keep this information a secret?

Only the Future Lawmakers had money, and they didn't have the kind of money I had. If they'd offered my PIs something more, I could easily top their offer tenfold.

Then an icicle scraped along my skin.

One thing trumped money.

Life.

I'd seen that in action when my father threatened Dr. Pelletier.

Someone had threatened my PIs.

What else could have happened?

Time to make a phone call to my lead PI. I dialed.

"Morey here."

Jason Morey. Aged forty-three. My father's go-to investigator. He supervised a team of ten who were currently working on our cases. We'd paid them millions over the years. Fucking millions.

"Brad Steel," I said.

"Hey, Steel. What can I do for you?"

"You can tell me who's been threatening you."

A pause. Then, "What the hell are you talking about?"

I cleared my throat. "You and I both know you and your men are the best in the business. It's been nearly a year since my best man was killed at my wedding. Months since my wife's friend was brutally murdered. Since my son was threatened. Yet you've given me nothing."

"We've been through this. Whoever is responsible covered their tracks. Like you said, it's been a year. The trail's gone cold, man."

"You'll never convince me you're *that* incompetent, Morey."

"What the fuck is that supposed to mean?"

"It means exactly what it means. You're the best. My father's top guys. He's told me stories about how you've uncovered needles in haystacks in the past. But this stuff is eluding you? Doesn't make sense."

"Look, I—"

"Save it. We've paid you millions. So either someone out there has paid you more *not* to tell us what's going on, which I doubt, or your lives have been threatened."

Silence on the other end of the line.

Yup. Bingo.

"Spill it, Morey."

"I can't."

"Sure you can."

"Your phone might be tapped."

"I have the best security team in the business. Nothing is tapped in my home."

"What if someone got to your security team?"

My blood ran cold. If someone could get to my PIs, someone could get to my security team.

My father's MO was starting to make sense to me.

And that was fucked up.

What the hell was happening? I was one of the good guys. I had integrity, good faith, good ethics.

I worked hard every day, to the point where I sacrificed time with my wife and son.

And in the end, that wasn't enough.

No. In the end, I was being forced into shoes I didn't want to wear. I was becoming my father.

Fuck it all to hell. Jason Morey was making me question everyone around me. Was this how my father had lived his whole life?

"Meet me, then," I said.

"Tonight? It's already ten."

"It'll be worth your while. There's a pub in the city. It's a dive, but it's safe."

"How do you know?"

"My father told me about it."

★ ★ ★

An hour later, Morey and I sat at a dark table in the pub. A couple of guys sat at the bar, but otherwise the place was empty. We ordered two bourbons.

This was it.

This was a turning point for me. If I couldn't get Morey to level with me, I had to do something drastic.

"Spill it," I said.

"I can't."

"You can. Who's responsible for the murders? For the threats against my son?"

"I don't know."

"Bullshit."

"It's not bullshit, Steel. I actually don't know."

"So you suck as a PI? Is that the shit you're slinging?"

He took a sip of his drink and shook his head. "No. I don't suck. I could have solved this case a year ago."

"I figured as much. Tell me what's going on."

"Someone came to me. Masked. Put a gun inside my mouth and told me if I investigated your case, he'd rape my pregnant wife and make me watch as he cut out the child." He shuddered. "You don't recover from that kind of shit."

Chills ran through me, but I held my face in check.

Whoever we were dealing with was a psycho. A fucking psycho.

"Your wife and kid are okay?"

He nodded. "So far. But these lunatics visit me a couple

times a month to reiterate what they're capable of."

"Where do they visit you?"

"Sometimes at my office. Sometimes at home."

"When Lora's home?"

"Yeah. Sometimes."

"How do you keep it from her?"

"They . . . " Morey shakes his head. "I can't fucking believe this."

"What? What does he do?"

"They inject her with something. She stays out for a couple of hours and then doesn't remember anything."

"Fuck."

"It's terrifying. The first time they did it, she was still pregnant. I was so scared something would happen to the baby. But she's all right, thank God."

"Why didn't you just call me and say you can't do the work? You're still taking my money, Jason."

"That was part of the deal. I take your money. Tell you I'm working on it. That whoever did it has covered their tracks like a pro."

I didn't like where this was headed. In fact, I already knew the answer to the next question.

"And my money? Where does *it* go?"

He closed his eyes and took another drink. "They take most of it. Leave me enough to show that I'm working plus a little extra."

Fuck.

Fuck, fuck, fuck.

How much had my father and I paid Morey and his guys in the last year? I didn't have the exact number, but off the top of my head, it was around five million.

"Who the hell am I subsidizing, Morey?"

"That's just it." He looked around nervously and then whispered, "I don't know."

"Why haven't you left town?"

"I tried. I was packed and ready to go. Lora went into labor."

"And now?"

"I've been told to stay put."

Now what?

"When was the last time the psychos visited you?"

"I don't know. A week ago, maybe?"

"Here's what's going to happen," I said. "Lora and the kid are leaving town. Tonight."

"But—"

"No buts. Get Lora and the baby and head to the airport. I'll have tickets waiting for her."

"This is insane. I'm not sending my wife anywhere."

"You want her safe? Or you want her with you? You have to choose, Morey. If it were me, I'd want my wife safe."

No truer words.

"Safe. Safe, of course."

"You choose the place. I'll make the arrangements."

"Okay. Okay. Then what?"

"I'm going to transfer some money to you. Enough to make them take notice. And the next time the psychos visit you, I'll be there."

CHAPTER TWENTY-TWO

Daphne

The deli owner's daughter held the stuffed dog and gazed at the perfectly sewn-up seam.

So many secrets held inside this doggie.

So, so many.

That last one had been a doozy. Three names. Three names to be locked up forever.

She wouldn't forget, but she needed backup just in case something happened to her. The three names were safe here.

Safe here, along with the other secrets.

The one about the girl named Sage. The one about the girl named Patty.

And all the ones about the young woman named Daphne.

All the secrets.

★ ★ ★

I snuggled Puppy to my face. Why hadn't I brought him home before now? Yeah, it was a little juvenile to keep a stuffed animal from childhood. So what?

Brad had left an hour ago to go out. At ten. I sighed. I was used to his comings and goings at odd hours, but still I hated it.

Ennis was still in Brad's office, reading through winemaker résumés.

The door was ajar, so I entered.

"Hey," I said. "You want me to have Cliff go to town and bring your stuff from the hotel? It's late. You may as well spend the night here."

"Cliff isn't supposed to leave you unguarded," he said.

I let out a soft scoff. "This place is like a vault. No one can get in."

"I'll be fine. If it gets too late, I'll just crash here and pick up my stuff tomorrow."

"Okay. Whatever you want." I nodded to the folder. "Any good prospects?"

"A few. It's nice to have a project."

"Ennis . . . "

"Yeah?"

"What happened in London? With your job, I mean." Yeah, still wasn't my place to ask, but I was curious. I cared about Ennis, and I knew enough about him to know he wouldn't just up and leave.

"Nothing. I quit."

Okay . . . maybe he *would* up and leave. "Why?"

"Simple. I asked for some time off to come here, and they said no."

"Why'd they say no?"

"Because I haven't worked there very long. They asked if it was an emergency, and I said no. I should have lied. Anyway, they said I couldn't have the time off, so I quit."

"Was that wise?"

"I didn't come here for judgment, love. I told you how freaky the dream was. I had to come."

I nodded. "I miss her too."

"Daph, this isn't about missing her. It's about finding the truth."

"If anyone can find the truth, Brad can."

"That's what I'm counting on," he said. "Besides, maybe I'll stay over here. Get myself one of those green card jobbies and work here in the States."

"Won't you miss your home?"

"Of course. But I was ready to stay for four years to study. I only went home because Patty jilted me."

"And you came back because of Patty."

"I did. Which makes me think this is where I should be now."

"Do you think you'll go back to school?"

"I might. My student visa is still valid."

"What if we could find something for you to do around here? On the ranch?"

"I don't think I'm qualified to do anything here."

"Brad already offered you the job as winemaker."

"And I told him I wasn't qualified."

"But you're qualified to *choose* a winemaker?"

"More qualified than Brad is."

I nodded. "All right. Assistant winemaker, then. That'll be your job."

He laughed. "Are you allowed to go around offering jobs on the ranch?"

"Why not? I'm mistress of the ranch, aren't I?"

"I'd love to stay here, but let's see what Brad has to say, okay?"

"All right. Wherever you end up, make sure it's somewhere close. I've missed having a friend around."

"You got it." He shuffled a stack of papers. "These five look like they have the most promise. Where'd Brad go?"

"Out."

"Out where?"

"He didn't say."

"Does he go out this late a lot?"

"More often than I'd like for him to, but not every night, if that's what you mean."

"I'm sorry, love."

I sighed. "His father passed away, and now this place is his to run. He's terribly busy. I understand."

"But . . ."

"But . . . I miss him, of course. I need him. I feel completely self-indulgent saying so. I have so much help around here with the baby. I don't have to cook or clean house. All I have to do is take care of Jonah. It's a dream life, really."

"You know what, love? It sounds like you need a hobby."

"I help Mazie in the greenhouse sometimes."

"Sure, but the greenhouse is Mazie's hobby. What would you enjoy doing?"

"I guess I'd like to finish school. Learn how to write."

"I bet you already know how to write."

"You know what I mean. I want to write something that moves people."

"Do you keep a journal?"

"Funny, Brad just asked me that a few days ago." Of course, he'd asked me if I kept one while I was hospitalized. Ennis still didn't know about that year, and I didn't feel like enlightening him at the moment.

"Did he?"

"Yeah. Weird, I've never kept one."

"You should start. Write down your feelings. What's going on in your life. You want to write? Then write."

"No one wants to read what's going on in my life." God, no.

My life had had its share of heartache and headache.

"This isn't for anyone's eyes but yours. It's a start. It'll get you used to writing."

"Okay. Fair enough. But journaling will take about an hour a day."

"Can you register for a few courses at a local college?"

"The closest would be in Grand Junction. I don't want to be away from Jonah during the day."

"You have your mother-in-law."

"I know."

"So he's in good hands."

"But he's my baby. I don't want to miss a minute with him. Plus, he's still nursing."

"All right. I can see this is a losing battle. Tomorrow we'll go to the bookstore in town."

"What for?"

"To get you some books on creative writing, of course."

I smiled. I liked the sound of that. I liked the sound of that a lot.

CHAPTER TWENTY-THREE

Brad

I got home after one a.m. Daphne and the baby were asleep, and Ennis's car was still at the ranch. He was asleep in one of the guest bedrooms. I yawned as I walked into my office. On the desk was a pile of résumés with a note from Ennis to interview those five.

In the morning, Ennis would find out I had a new job for him. He was going to interview the candidates, because I was going out of town.

Only to Grand Junction, but I couldn't tell anyone exactly where.

I'd be staying at Morey's place until the psycho who was pilfering my money and keeping Morey from investigating my friends' deaths showed up.

And he'd show up. In the morning—well, later *this* morning, as soon as the banks opened—I planned to have a large sum wired to Morey. Larger than ever before. If that didn't draw out the villain, I didn't know what would.

I jerked when the phone rang.

Who the hell would call at this hour?

"Steel," I said into the phone, picking it up before it rang again and woke someone.

"It's me, son."

"Dad, why the hell are you calling me at this hour?"

"An offer will come in first thing tomorrow on one of our private Caribbean islands. I want you to take it."

I shook my head, trying to make sense of his words. "What? Who wants to buy it?"

"A corporation, and they're offering a mint for it. We'll make over ten times what I bought it for a couple years ago."

"What does a corporation want with a Caribbean island?"

"How the hell should I know? And who cares? You're making money on the deal."

"Is money the only thing, Dad? Shouldn't we know who we're selling to?"

"All we need to know is that they have the cash, and they do."

Something stuck in my gut. This didn't feel right.

"Can we possibly discuss this in the morning, Dad?"

"I'm flying out at four a.m. I wanted to reach you before then."

"Oh? Where are you going?"

"I'm going to Jamaica."

"Jamaica? What the hell—"

"I'm following a lead, Brad. A lead on what happened to Sean Murphy and Patty Watson."

"Dad, I just talked to Morey tonight, and—"

"I know. I just found out as well. He's being threatened. I'm trying to find out who they are."

"I'm one step ahead of you, Dad," I said. "I'm going to sniff those psychos out myself."

★ ★ ★

I arrived in Grand Junction at Morey's home the next afternoon. The money had been wired first thing in the morning, and I'd been in touch with Morey, whose phones were most likely bugged, so we'd only talked about the investigation. In the meantime, I parked my truck several miles away and called a cab to take me to Morey's.

Once inside, we settled in for what could be a long haul.

"Do they expect you at your office?" I asked.

"They come to either place. Once they realize I'm not there, they'll come here."

I nodded. Not much to do but wait.

In the meantime, I inspected his residence for any indication of surveillance equipment.

"I've already checked from top to bottom," he said. "There's nothing."

"You sure?"

"I'm a PI, Steel. Of course I'm sure."

Good point. He probably could ferret it out easier than I could.

"How soon after a transfer do they come around?"

"Within twenty-four hours. Usually sooner."

I nodded. "Good. We'll be ready."

"What do you plan to do?"

"Unmask them, for one."

"They'll have guns."

I nodded to my ankle. "So will I, and so will you."

"Already armed," he said. "The problem isn't my ability to defend myself. It's the fact that there's always three of them."

I raised an eyebrow. "Three?"

"Yeah. Always three big guys wearing black ski masks."

No. Couldn't be.

Larry was in law school in Arizona. Tom was a new father and law student in Boulder. And Theo... Well, I never knew for sure where Theo was. And why wouldn't they want me to figure out who had killed Murph and Patty? Who had threatened my son? Besides, if they wanted my money, they'd ask.

Except... the last time they'd asked, I'd made it clear they were cut off.

No.

I was grasping at straws. The number three didn't automatically mean the Future Lawmakers.

So why did my mind automatically gravitate to them?

They'd been my friends. I'd invested in their success.

But now they were getting into drugs. Perhaps they'd been into drugs all along. Time to give my father's files another perusal. Too bad I hadn't brought them with me. I longed for something to do.

"Got any books around here?" I asked Morey.

"A shelf in the extra bedroom." He gestured toward a short hallway. "Help yourself."

I rose and walked toward the room. A small shelf of paperbacks stood beside the bed. Mostly commercial fiction, and none of it looked interesting. I finally grabbed the thinnest one. If Morey was correct, the derelicts would be here soon. No sense getting invested in a long novel.

Twenty-four hours later, we were still waiting.

"I don't get it," I said.

"Don't ask me," Morey replied. "Though I can't say I'm sad they didn't show."

"I'm sure you're not, but I need to find out who these people are. They've been stealing my money and keeping me from finding out the truth."

"I know. I'm sorry."

"I don't give a rat's ass about the money. I want the fucking truth. I want to know who killed my friends and why."

"You still think that woman had something to do with it?"

"Wendy? I wouldn't rule her out."

"She's out now, right?"

"Yeah. In Denver, back in school. I've got someone watching her twenty-four seven."

"Someone you trust?"

I regarded him. "I'd say yes, but until yesterday I thought I could trust you."

"Good point."

My piece itched against my ankle. I could pull it out and threaten Morey. He could easily be playing me.

But I wasn't George Steel.

At least not yet.

CHAPTER TWENTY-FOUR

Daphne

I missed Brad. He hadn't called, but he'd warned me he might not be able to for a day or two. Why worry? I had my wonderful baby and a friend visiting. Life was good.

I'd already devoured one of the creative writing books Ennis and I had found in town yesterday, and I wanted to write. I wanted to describe the beauty of the ranch and how it made me feel. So I strapped baby Jonah into his stroller and decided to take a walk on one of the paths outside the ranch house.

But what would I write on?

I laughed aloud. Ennis and I should have purchased some notebooks while we were in town. I left little Joe in Cliff's care to search for what I needed.

This place had everything. Surely there was some paper around the house. Mazie was out in her greenhouse, and Ennis had gone into town. Belinda was in the kitchen, but she wouldn't know where anyone kept paper.

I started a search.

I opened every drawer I found. Even stationery for writing letters would do. I wasn't picky. After coming up empty-handed, I headed into Brad's office.

I normally stayed out of this room. It was where Brad worked, and I had nothing to do with that. But if there was one place where surely I'd find some paper, Brad's office was it.

The folder with Ennis's recommendations for our winemaker sat on top of Brad's desk. To the right of it sat a yellow legal pad. "Perfect," I said aloud.

Brad had scribbled some notes on the pad, though. I shouldn't take it. But where there was smoke, there was fire. Or rather, another legal pad. I opened the large drawer on the bottom left of his desk first.

I cocked my head.

A notebook sat in the drawer.

A pink notebook that seemed vaguely familiar.

★ ★ ★

The deli owner's daughter picked up the notebook and opened it.

I'm supposed to keep a journal. Write something down every day. I don't know what to write, though. I want to go home. I miss Mom and Dad. I miss Sage. The only thing I have from home is Puppy. I sleep with him every night, but it's not enough. I just want to go home.

Hmm. Interesting. She didn't recognize the handwriting. The deli owner's daughter had a stuffed dog where she kept all her innermost secrets—secrets that could destroy Daphne, whom she kept them from.

What of this journal?

Should she keep this a secret as well?

Something inside her said yes. Not just yes, but an emphatic yes. But this notebook was too big to stuff inside an already stuffed dog.

Where to hide it?

She looked around. This place seemed familiar. Yes, she had been here before. On the phone, actually, when she'd discovered the three names that were now hidden inside her own head and inside the stuffed pup.

The deli owner's daughter was used to turning up in unexpected places. It was how her life went. If she wasn't working at the deli, she was always in a strange place, and she was never sure how she'd gotten there.

It was just life, and she was used to it. She had a job to do. To protect Daphne.

Pull. Slice. Wrap. Hand to customer and smile. "What else can I get for you today?"

The logic of the deli made her life easier. Life without emotion, without fear, was what she was all about.

Now, the problem of the notebook.

It was one thing to memorize information, write it down, and hide it inside a stuffed animal. It was quite another to hide something as big as this notebook.

Perhaps she should just destroy it.

She'd thought about burning things before, but she could never find a match. Especially in the white place. The sterile place. She'd constantly looked for a match there, but she'd never found one.

Almost like they didn't exist in that place.

But here? Perhaps she could find a match. She hastily opened all the desk drawers. No matches. She took the notebook and ambled out of the room and down a hallway. Her nose led the way. Something smelled irresistible, kind of like the yeasty aroma of fresh bread. She knew the fragrance well. The deli baked its bread fresh daily.

This was a white bread, a crusty white bread. It smelled a lot like the pioneer loaf at the deli.

Her nose led her to a kitchen. Good. It was empty. The smell was coming from the oven. She peeked inside. Yes, a loaf was rising and had just started to become golden on top. She closed her eyes and inhaled, taking care to keep her face far enough away from the heat so as not to burn.

But back to the task at hand. Matches.

She methodically opened each drawer and riffled through the items.

Eureka! Finally a box of kitchen matches.

She'd have to go outside to burn the notebook. Safety came first, just like at the deli. Never start a fire in a confined space.

French doors beckoned. She opened them, and two dogs ran up to greet her. Did she know these dogs? Yes, they seemed familiar. She knelt down and petted them on their soft heads. They licked her face.

A moment later, though, she shooed them away. She had a task to complete.

She walked out onto the green grass. It wouldn't do to start a fire on a wooden deck. The dogs nosed around, but once she lit the match, they eased away, bothered by the flames.

She lit a corner of the notebook and watched the orange flame spread. Good thing it wasn't a breezy day. The fire took with no trouble at all, and soon all that was left of the pink notebook was a pile of ashes.

She waited for the ashes to cool, and then she stood and ground them into the grass so no one would see them.

Pull. Slice. Wrap. Hand to customer and smile. "What else can I get for you today?"

Another task completed without emotion.

Nice job. Very nice job indeed.

★ ★ ★

The afternoon sun warmed my face.

"Daphne, there you are."

I turned. Mazie stood on the deck. I waved to her.

"Belinda said you were looking for some paper." Mazie held up several notepads. "Here you go."

Right. I *was* looking for some paper. So why was I outside?

I walked toward Mazie and took the pads. "Thanks. I'm going to take Joe out on a walk and do some writing."

"Sounds wonderful. What are you going to write about?"

"I don't know. The beauty of this place, I guess." I inhaled. Hmm. Was that a faint smell of something burning? It smelled kind of like a campfire.

"Do you smell something?" I asked Mazie.

"No, but I'm a little clogged up today," she said.

"For a minute, I thought I smelled something burning." I shook my head. "I must be imagining it."

"One of the hands might have lit a wood stove or fireplace," she said. "Sometimes the smoke drifts over this way and we can smell it."

"In this warm weather?"

"You never know. It is autumn, after all."

I nodded. "I suppose so. That must be it."

She smiled. "Enjoy your walk, Daphne."

CHAPTER TWENTY-FIVE

Brad

The next day, I was back home. Morey had instructions to get in touch with me if the derelicts came to him, but so far, nothing. He'd assured me they'd always come well within twenty-four hours of a transfer, so this was strange.

Unless he was lying, in which case, I'd find out, and he'd pay.

For now, though, I had to get back to ranch business and my investments. That stuff didn't stop just because I was trying to solve murders—murders that someone was working very hard to keep me from solving.

The offer on the island had come in this morning via courier. The buyer was an entity called Fleming Corporation. They were paying a substantial sum in cash, the property was in escrow, and title was ready to pass as soon as I signed the power of attorney for the lawyer in the area to handle it.

My father had advised me to sign.

That in itself was reason to look into this further before completing this transaction.

If only I had the time.

But this was an island in the Caribbean. Thousands of miles away, and I had other fish to fry. Yeah, maybe it'd be nice to build a resort, make a load of money, have somewhere to vacation for free. I liked the idea, but I didn't have time to build a resort. I had things that were much more important, and if I accepted this offer, I was making a huge-ass return on the original investment.

I signed and called the courier to pick up the package.

I still had its sister island if I wanted to go forward with the resort plan. Right now? Fleming Corporation could have the other. It was one less thing on my plate.

I made several other phone calls and was ready to head to the actual office, when I thought of Daphne's journal. I'd never finished reading it. My hand hovered over the bottom drawer of my desk where I'd hidden it. I sighed. I didn't have time to get involved in the journal now. I'd already spent two days dealing with Morey. Time to do ranch work. Ennis and I had an appointment with a potential winemaker in an hour.

The journal would still be here tomorrow.

★ ★ ★

Since I didn't know shit about making wine, I let Ennis ask most of the questions in the interview. I had to hand it to him. He did a damned good job. By the end, I was ready to hire the guy, but Ennis said we should talk to the others first.

"I've got to get someone started soon, though," I said. "The grapes are nearly done being harvested."

"All right," he said. "What do I know? Give him the job, then."

I ran out of the office and caught our new winemaker before he left. Bruce Gershwin was ecstatic to have the job.

"Ennis will be working with you as your assistant," I said.

Ennis raised his eyebrows. "I will?"

"If I have anything to say about it. Daphne tells me you're thinking about staying in the States."

"If I can get a green card."

"Consider it done," I said. "I'll have my attorneys handle it."

"This is a big step," Ennis said.

"If you're going to turn me down, tell me now," I said. "That way, Bruce can bring in his own people."

"I don't have any people," Bruce said.

"Seems like kismet, then. What do you say, Ennis? You can both hire who you need."

Ennis stood and held out his hand. "Deal, Brad. Thank you."

"Good." I picked up the phone and had a brief conversation with my HR manager. "Lynne is expecting both of you in HR, on the second floor. She'll set you up with your benefits and such. Get your W-4s signed and all that. Oh, Ennis? You'll be getting the same salary as Bruce."

"I will?" His eyebrows nearly flew off his forehead.

"Yeah, is that a problem?"

"Hell, no, but—"

"Good. Go get settled with HR."

Once they were gone, I went over several accounts. I was jarred when the phone rang.

"Steel," I said.

"It's Morey."

"Did they show?"

"Nope. It's the weirdest thing."

"Maybe they flew the coop. Now it's time to do some real research into who killed my friends."

Morey sighed. "Find another PI, then. I'm out."

But you're the best.

The words were on the tip of my tongue, but I didn't let them come out. Truth was, he wasn't the best, or he'd have done the job he was hired to do. Instead, he let himself be threatened by three masked men who stole my money.

"Understood," I said.

"I'm leaving town," he continued. "Lora and the kid are safe with her parents. I'm going to be with them. Colorado has left a bad taste in my mouth."

I couldn't fault his observation.

"Do you have any idea who these guys were?" I asked.

"Not a one."

"Would you tell me if you did?"

Silence.

I had my answer.

The guys had scared him shitless. My best PI—my father's best PI—had been bested by three masked psychos.

"I'll pay you back," he said. "If it takes the rest of my life."

It would, but I didn't say so. "Don't concern yourself about it. Go live your life."

"I'm leaving tomorrow."

"What time?"

"Noon. Flight out of Grand Junction to Syracuse."

"All right. Good luck, man."

"Thanks. Again, I'm sorry."

"Not a problem."

But it was a problem. I'd be paying a visit to Morey.

Tonight.

CHAPTER TWENTY-SIX

Daphne

Brad was away again for dinner.

I should be used to it, but I wasn't.

Good news, though. Ennis was staying in Colorado! Not only that, he'd be working here on the ranch as assistant to our new winemaker. I could see him whenever I wanted to, especially since Brad had invited him to stay at the house until he found a place of his own.

Finally, I had a friend just down the hall who I could always see.

A friend.

I'd had so few in my life, and two of them had moved on without even writing to me. But not Ennis. Ennis was here. He was staying.

He smiled across the kitchen table at me. Mazie wasn't hungry, so she'd skipped dinner, and of course Brad wasn't here. Just Ennis and me, and it felt good. Not as good as if Brad had been here, but good nonetheless.

"Has Brad checked with the Peace Corps yet?" I asked Ennis. "About Patty?"

"Not that he's told me. I'm beginning to see what you mean. He's always doing something. I had to force him to sit down at that interview today, and then he went and hired the very first guy."

"He also hired *you*," I said. "And I think that's terrific."

"Gives me an excuse to stay here, yes," he said. "Still doesn't feel right to be here without Patty."

"Maybe it's time to let her go," I said. "Maybe we both need to let her go, Ennis."

He nodded. "You're right, love. I just didn't want to think our relationship meant nothing to her, and when I had that dream, I had a sliver of hope and a sliver of dread at the same time. I don't want her dead, of course, but part of me wants to believe I meant something to her."

"Of course you did."

"Perhaps. But the Peace Corps apparently meant more. Something she never even discussed with me. It doesn't make any sense."

"It doesn't. But like I said, Patty isn't the first friend who's left me in the dust never to be heard from again, which makes me think maybe it's not that abnormal of a thing."

I jumped when the doorbell rang.

"I'll get it." Belinda hustled out of the kitchen.

She returned a few minutes later with Brad's friend Theo Mathias in tow.

"Hello, Daphne," he said.

Theo was a good-looking man, but he had an edge. A sharp edge that I couldn't quite define. Ever since I'd first met him, when he'd been wearing those weird Halloween blue contact lenses, I'd gotten a weird feeling from him.

Tonight was no different.

"Hi there. Brad's not home."

"I know. Belinda told me. I wanted to come in and say hi."

"Sure. You want to join us? Belinda always makes plenty. This is Ennis Ainsley, by the way. You might have met him at the wedding."

"Sure, good to see you." Theo thrust out his hand.

Ennis stood and shook it. "You too. Have a seat."

They both sat down, and Belinda brought Theo a plate of dinner.

"When do you expect Brad to be home?" Theo asked me.

I suppressed an eye roll. "Late, probably." If I didn't get a call that he was staying in the city. Those calls came a lot.

At least he called.

"Do you mind if I stick around? I've got some business to talk to him about."

"Did you try his car phone?" I asked.

"Yeah. He didn't answer."

"He's probably in a dinner meeting," Ennis offered.

I loved this man. If Brad hadn't swept me off my feet, I couldn't think of a better man than Ennis Ainsley. But I was Brad's, through and through. Even though I no longer thought of him as perfect, he was still mine, and I still loved him just as much as ever.

"What kind of business are you in?" Ennis asked Theo.

Good question. I had no idea. Honestly, I'd never thought about it before.

"This and that," Theo replied.

"Ennis is working with us now here on the ranch," I piped in. "Brad's starting a new wine business, and Ennis is helping."

"Oh?" Theo raised his eyebrows.

"Guilty," Ennis said.

"Good for you. Great business, wine."

"Are you familiar with the business?"

"Only in an ancillary way," Theo said. "People will always want alcohol."

"Good winemaking is an art," Ennis said. "It's not just about the alcohol."

"True enough." Theo brought a bit of food to his mouth, letting it hover while he spoke. "Just saying the fact that it's alcohol certainly won't hurt you."

"Are you in the alcohol business?" Ennis asked.

"I have been, in the past. Anything that helps people escape the everyday doldrums is good business."

"Everyday doldrums?" I said.

"Of course," Theo said. "People need an escape. Tom, Larry, Wendy, and I have specialized in escape. Getting people what they want, you know?"

"Wendy?"

"Yeah. You know we all started a business back in high school, right?"

Sounded vaguely familiar. "She's back in school now." I dropped my gaze to my lap.

"She is. Doing well, from what I hear."

"Do you keep in touch with her?" I asked.

"I keep in touch will all my friends from high school," Theo said. "You never know when you might need an old friend."

"What kind of business do you want to talk to Brad about?" I asked.

"A new venture," he said. "Nothing that would interest you."

"Anything my husband does interests me."

"It's still in the preliminary stages," he said. "Tom, Larry, and I have made a commitment. We'll be going into some intensive training next summer."

"Oh?"

"Yeah. Tom and Larry wanted to finish the school year first. The training will last three months, so they'll be back to continue their law school in the fall."

"I see." Though I didn't see at all. "And you want Brad to go in with you?"

"If he's up for it."

"Brad doesn't have three months to go off for some kind of training. He has a ranch to run. And he has a son."

"Tom has a son too."

No way. No way was Brad leaving us for three months next summer. Who would run the ranch?

"Brad won't be interested," I said, sounding much more confident than I felt.

After all, Brad wasn't here right now. He was out. Working. Away from his family.

Theo finished his dinner and stood. "Thanks for dinner. Tell Brad I'll be in touch."

"Of course." I stood. "I'll see you out."

I didn't want to see him out. I got such a bad feeling from him. That sharp edge that permeated his demeanor.

But I faced him. Took a good look at Theodore Mathias.

And jerked at what I saw.

CHAPTER TWENTY-SEVEN

Brad

I was wearing a black ski mask.

Black pants, a black sweatshirt, black gloves—thin fabric so as not to hamper my shooting—and a black fucking ski mask.

I opened the door to Morey's house in the city. It was unlocked, as I'd had a locksmith come by earlier to take care of that.

He was no doubt in bed, so I crept upstairs.

Yes, there he was. I grabbed my piece from my holster and held it to his temple.

"Wake up, Morey," I said gruffly.

When he didn't respond, I pressed the gun more firmly into his flesh. "I said wake up!"

He jerked and then gasped.

"That's right," I said. "Did you think we forgot you? Forgot about the money?"

"Fuck. What is it?"

"You know what it is. We want our share."

"Where are the other two?"

"Downstairs," I lied. "Make the arrangements."

"It's the middle of the night."

"It's ten p.m."

"I have to leave for Denver in the morning. I went to bed early."

"Start talking," I said. "We know you've been talking to Brad Steel. What did you tell him?"

"Nothing. Nothing, of course."

"Right. Don't fucking lie, or I'll blow your fucking head off."

"He figured it out. He knows I haven't been working his case."

"He figured it out? Or you *told* him?"

"I swear. He figured it out. He knows I'm the best. I told you this would happen. Steel's not stupid. He might not be the shrewd guy his old man was, but he's far from foolish."

I wasn't as shrewd as my old man, huh? The words stung, not because they were true—they weren't—but because Morey thought they were. The PI had a lot to learn.

I'd kept myself from pulling a gun on him previously because I'd decided I wasn't my old man.

Turned out, maybe I was a chip off the old block after all.

I didn't like the idea, but I'd learn to live with it. You could learn to live with a lot of things given no choice.

At this point, I had no choice.

I had to protect my wife and child. Preserve the legacy, even if it meant my own descent into hell. I didn't matter anymore. Only Daphne and Jonah. The other children we'd have.

My legacy was for them.

I'd make sure they never had to resort to what I was resorting to now.

This was my first step. "You didn't tell him, then, that you know who was behind the murders and the threats to his son."

"I didn't. I swear I didn't."

Right. My hunch had been correct. He knew. Now, how

to get him to fess up without him figuring out I was under this mask?

"Get up," I said harshly.

"Your gun."

"What about my gun? It's not going anywhere." I nudged him in the temple.

He moved slowly, his eyes wide. He sat up.

"Please. I'm done. I'm leaving town. When you didn't come around within twenty-four hours, I figured you were done with me. I won't be an issue. Just let me go."

"You know a little too much for that. How am I supposed to let you live?"

"Because my word is as good as gold."

"Is it? You told Brad Steel you'd investigate his case. Your word wasn't so good then, was it?"

"Please. Just let me be. I have a family."

"So does Steel."

"I know that. He ... Since when do you even care about Steel's family?"

"I don't." Dumbass move on my part. "I told you to get the fuck up."

He rose, trembling. He wore a T-shirt and pajama bottoms. While still holding the gun on him, I fished a piece of paper out of my pocket. "Here's where you'll send our portion of that last deposit." I handed it to him.

"This is a different account number."

"So?"

"So ... in all the time we've been doing this, nothing ever changed."

"Things change sometimes, asshole. Why do you think we haven't been here? We were working on moving things around."

Good save on my part.

"Right. Okay. I can't call in the transfer until morning."

"Yeah, you can."

"But—"

"Why do you think we moved things around? To get round-the-clock service, that's why. Make the fucking call."

In reality, my father had set up round-the-clock service years ago. Whoever the psychos dealing with Morey were, they didn't have my connections. At least not yet.

Good to know.

Morey walked slowly to the phone sitting on a table in the corner of his bedroom. I held the gun firmly at his head as he dialed and made the transfer.

"Where's your gun?" I asked.

"Same place it always is," Morey said.

Yeah, he was good. A good PI had good instincts. At least I'd gotten my money back. Far from all I'd paid him in the past year, but the big chunk I'd deposited to draw out his tormenters.

Too bad it hadn't worked.

"I want all your files," I said.

"I've given you all the information I came up with."

Another thing I'd been afraid of. "Why don't I believe you?"

He trembled. "I'm leaving town, damn it. Why do you have—"

"Shut up!" I rammed the gun into his nose.

He winced.

"I happen to know you haven't forked over everything. Get the damned files. Now."

Another hunch paid off.

"In my office. Downstairs."

"Let's go, then."

I held the gun on him while we walked down the stairs and to the spare room he used as an office on his first floor. Would he notice the two others weren't there? Maybe, but I kept the gun trained on him. I was his worst nightmare at the moment.

He opened a file cabinet and pulled out several manila folders. "This is everything."

"Everything, huh?"

"Everything you don't already have."

"Just so I'm certain, you're going to sit down at your little desk here and write down everything you know about this case. Every fucking thing. Got it?"

"But—"

"You want to live to see your wife and kid again?" I nudged the gun against his temple.

"But what's the point? You already have—"

"I'll take that as a no." I cocked the gun.

"No! Please. I'll do it. I'll write it all down. Everything I can remember."

"Good. You do that."

"It's a lot of information."

"Of course it is. Now start writing."

CHAPTER TWENTY-EIGHT

Daphne

I'd taken Dr. Pelletier's advice to heart. I'd tried to stop observing every little detail about everything.

But it was a difficult habit to break. I was still determined not to lose a moment of time.

Theo stood before me, his demeanor as unreadable as it always was.

Except something stood out. Something I'd never noticed before, no matter how observant I'd been.

Theo Mathias had cold eyes. They were dark brown, yes, but they were as cold as they'd been the first time I'd met him, when he was wearing icy blue contact lenses.

"I'll be sure to tell Brad you stopped by," I said again.

"Thank you, Daphne." He reached toward me and pulled me into an awkward hug. "Good to see you."

"You too."

Then he was gone, as mysteriously as he'd come.

★ ★ ★

Something warm cupped my cheek. "Hey, baby."

I opened my eyes and smiled. "Brad."

"Sorry, I didn't want to wake you, but once I saw you lying there so beautiful, with your hair splayed on the pillow like a silky curtain, I had to wake you. Had to see your smile."

"I'm glad you're back. What time is it?"

"Four a.m."

"Why didn't you stay in the city?"

"That would have made more sense, but I couldn't stay away from you any longer. I need you, Daphne." He pressed his lips to mine in a soft kiss.

"I need you too. So much. Come to bed?"

"Absolutely." He rustled around, undressing, and then slid into bed next to me, opening his arms.

I snuggled into them and kissed his warm neck, inhaling his spicy scent. That scent I'd never get enough of.

"Make love to me," I murmured.

He slid his hand under my pajama bottoms and ran his fingers over my folds. "Mmm. You're already wet."

"Always for you, Brad. I'm always here, always waiting for you."

"So warm and soft." He withdrew his fingers and traced my lips with them.

I licked them, tasted myself on him. My own flavor. Tangy and sweet.

"That's hot," he said.

I closed my eyes, embarrassed.

Then he kissed me, slid his lips over mine, and I opened for him. The kiss was soft and gentle at first, but soon it morphed into a wild kiss of need and desire. Brad lifted my T-shirt and grabbed one of my breasts. My nipple hardened instantly.

I wanted his mouth on me. Everywhere on me.

He continued the kiss for a few more blissful moments, and then he broke it, gasping.

"God, what you do to me. You're everything, Daphne.

Everything beautiful in the world. Knowing you're here makes everything easier."

Makes everything easier?

Was something bothering my love?

I didn't have time to ponder the question further, though, because he slammed his lips down onto mine once more.

I lost myself in the kiss. I let everything in me become that kiss, that beautiful joining of lips that showed me passion beyond measure.

My body throbbed. I felt my own juices against my inner thighs. I was ready, so ready.

He squeezed my breast again, this time harder. I broke the kiss and cried out.

"Okay?" he asked.

I nodded. It hadn't hurt. It was just harder than he usually squeezed.

He crawled downward a bit and took a hard nipple into his mouth. The tingling. My milk was letting down.

It would make a mess.

I didn't care.

"So sweet," he murmured against my flesh.

My milk? My nipple? Or me?

Didn't matter.

Didn't matter at all.

"Need you," I said.

"Mmm. Need you too, baby."

Could I ask for what I wanted? Did I have the gumption?

"Brad," I said, panting. "I want you to . . . go down on me."

He dropped my nipple and smiled. "My pleasure."

He crawled farther down my body and removed my pajama bottoms. Then he spread my legs.

"God, you're beautiful. So wet and ready for me." He touched my clit.

Just a tiny touch, and I nearly flew off the bed.

He smiled. "So responsive. So hot." He slid his fingers over me and inserted one.

I nearly flew off the bed again.

"Does that feel good? My finger inside you?"

"Yes. God, yes."

"You want my mouth on you, baby?"

"Please."

He twisted his finger slightly, hitting something inside me that made me insane. I lifted my hips without meaning to.

"There are all kinds of places inside you," he said. "All kinds of pleasure points."

Cool. Great. Now get your mouth on me.

As if he could read my mind, he lowered his head and flicked his tongue over my pussy, his finger still moving in a strange figure eight kind of way. God, he was hitting something. Something amazing. When he added his tongue to the mix, swirling it around my clit and then sucking my folds into his mouth, I knew I wouldn't last long.

"Mmm," he said against my vulva. "I haven't taken enough time with you lately. There's so much to show you. To teach you. So, so much." He licked at me once more, twisting his finger and then adding another.

"You like that? How I stretch your pussy open?"

"I like everything you do to me, Brad."

"I like doing it. I love doing it, Daphne. I love bringing you pleasure. It pleases me to please you."

I trailed my fingers over my chest and cupped my breasts. Then I touched my nipples. God, so sensitive. I gave one a pinch and nearly flew off the bed for a third time.

"Feel good?" Brad asked. "Does it feel good to touch yourself?"

"Yes," I said on a moan. "Feels so good."

"Make it feel good, baby. I'll eat your pussy, finger-fuck you, and you make those sweet little nipples feel good, okay?"

His words were crass. But God, they turned me on. How could I be turned on by mere words?

It added a whole new level to what I was feeling.

I closed my eyes, pinched my nipples, reveled in what Brad was doing between my legs, and before long, the feeling I'd come to know surged like an electric current through my body.

"Brad! God, Brad!"

My hips undulated, seemingly of their own accord, as I moved with the rhythm of my body, moved with the rhythm of Brad's tongue and fingers.

The climax was swift in coming but stayed longer than normal.

"Keep going, baby. That's it. Keep going."

As if in obedience to his words, I did. I kept it going. I came. I came. And I came again.

I was lost in a kaleidoscope of swirling emotion and colliding physical sensations.

And then—

Brad was inside me, thrusting. His cock so hard, stretching me into another climax and then another.

"This," he said through gritted teeth, sweat dripping onto my neck from his brow. "This. This is why I do everything. For you. All for you, Daphne."

My orgasm finally subsided, but still he pumped into me.

Harder and harder and harder, his words still hovering around us.

This is why I do everything. For you. All for you, Daphne.

CHAPTER TWENTY-NINE

Brad

Once she'd fallen asleep, I returned to my office where I'd hastily stashed the notes from Morey. I'd thrown them in the bottom drawer where I kept Daphne's journal.

It had taken every ounce of willpower not to read them as soon as he gave them to me. I'd resisted only because I needed to get home to Daphne. Needed to make love to her. Needed to remember why I was doing all of this.

Had I read them first?

I might have forgotten. Neglected her again.

I had to stop doing that.

Now, though... Now I was going to find out who had taken our friends from us.

I picked up the notes and began to read his hasty scrawling penmanship.

None of the names were familiar to me save one.

The one I'd always known was behind this terror.

Wendy Madigan.

A scream lodged in my throat. I couldn't wake Daphne and the baby. Couldn't wake Ennis and my mother.

How had she managed this while she was locked up and drugged?

She'd had help. From whoever had been using my name to

sneak in to see her. Had it been Theo? I didn't know, though he seemed the most likely suspect. Tom was busy with law school and his new son. Larry was busy with law school and his new fiancée.

Neither of them were anywhere near Grand Junction.

And none of their names appeared anywhere in Morey's report. Only Wendy's name. She hadn't been acting alone, but she hadn't been acting with those three, either.

How had this happened? How had I let it happen?

I'm so sorry, Murph. I'm so sorry, Patty. Fuck. I'm so damned sorry.

My head fell into my hands as my gaze dropped to the open drawer.

And a brick hit my gut.

Daphne's journal was gone.

Who had taken it? Had she read it herself? Even so, if she had, what could I do? It belonged to her, and I'd kept it from her.

Daphne.

Daphne and my son.

To keep them safe from harm—all harm—I'd do whatever I had to.

Some of it wouldn't be pretty, but I'd do it anyway.

And I finally understood my old man.

CHAPTER THIRTY

Daphne

Five years later...

The deli owner's daughter cut the seam on the stuffed dog's belly methodically.

Inside were all the notes she'd hidden over the years—hidden from Daphne to protect her.

The rape.

The suicide of Sage Peterson.

The names of Daphne's rapists.

The burning of her journal.

Brad's infidelity with the woman named Wendy.

The subsequent pregnancy, resulting in Ryan.

The deli owner's daughter had taken over for the whole nine months that time. As far as Daphne knew, Ryan was her child.

And other secrets. Other secrets only the deli owner's daughter knew.

She stuffed the notes back into the toy. Then she went to a dresser drawer, opened it, and withdrew a small pad of paper and a pen.

She scribbled a quick note and inserted it into the opening of the stuffed dog. She resewed the seam perfectly.

Pull. Slice. Wrap. Hand to customer and smile. "What else can I get for you today?"

For now, her work was done.
She closed the shop.

CHAPTER THIRTY-ONE

Brad

Seven years later...

"I'm pregnant, Brad."

My beautiful wife stood before me, her body and face unlined and as youthful as when I'd first laid eyes on her. She'd given her life to our three children—even though one of them hadn't come from her body—and still she was as radiant as she'd been at eighteen.

I'm pregnant, Brad.

My heart dropped to my stomach. Joy filled me—joy encased in dread.

My wife was pregnant. We'd made another child together. I loved my children, and I'd love another just as much. My heart was big enough for Daphne and all my children.

But this was not good news, for reasons I alone knew.

"What happened? Weren't you taking your pill?"

"Of course I was. Things happen sometimes."

Things happen sometimes.

I'd considered a vasectomy seven years ago. When Wendy gave me her ultimatum. When I'd made one of the biggest mistakes of my life.

But I had a beautiful third son to show for it, so I couldn't be unhappy at the turnout.

Except for what it had cost my wife.

She'd spent days in bed sometimes when the depression took her. She was perfect when she came out of it, though.

Should have gotten the fucking vasectomy. Part of the bargain I'd struck with Wendy was that Daphne and I would no longer have sex. I didn't have a choice. Wendy had shown me irrefutable evidence linking me to horrific illegal activities. All counterfeit, of course, but they'd hold up in any court of law.

Not even all my money could get me out of what she'd fabricated. I'd looked into everything.

Making the deal had been one thing, but I had no intention of keeping the promise. What Wendy didn't know wouldn't hurt her. Daphne had been on the pill since Talon arrived anyway, and it had worked just fine.

Until now.

Daphne's lips turned into a slight frown. "You look like you're about to be sick, Brad. This is good news, isn't it? It is for me. Maybe I'll get that girl I've always wanted."

I forced a smile. "Yes, of course, baby. It's good news. Have you been to the doctor?"

"Last week. I just got the call. I missed my period last month—"

"You did?"

"Yeah. I didn't think anything of it because of the pill. But I've been more tired than usual, and I started feeling nauseated about a week ago. A feeling I knew well. Still, I figured it was just a little bug or something, but I decided it wouldn't hurt to rule out pregnancy. Turns out my hunch was right."

"But the pill."

"The doctor says nothing is a hundred percent except abstinence."

Or a vasectomy. Fuck. Why hadn't I done it?

I'd been a fucking coward. I didn't want any doctor going near my balls. That was what I told myself at the time.

But it wasn't the real reason.

I was still fighting against Wendy. Against the control she had over my life.

Fucking bitch.

She could tell me not to sleep with my wife, but she couldn't be here twenty-four seven to make sure I didn't.

I loved my wife. Not being able to make love to Daphne? I might as well be dead.

My mind raced. What now? As soon as Wendy found out about the pregnancy, she'd know I'd broken my promise.

This was a child, though. Wendy wouldn't hurt a child. At least not one of mine.

I felt certain.

"Mom? Dad?" Jonah, nearly thirteen, stood in the doorway of my office.

"What is it, son?"

"I want to meet Bryce in town. Can one of you drive me?"

"We're kind of busy, Joe," I said. "See if Belinda can take you."

"She's not here. She must have gone out on errands."

"Your grandmother?"

"She's busy in the greenhouse."

"Sorry, Joe, we're bus—"

"It's okay, honey." Daphne smiled. "I'll drive you. I want to pick up some stuff at the pharmacy anyway."

Jonah flashed his signature Steel smile—so like mine. All three of my sons favored me, but Joe ... He was almost like my clone.

"You're the best, Mom. I'll wait for you in your car."

"Fine," Daphne said. "I'll only be a minute."

Once Joe was gone, she continued, "I didn't expect you to be so upset, Brad."

"I'm not upset, baby. But Ryan is seven. Are you sure you want to do this all over again?"

"Of course I do. You're not suggesting . . ."

"No." Even if I dared to suggest abortion, Daphne wouldn't go for it. She'd had Joe at nineteen because she refused to have an abortion. She felt very strongly about it.

"Good," she said adamantly.

"I guess we're having a baby, then," I said, trying to sound happy about it.

Indeed, I *was* happy about it. I loved all my kids, and I'd love this one. I'd been working my ass off for the last thirteen years to provide something amazing for them—a world where they could all live good lives and keep their integrity.

The integrity I'd had to say goodbye to long ago.

"I'm going to drive Joe into town, like I said." Daphne looked wistful. "Take the hour I'm gone to get used to the idea."

I stood as she walked out of the office.

"Mommy!" Ryan ran up to her in tears. "I scraped my finger!"

Daphne knelt down to his level. "Let Mommy have a look."

"It hurts!"

"What did you do, sweetheart?"

"I scraped it outside. On the deck. There was a nail sticking out."

"Brad, I asked you to fix that!" Daphne glared at me, anger in her dark eyes. Then she focused on her son.

Yes, he was her son.

He hadn't come from her body, but she loved him like she loved Jonah and Talon. Anyone witnessing her right now could see it.

"Let's get you a bandage, okay?" She stood and pulled Ryan into her arms.

He leaned his head on her shoulder and sniffled.

"Brad, can you please drive Jonah into town? I need to take care of this."

I nodded.

My Daphne was the most amazing mother in the world. Just as she would be to the new child she carried inside her.

I'd make sure she had the best care, as I always did. This child would be healthy and happy like the other three.

It would cost me.

I just didn't know how much yet.

I grabbed the keys to my truck and found Jonah waiting in Daphne's car. "Change of plans, bud. I'm driving you. Mom had an emergency."

"Is she okay?"

"She's fine. Your brother scraped his finger on one of those loose nails on the deck."

Jonah laughed. "I bet you're in trouble now!"

"I was supposed to fix those yesterday. Can you do it when you get back from Bryce's?"

"Yeah. I'll do it. Anything for Mom."

My boys were devoted to Daphne, nearly as devoted as she was to them. It was beautiful to behold.

I did my best. I taught them ranch work, orchard work. They even hung with Ennis in the winery from time to time. He'd taken over for Bruce after a couple of years, and he was our master winemaker now. A Brit. Go figure. He sure made great wine, though.

I kept them busy while they were home and saw to it that they kept their grades up at school. They went to public school in Snow Creek. No Tejon Prep in Grand Junction for them.

I'd paid dearly for going there.

In fact, my boys knew nothing of my high school days. I'd told them I went to Snow Creek Schools, just like they did.

I didn't like lying. I'd never developed a taste for it, but damn, I'd become good at it over the years. I still wasn't quite as good as my old man was.

My old man.

He'd called me thirteen years ago and said he was going to Jamaica.

I'd never heard from him again.

He could be dead, for all I knew. Hell, everyone else thought he'd been dead for over thirteen years.

I hadn't given him a thought in a decade.

But now? I wanted his advice.

Because when Wendy found out about Daphne's pregnancy, there'd be hell to pay.

CHAPTER THIRTY-TWO

Daphne

I didn't have favorites.

Jonah was my first, and boy, was he ever his father's son. Not just in looks but in temperament.

Talon had a gentleness about him that reminded me of myself as a child. I'd been shy and somewhat introverted. Talon cared so much about others. He brought in baby birds and abandoned kittens.

And dogs. They were his real weakness. Every stray that came by became a new project for my Talon.

Then there was Ryan, whose wound I was cleansing with Bactine at the moment.

"It stings, Mommy!"

"I know, sweetie, but it only lasts a minute." I pressed a bandage onto his finger. "All better?"

He smiled. What a radiant smile this little boy had. He was more pretty than handsome, with delicate features and full red lips. Definite male model material. Not as rugged in looks as Joe and Talon.

I didn't remember much about being pregnant with him. I'd been so good about losing time over the past years, but that chunk of time was one that eluded me.

I didn't worry so much about time loss these days, though.

I was a busy ranch wife and mother of three.

I patted my belly. Soon to be mother of four.

Three children were more than a handful. Add in a fourth and ...

Of course, the boys were bigger now. Jonah was nearing thirteen and didn't need me as much. The thought saddened me a little, but it was the way of things. My little dove would leave the nest eventually, and I had to get used to the idea.

This baby, in some ways, would make up for that. I'd have a new little one who needed me. A new little angel to devote myself to.

This would be my girl.

I knew it in the depths of my soul, just as I'd known the others were boys. All except Ryan. I didn't remember having those thoughts while pregnant with him.

I didn't remember anything at all.

Obviously I'd been lucid. I'd taken care of my other two children, who had thrived, so I must have been doing something right, even though I didn't recall what.

I kissed Ryan's tear-stained cheek. "Go find your brother and play, okay?"

He nodded.

Just a bandage and a kiss and all was better.

How wonderful to be a child—to have no worries other than being sheltered, fed, and loved.

And my children were all loved beyond measure.

I was loved beyond measure, as well. Not just by my children but by my husband.

I just wished it were enough to heal me, to keep me from ever losing another second of my life. I'd stopped going to therapy after Talon was born. I was struggling with potty-training Joe, and Talon had colic and required a lot of attention.

I didn't regret a minute sacrificed to my children.

But I feared I might have sacrificed myself a little bit.

Perhaps it was time to return to therapy. The boys were older now, and we had full-time help. I patted my belly once more.

"I'm going to fix myself," I said to my unborn daughter. "I'm going to fix myself for good this time."

Summer was my favorite time of the year. The boys were home from school, all my favorite flowers were in bloom, and now I was blooming as well with a new child growing inside me.

The boys and I were set to take a trip to Disneyland in a few weeks. I was determined to get there, even with morning sickness. My first pregnancy had been tough, and I'd ended up on bedrest. Talon, my second, had been much easier. I still had morning sickness, but after the first trimester, I was much better. My body cooperated a lot more, and I didn't need to be on bedrest. He'd come early at thirty-six weeks, but he was still an eight-pound bouncing baby boy.

Then there was Ryan. I wished I knew how that pregnancy had progressed. Brad never talked about it. Whenever I brought it up, his response was always, "Daphne, we always said we'd never speak of it again."

Not speak of my pregnancy?

Seemed like a strange deal to have made, but since I didn't remember any of it, perhaps I had. I stopped asking after a while. Now that I was facing another pregnancy, though, I needed to know how my last one had gone.

Easy enough. My doctor would have the records. I'd ask

him when I went in for my next visit in a few weeks. Until then, I'd enjoy the beginning of summer.

The beginning of a new life growing inside me.

★ ★ ★

The deli owner's daughter opened the door to the shop and looked around.

She'd been gone a long time. Everything seemed in order, and she smiled, touching her belly. Daphne's child grew within her, but her main duty was to Daphne herself.

Pull. Slice. Wrap. Hand to customer and smile. "What else can I get for you today?"

Daphne would never ask her doctor for the medical records concerning Ryan's pregnancy. The deli owner's daughter would make sure of it.

CHAPTER THIRTY-THREE

Brad

Joe and Bryce Simpson had been the best of friends since Tom and Evelyn Simpson had moved back to Snow Creek a few years after Tom had finished law school. The boys were around six at the time and went to first grade together.

They'd been drawn to each other like magnet and steel, no pun intended.

I hadn't been thrilled at first, given my history with Tom and the fact that he'd been in the drug business, but soon the two of them had become inseparable. Once Tom assured me he was out of the drug business for good, I'd given Jonah a little more leeway. Eventually he was accompanying Tom and Bryce on their weekend camping trips more often than not.

Until I put a stop to that.

Joe had raised a ruckus, but I was adamant. He could still hang out with Bryce, still be friends, but the overnight visits were over. A young friend of theirs had drowned on Tom Simpson's watch several years ago. Was it an accident? Maybe. Maybe not. One thing was certain, though. My son wasn't doing any more camping trips with the Simpsons.

The son is not responsible for his father's sins.

My mantra, these days. Bryce needed Joe. He was a good kid.

Besides, I had to believe my mantra, because I had to believe I wasn't responsible for my own father's sins.

I'd learned more than I wanted about George Steel in the decade since he'd disappeared, seemingly for good this time.

I'd spent the better part of that decade cleaning up his messes, and he'd left some big ones. Cleaning up after him meant leaving my scruples at the door most of the time.

Damn. That had never been my intention. My intention had been to create a legacy—one built on hard work and integrity—for my own children.

Instead, I'd created one built on secrets, lies, and the occasional crime.

My children would do better. By the time they were ready to take over the family business, I'd see that they'd never have to get their hands dirty.

Then there was Daphne. My Daphne, whom I'd promised to protect no matter the cost.

And the cost had been high so far.

It would only get higher.

Dr. Pelletier and I kept in touch. He no longer saw her for therapy, but I kept him on the payroll just in case I needed him, and there was another reason. I wanted to pay him back for how my father, and then I, had treated him in the past. He truly had helped Daphne. She never knew what her actual diagnosis was. Dr. Pelletier had wanted to tell her, but I'd begged him not to. It would only open a can of worms, which might lead to her discovering what had truly happened to her when she was only sixteen years old.

I couldn't do that to her.

I just couldn't.

She loved Ryan as much as the sons from her own body.

We agreed never to speak of that time, and though she sometimes asked, I never indulged her.

I relived that time eight years ago more often than I wanted to, and still, I couldn't regret it.

It had brought me my third son—Ryan favored me but had finer features and slightly lighter eyes and hair than his brothers.

But it had cost me so much in other ways.

Some of which I hadn't even discovered until recently.

Which gave me another reason to keep Joe from going on sleepovers with Bryce and his father anymore.

Tom, Theo, and Larry had indeed gotten in bed with gangsters. They'd become rich men because of it, and they'd been witness to heinous crimes.

Perhaps even taken part in the crimes, but I chose not to think about that.

What could I do about it anyway? Wendy had made sure I could never do a damned thing.

I pulled up into the Simpsons' driveway at their house in town. Tom Simpson ran a satellite office for a major Denver law firm here in Snow Creek. He made a good living.

Still, it was nothing compared to what he stashed away from his other business.

"Here you go," I said. "When do you need to be picked up?"

"I don't know. I can just stay the night."

"No," I said adamantly. "You know the rules."

Joe shook his head, scoffing. "Geez, Dad, I used to spend the night here all the time when I was way younger. I miss those camping trips, you know?"

"You want to go camping? I'll take you camping. Anytime."

He scoffed again. "You never have time."

"Running our ranch is a huge deal. You know that. Besides, you're going to Disneyland with your mother in a few weeks."

"That's for kids. Tal and Ry will love it."

"So will you. You're not quite grown up yet, Jonah."

He didn't reply. Just got out of the truck and slammed the door.

Evelyn Simpson opened the door to the house and let Joe in, and then she came out. I rolled down the window.

"Hello, Brad," she said.

"How are you, Evie?"

She sighed. "Tom's on another trip, and I just got some bad news."

"Oh?"

"A little girl from the kids' school is missing. She's nine, and she hasn't been seen since yesterday."

My skin chilled. "What's her name?"

"Raine Stevenson. She's from the town over but goes to school in Snow Creek. Bryce doesn't know her, but Talon or Ryan might."

"Have the police been called in?"

"I assume so. I'm just beside myself. I just can't even imagine. I wish Tom were home."

I had a feeling I knew exactly where Tom was. Or maybe not. Tom and Theo were too smart to shit where they ate.

Right?

Hell, I had no idea at this point. They'd all gone crazy a long time ago. Tom's wife stood here next to my car, her eyes sad and sunken.

Run away, Evie. Take Bryce and run.

But I couldn't say anything. Not without losing everything dear to me.

"Listen," I said, "if you're worried about staying alone with Tom out of town, you and Bryce are welcome at the ranch anytime. We have all kinds of room."

"I'd hate to infringe on Daphne."

"She loves Bryce and you. Don't you worry about that."

Evelyn sighed again. "We'll be all right."

"I mean it. The offer stands. Anytime."

"You're a good man, Brad. Thank you. I can run Joe home later if you want."

"If it's not too much trouble, that'd be great. Otherwise I can come pick him up."

How easy it would be to tell her Jonah could stay the night. After all, Tom wasn't home, and Joe and Bryce would love it.

But I couldn't. Not without doing a lot of explaining to a lot of people—explaining I wasn't prepared to do.

"I'll be happy to drive him home."

"Why don't you and Bryce come for dinner?"

"Daphne won't mind?"

"Of course not. She'll be thrilled. I'll tell Belinda when I get home."

"Thanks, Brad. It'll be nice to get out of the house."

"Do you happen to have the Stevensons' number?" I asked.

"I don't. Like I said, Bryce doesn't know the little girl. Why?"

"I just want to see if there's anything I can do to help."

And I wanted to find out the details. Where she was when she disappeared, for one. I had a bad, bad feeling about this.

CHAPTER THIRTY-FOUR

Daphne

Dinners at our home were major events with three boys, a hungry dad, plus Mazie and me. Tonight we had Bryce Simpson and his mother as well, and I'd invited Ennis to join us.

Belinda had grilled burgers, the boys' favorite meal in the summer.

We sat outside at the table on the redwood deck.

"Tom's out of town again?" I said to Evelyn.

She nodded and swallowed her bite of burger. "I'm used to it."

"I know."

Evie and I had that in common. Husbands who were out of town a lot. I often wondered how Brad kept this ranch running. Chalk it up to his amazing staff, one of whom was sitting across from me. Our winemaker.

Ennis opened a bottle of young Cabernet Franc. "Tell me how you like this, loves. It was only bottled last year. I'm hoping it's a fruity and noncomplex table wine."

I bit my lip. Now what? Brad had asked me to keep the pregnancy under wraps for now. One sip wouldn't hurt, I guessed, and then I'd say I didn't feel like drinking. Wine all tasted the same to me. Good, but nothing special.

Brad had taken a phone call and was inside. Typical. Still, I loved him fiercely. I always would.

Evie took a sip. "Mmm. It's good. Good with burgers."

"That's what I'm going for. A basic table wine with basic food. I love producing fine wine, but I think Steel Vineyards needs some go-to offerings as well. I can use the franc grapes, and I'm also experimenting with some blends."

"I'm no expert, Ennis," I said, "but it's delicious."

"That's what you say about every wine I bring over here." He laughed.

"Sorry. I'm not an oenophile."

"I'm not either, Ennis," Evie offered, "but this is lovely. Subtle on the taste buds and with a fruity finish and just the right amount of acidity."

"Not an oenophile?" Ennis said. "You described this wine perfectly. The acidity is why it goes so well with food. Makes your mouth water a bit."

"I'm impressed," I said to Evie.

"Don't be. Tom gave me a wine book for Christmas a couple years back. I have no idea why. He hates wine."

"Maybe because he knew you liked it," I said.

"Maybe." She smiled. "He's good that way. He may be busy and leave me alone with Bryce a lot of the time, but I know he's doing it all for us. He always remembers the little things."

I nodded. Evie was lucky.

Brad wasn't quite as good at remembering the little things. He had a lot more on his plate than Tom did, though. Tom might be a busy lawyer, but Brad had a multimillion-dollar ranch to run.

That was what I told myself, anyway.

Talon and Ryan had finished eating and were in the yard

playing with the dogs. Joe and Bryce were each on their third burger. Getting ready for their teen years. Their appetites were off the charts now. Both of them would be thirteen in a matter of days. They were only a week apart, Joe being the older of the two.

They were very much alike. Both tall and broad, like their fathers, but where Joe was dark-haired and dark-eyed like Brad, Bryce was blond and blue-eyed like his own father.

Both handsome as all get-out and already interested in girls. Jonah had just come home earlier in the week with a poster of a blond and silvery-eyed model named Brooke Bailey wearing a royal-blue one-piece swimsuit. I wasn't thrilled, but Brad had let him hang it above his bed.

I tried not to think about what he did at night while gazing at the leggy model.

Some things mothers just didn't need to know.

My two youngest were still my little boys. Oh, they'd be teens before long, but for now, I reveled in their little boy hugs and the little boy scent of their hair. The muddy footprints they tracked in, and their little treble voices calling for me.

Joe's and Bryce's voices had already begun to drop. Within a year, those baby voices would be completely gone.

Brad walked back outside.

"Done with your phone call?" I asked.

"Yeah. Sorry about that."

"Don't worry about it." That was what I always said.

Brad was Brad. He was a provider, and he took his role seriously.

I was dying to tell Evie about my pregnancy, but Brad asked me not to, so I didn't.

The only person who knew, other than us, was my doctor in town.

"Did Brad tell you about Raine Stevenson?" Evie asked me.

"No. Who's Raine Stevenson?"

"A little girl in town. She's been missing since yesterday."

"Missing? You mean she ran away?"

"Unlikely. She's only nine."

My heart dropped. "Then what happened?"

"No one knows."

"Do the boys know her?"

"Joe and Bryce don't. Maybe Talon or Ryan does."

Should I call the boys to the deck and ask? No. If this little girl was their friend, I didn't want to upset them.

I looked to Brad. He said nothing.

So I said nothing.

Story of my life.

I was used to it.

CHAPTER THIRTY-FIVE

B r a d

I listened with half an ear.

The phone call I'd just had pervaded my mind.

The little girl hadn't been found, and the police had no leads.

And Tom Simpson was out of town.

I didn't like how these cards were stacking up.

You could be wrong. You could be totally barking up the wrong tree.

But I wasn't. I felt it in my gut.

No child had disappeared from Snow Creek in four years—not since a child had presumably drowned on Tom Simpson's watch.

It was a mess. I'd helped Tom pay off the parents to move out of town, so he could keep his good name, and no one else was the wiser.

Except I knew.

And I had to live with that.

Justin. That was the kid's name. A boy who was being bullied at school, and Joe and Bryce had befriended him.

They were good boys. Really good boys. That was how I knew my son would not grow up to be like me.

Thank God.

I hadn't wanted to grow up to be like my old man, but here I was, a damned clone of him.

Using my money to make things go away.

I'd done some research after the drowning—research into what the Future Lawmakers and their gangster cohorts were really into.

What I'd found had nauseated me.

Still did.

I wasn't sure Justin had actually drowned, but I pushed it to the back of my mind.

I didn't let myself think about it for one reason and one reason only. I could do nothing. Wendy had seen to that.

All my resources, and I couldn't stop the horror that these men—whom I'd once considered friends—were doing to others, to the most vulnerable.

I checked my watch.

It was time.

I stood. "Excuse me for a minute, please."

Daphne and Evie nodded.

I walked into the house and down the hallway to my office.

I dialed the number—the number that was engraved in my mind.

"Hello, Brad," the icy voice said.

I cleared my throat. "Wendy."

"Right on time, as usual."

"We have a deal, don't we?"

Our deal was she'd stay out of my life and my son's life as long as I called her weekly and told her all about him. I opened my desk drawer and took out the gold ring I hadn't worn in years. For some reason, I always fidgeted with it when I talked to Wendy.

I wasn't sure why.

Maybe because she had designed it. Maybe because the ring represented a time when Wendy actually meant something to me.

As a horny teenager, I'd thought I loved her.

Now I hated her.

Hated her for what she'd done to me. To Daphne.

What she had the power to do.

"How's my son?"

"He's fine. He's happy that school's out. He's playing with Talon out back right now."

"Are you still taking him to Disneyland in a few weeks?"

"Daphne is taking them. I can't make it."

"Oh?"

"You know how busy the ranch keeps me."

"And you trust Daphne to care for my son?"

"Damn it, he's *her* son. She adores him as much as she does Joe and Talon. Ryan is in the most loving hands on the planet."

"If I thought he wasn't, trust me, he wouldn't be there."

"We made a deal a long time ago, Wendy."

"We did. And I never renege on my deals."

"Neither do I."

Except I had. I'd continued to make love with my wife. What Wendy Madigan didn't know wouldn't hurt her.

But now, Daphne was pregnant.

And Wendy would eventually find out.

My only solace was that she kept herself busy as an investigative reporter and also with the Future Lawmakers. She'd stayed in business with Tom, Theo, and Larry.

And the gangsters, I assumed. The gangsters who were

in such a dirty business, I couldn't allow myself to think about it. How had I been blind to it for so long?

I shuddered at the thought. All those times I'd allowed my son to go camping with Tom Simpson.

All those fucking times . . .

"I want to see him," she said.

She said that every time. And every time, I told her, "You know the rules, Wendy. You agreed to them."

Ryan was her one Achilles' heel. For most of her life, I'd held that title, but now Ryan trumped even me.

"Do you ever wish things could be different?" she asked.

"Of course."

But I meant something entirely different than she meant. I wished I'd never gotten involved with her in the first place. I wished Daphne and I and our family could live in peace.

But then you wouldn't have Ryan.

Always the same argument with myself. I was stuck between a rock and a hard place. Really stuck.

Wendy had dug her claws deep into me, and there was no escape. I'd given up any escape from her the night I'd found her in Talon's nursery, a knife hovering over him.

★ ★ ★

"Put that knife down, Wendy."

I ran to the crib and picked up the sleeping Talon. He was a good toddler. He slept well. I shook him gently and kissed his little forehead, begging him silently to stay asleep.

Fuck. This was my fault. We hadn't had any trouble in years, and Cliff had the week off.

I'd gotten careless.

Wendy never could have gotten past Cliff. As it was, I had no idea how she'd bypassed the security system.

"I'm ovulating."

"Do you think I care?"

"You're going to fuck me, Brad. You're going to give me that baby we lost all those years ago."

"Dream on. Now get the fuck out of here and leave us in peace."

"You either give me a child, or I take one of yours. This one." She raised the knife.

I could easily disarm her, but I'd have to put Talon down. If he woke and cried out, Daphne would come in and find Wendy.

I couldn't let that happen.

"I'm happy in this life," I said. "Why can't you let me be happy?"

She laughed. Softly enough not to wake Talon, though, thank God. Did she truly have a tiny bit of compassion for my child?

"You and I both know you'll never be happy the way you could be with me. But I've accepted your choice. I accepted it long ago, Brad. Now you're going to have to accept mine."

"I don't have to accept shit."

"I'm going to have your child."

"No, you're not."

"I think you'll change your mind."

"When pigs fly, I might."

She laughed again softly. "You always had a sense of humor. I love that about you. I've always loved you, Brad, and I always will."

She said those words a lot, and I never knew what to say in response. I didn't love her. Looking back, I wasn't sure I ever did.

If so, only as a teenager loves his first love.

Antisocial personality disorder. That was what Dr. Pelletier had diagnosed for Wendy.

I'd since looked it up. People with the disorder show long-term patterns of disregarding the law, violating the rights of others, and manipulating and exploiting others.

Dr. Pelletier was right on the mark with Wendy.

This was the woman who'd held a gun on my best friend and had later orchestrated his murder. The woman who'd arranged the rape and murder of Daphne's friend Patty Watson. The woman who'd made two threats against my newborn son. All of this while she'd been locked up in a mental facility.

"But," Wendy continued, "your sense of humor won't get you out of this one."

I didn't reply. She couldn't have anything on me. I'd been so careful in my dealings since my father had disappeared from my life once again.

"Nothing to say?" she asked.

"What do you want me to say? You're threatening me. I don't respond to threats, Wendy. You should know that by now."

"Always the same Brad Steel." She sucked in a breath. "Fuck. This is why I can't ever get enough of you. Your overwhelming arrogance turns me on."

"Arrogance, huh? I'm simply confident, Wendy."

"Oh, no, Brad. You go way beyond confidence. You always have. You just don't see it. It's not your fault, of course. You grew up the only son and heir to a million-dollar ranch and other investments. And your physical attributes . . . Well, they speak for themselves. You grew up with the ultimate silver spoon in your mouth."

"There's a lot you don't know about my upbringing."

True words. My father had been hard on me from the beginning. It wasn't something I advertised.

"Maybe, but it doesn't take a genius to read between the lines."

Interesting choice of words. Wendy was a genius. Her IQ was around 165.

"I'm going to put my child back to bed, Wendy. Then you and I will go to my office. Is that clear?"

"What will your dear wife think if she wakes up and finds you gone?"

"She won't think anything of it."

More true words. I was gone more than I was home. If Daphne woke up, she'd go right back to sleep. There was a time when she would have risen and looked for me.

That time was in the past.

Way in the past.

I'd wanted so much more for us . . .

I watched Wendy as I laid Talon back in his crib gently. He stretched a little but didn't open his eyes. When I was satisfied he wouldn't cry out, I spoke.

"My office. Now."

She followed me. She always followed me when I got stern. I didn't labor under any delusion that I still held power over her, though.

No, she had to be handled with kid gloves.

This woman was capable of anything.

I closed my office door and locked it from the inside. Then I sat behind my desk and gestured for Wendy to sit in one of my leather chairs.

"Nice digs, Brad."

"Talk," *I said simply.* "You broke into my home, held a knife to my son, all presumably to get my attention. You have it, so talk."

"Your attention isn't all I came for."

"I'm not fucking you, Wendy."

"Maybe not tonight. But you will."

"I've been more than patient. You promised me, when you were released from Piney Oaks, that you were going to make a good life for yourself. That you were healed."

"I was never ill, Brad."

"Your doctors say otherwise."

"Pfft. What do doctors know? Only I know what goes on inside my head, and I've never been mentally ill. Only desperately in love."

I resisted an eye roll. Not a good time to piss her off. One scream could wake my household, and if Daphne found Wendy here . . .

I sighed. Daphne was doing so well. Her therapy was helping, and she hadn't dissociated. She loved her children with the fierce devotion of a lioness.

She loved me that fiercely as well, despite everything.

I should have known I couldn't escape the inevitable.

Should have.

But apparently didn't.

I'd allowed myself to take a breath. To think that maybe my life could move forward with my wife and children. That we could be happy.

Dumbass.

"Start talking," I said. "And don't leave out a single dirty detail."

CHAPTER THIRTY-SIX

Daphne

"I've been thinking," I said to Evie. "Would you be okay if we took Bryce to Disneyland with us?"

Bryce and Joe stopped eating.

"Wow, Mom, could I?" Bryce asked.

"That'd be great," Joe agreed.

"I suppose it must be a good idea if it got the two of you to stop eating for a second." Evie laughed.

"Please think it over," I said.

She nodded. "I don't know how Tom would feel."

"If you're worried about the cost, we'd pay for everything. We already have a three-bedroom condo reserved, so we'll have plenty of room."

"I should check with Tom."

"Please do. It would actually be a godsend. We'd have an even number for rides, so I wouldn't have to go on any of them."

A godsend indeed. With the nausea already beginning, getting on roller coasters with my children sounded awful. I couldn't consider canceling the trip. They were all looking forward to it so much, especially Talon and Ryan. Joe was beginning to think he was too old for such things, but once he got there, I knew he'd love it.

He'd love it especially if his best friend came along.

"Please, Mom," Bryce said. "You can talk Dad into it."

"I'll try," she said.

"Great!" His blue eyes lit up. "I can't wait to get out of this damned town."

"Bryce!" Evie admonished.

"Sorry," he mumbled.

"Don't worry about it," I said to her. "I gave up trying to keep my boys from using those words years ago. Brad talks like a sailor most of the time."

"So does Tom, but I do what I can."

"I figure there's more to worry about, you know? I'm raising good, decent young men who know right from wrong and who have amazing work ethics. What do a few words matter? Of course they know if they say them at school, they have to deal with whatever punishment their teachers decide on."

I firmly believed that. Brad was a good father when he was around. He'd had the boys working on the ranch as soon as they could walk and talk, but he also taught them to value time with family.

A value he himself sometimes had issues with.

But at least he was teaching our sons how to be the man he tried to be.

I patted my pregnant belly absently. Our daughter. I'd been right about Jonah and Talon. Unfortunately, I didn't remember Ryan's pregnancy at all, but I'd bet I knew it was a boy.

And this one?

This was a girl. Not a doubt in my mind.

A girl that might have a rough start.

My skin chilled. Where had that thought come from?

All of my babies had been healthy as horses so far. No reason why this one would be any different. I was thirty-one years old, still a young woman.

"Dad'll let me go, right?" Bryce interrupted.

"We'll see," Evie said. "Why don't the two of you go play?"

"Play? We're not kids, Mom."

"Then . . . hang out, or whatever it is you do. I want to talk to Daphne about a few things."

"That's a cue," Joe said. "They're going to talk about boring mom stuff."

"That's right," I said. "Boring mom stuff."

The two preteens ambled into the house, most likely into Jonah's room, where they'd either read comic books or talk about girls. Probably a little of both.

"What do you want to talk about?" I asked Evie.

She sighed. "You know my sister, Victoria Walker?"

"Sure. I mean, not personally, but I know of her."

"She has a son. He's Talon's age. His name is Luke."

"Oh. Talon's never mentioned him."

"They're probably not friends. I don't know. Luke is . . . Well, he's been having some trouble."

"What kind of trouble?"

"I hesitated to bring this up, since it's summer break and all, but school will be back in session before we know it. Luke is having trouble with some bullies."

"Oh. I'm so sorry."

"I'm worried. Remember what happened to that last little boy who was being bullied."

"The boy who drowned?"

She nodded. "Tom has never gotten over that. It haunts him, Daphne."

"I can imagine."

"Luckily, his parents never blamed Tom. But that horrible time has been going through my mind since Vicki told me about Luke and his problems."

"What happened to Justin was an accident," I said. "There's no reason to worry about Luke."

"I just thought . . ."

"What?"

"Do you think you might . . . ask Talon to have Luke over or something?"

"I don't know, Evie. I appreciate that he's your nephew and all, but I don't tell my kids who to be friends with."

"I know. I don't either. I'm just so worried about Luke. Vicki's distraught. There's nothing worse than knowing your child is in pain."

I nodded. "You're absolutely right. I'll ask Talon if he knows Luke and wants to invite him over."

"You will? Thank you so much!"

I smiled.

I had a soft spot in my heart for anyone who was bullied. It was a horrible thing, and I'd gone through it myself.

Though I didn't remember it, so I didn't talk about it.

Apparently I'd ended up in a depression—which led to my hospitalization my junior year of high school—because I'd been bullied by two girls.

That all seemed so long ago now.

"I'll give you Vicki's number before I leave," Evie was saying. "This will mean so much to her. And to Luke."

"I can't make any promises," I said, "but I'll do what I can."

"That's all I can ask. Luke is so shy, and he's kind of small for his age. He's going through an awkward stage. He has a terrible overbite, and Chase and Vicki can't afford orthodontia right now. I've told them I'd be happy to help financially, but they won't hear of it."

"I'm sorry."

"Nothing I can do if they won't let me help. Tom is even on board. He really loves that kid."

Tom did seem to be a good father. I'd been grateful he took such an interest in Jonah when he was younger, taking him on all his father-son camping trips with Bryce. Jonah was upset when Brad stopped letting him go after that poor little boy had drowned, but I backed Brad up. Though Tom wasn't at fault for what had happened, I couldn't bear the thought of losing any of my boys.

The French doors opened.

"I'm sorry about that," Brad said. "Some calls just can't wait."

Seemed like all calls could never wait, but I didn't say so. We had company, after all.

"Where'd Bryce and Joe go?" he asked.

"Probably to Joe's room," I said.

"I see Tal and Ry are still out running around." He looked at his watch. "It's getting late."

"It's only nine," I said, though the sun had set and darkness was coming.

"Goodness." Evie stood. "I didn't realize it was so late. I should be going. I'll go find Bryce."

I stood then. "I'll find them. Just a minute."

As I suspected, they were in Jonah's room. I knocked.

"Yeah?" came Jonah's cracking voice.

"It's Mom. Can I come in?"

"Just a minute!"

Some shuffling, and then Joe opened the door. The poster of Brooke Bailey over his bed blared like a siren in the room. For a moment, I thought I could actually hear it. Then I noticed a magazine shoved hastily under his bed.

I sighed. I didn't need much of an imagination to figure out what two boys on the verge of teenhood were looking at.

"Your mom says it's time to go, Bryce," I said.

"Oh. Sure." He stood. "Thanks for dinner, Mrs. Steel."

"Anytime. You know that. I hope your father lets you come with us to Disneyland."

"Me too. Thanks a lot for inviting me."

"He has to say yes," Joe said. "Otherwise I'm stuck with my geeky little brothers."

"Geeky?" I shook my head. "Your brothers are not geeky."

"They still like doing little kid stuff."

"Yeah. That's because they're little kids. While you're such a grown man of twelve."

"Thirteen."

"In eleven days," I reminded him.

"Eighteen for me," Bryce piped in, leaving the room. "Thanks again, Mrs. Steel."

"Come on," I said to Jonah. "Let's see them out."

CHAPTER THIRTY-SEVEN

Brad

The phone call with Wendy had ended on a positive note. She was leaving soon on an assignment in DC and would be gone at least two weeks.

Two weeks of reprieve.

A perfect time for me to take my beautiful wife on a well-deserved weekend getaway.

"I don't know, Brad," Daphne said when I broached the subject. "You know how I am with morning sickness. Just the thought of Disneyland in two weeks has me about ready to spew. But I won't disappoint the boys. I'm not sure I'm up for anything else."

"I know, baby, but you're okay if you eat your crackers and stay hydrated. Let me do this for you. For us. I already booked a suite at the Broadmoor in Colorado Springs."

That should do it. Daphne loved the Broadmoor. We'd never had a honeymoon because of Murphy's and Patty's deaths, but a couple of years later, I took her for a weekend at the Broadmoor. First class all the way.

Talon had been conceived that weekend.

It was our special place.

"All right," she relented.

"I'll make it worth your while," I said. "I promise. Mom

and Belinda will take care of the kids, and we'll be back Sunday evening."

★ ★ ★

We began with a candlelight dinner at eight p.m. the evening we arrived. A perfect champagne moment, but Daphne couldn't drink due to the pregnancy, so we settled for sparkling spring water.

She was radiant in a pink sundress and white heeled sandals. I'd booked her a day of beauty at the spa tomorrow, but now, gazing at her by candlelight, I knew no one in the world could make her more beautiful than she already was.

I picked up my glass for a toast. "To my beautiful wife."

"And to you," she countered. "My husband, who's handsomer today than when I first laid eyes on him."

We clinked glasses and each took a sip.

This was good. This was right. This was what we needed.

Our meals arrived. Daphne had surprised me by ordering free-range roast chicken. I was sure she'd order a bowl of plain pasta, one of her morning-sickness staples. I'd already arranged it with the chef.

"Enjoy, baby," I said.

"I'm not sure why," she said, "but it sounded good."

"I'm glad."

She took a bite of the mashed potatoes. "Mmm. I wish I'd just ordered a plate of these."

"We can take care of that." I signaled to our waiter.

"No, it's okay. I want to try the chicken." She took a bite. "Hmm. Maybe not."

"Sir?" the waiter said.

"My wife needs a plate of just mashed potatoes, please."

"Is there something wrong?"

"No, no," she said. "I'm pregnant, is all."

"Congratulations."

"Thank you. I thought I could handle the chicken, but not so much."

"Let me box it up for you."

"Don't bother." She pushed the remaining mashed potatoes onto her bread plate. "I'm so sorry for the waste."

"Don't worry about that," he said. "Just take care of your baby. I'll be back with your potatoes shortly."

She smiled her dazzling smile at him. "You're so kind. Thank you."

I gazed at her.

She'd just made that waiter's night with a simple smile.

That was the power of my wife—that ethereal quality I'd never encountered in anyone else. Everyone saw it. Her father had been the first to use the word ethereal about her, and he'd been right on point.

Nope.

I did not want to think about Jonathan Wade right now. This was a time for Daphne and me to reconnect, to celebrate the baby we'd created.

Jonathan Wade, Wendy Madigan, promises I'd made and broken—none of that had any place here.

I sliced into my prime rib. Normally I didn't order beef anywhere, but I knew where this had come from. The Broadmoor served only Steel beef, which was humanely raised, of course.

Yeah, Daphne had turned me on to her humanely raised requirement over the years. She was so loving, my Daphne.

She loved all living creatures.

God, she deserved better than the life I'd thrust upon her. So much better.

Things were going to change.

I'd already put some processes in motion. My Daphne would live the rest of her life in joyful happiness. I'd see to it, no matter what.

"Oh, thank you so much," Daphne gushed when the waiter set down a plate of mashed potatoes in front of her. "You're a gem."

Anyone who made my wife's eyes sparkle like they were sparkling now was getting a huge tip.

I nodded to him. "Yes, thank you."

"You're very welcome, both of you. What else can I get for you today?"

Daphne froze, her lips parted.

"Baby?"

She didn't respond.

I turned back to the waiter. "Nothing. Thank you."

He nodded politely and then left.

"Daphne?" I said again.

She continued staring, as if looking through me.

I'd seen her this way before, but not in a long, long time. Usually a touch from me helped. I reached across the table and placed my hand over hers.

"Baby?"

She blinked. "I'm sorry. What did you say?"

Relief swept through me. "Nothing. Are you okay?"

"Of course. Why wouldn't I be?"

What to say next? I'd learned with these brief episodes to just go on as if nothing had happened. To do anything else would upset her.

"Just concerned about the nausea."

"I'm feeling okay." She inhaled. "These potatoes smell divine."

I nodded. "Good. I'm glad to hear it."

I watched in awe as Daphne cleaned her plate.

"Aren't you going to eat?" she asked.

I looked down at my own nearly full plate and chuckled. "I was having too much fun watching you."

"Silly. You've seen me eat before."

"Not like that, and not when you're in the first trimester."

"True enough." She licked her fork.

And my groin tightened. Only my wife could make licking mashed potatoes off a fork look sexy.

I pushed my uneaten dinner away.

"Let's go back to the room," I growled.

"Aren't you hungry?"

"Oh, yes. Very."

She smiled. Right now she had a full belly, which would ease her nausea for a while. I planned to take full advantage of the situation.

I signaled to the waiter. "Check, please."

"Of course." He took my plate. "Let me box this up for you."

"No, thank you. I'll be satisfying my appetite elsewhere tonight."

"Of course." His cheeks reddened as he grabbed Daphne's empty plate and made a quick exit.

"Now look what you've done," Daphne said. "You've embarrassed that poor man."

"He'll be well compensated. Don't you worry."

A few minutes later, he dropped off the check. I gave him a

generous fifty percent tip and scribbled my signature.

Then I met my wife's warm gaze.

"Let's go."

CHAPTER THIRTY-EIGHT

Daphne

We didn't make it back to the room.

Darkness had fallen, and as we walked around the back of the gorgeous brick building, we spied several couples cuddling on the wooden benches situated in the green courtyard.

I pulled Brad toward an unoccupied bench. "Let's sit."

"I can't do what I want to do to you out here," he said.

"Please. I want to sit here and make out like the other couples. I want to feel young again."

"We *are* young, baby."

He wasn't wrong. I was thirty-one and he was thirty-five. But we'd been yanked out of our young adulthood by an unplanned pregnancy thirteen years ago. We hadn't had the luxury of those first years together without children—getting to know each other while we couldn't keep our hands to ourselves.

We'd never made out on a bench.

"Please?"

He cupped my cheek, thumbing it softly. "I've never been able to say no to you. I suppose kissing you won't be *so* bad."

I turned my head slightly and kissed his warm palm. "Ha ha. I'll make it worth your while later."

"You don't have to make a deal, Daphne. If sitting on a

bench and kissing will make you happy, I'll gladly participate."
He sat down on the hard wood bench and pulled me close.

I wrapped my arms around his neck. "Have I ever told you how amazing your lips are?"

He chuckled. "I'm not sure you have."

"I've been remiss, then. You have the fullest, darkest, most kissable lips I've ever seen on a man. Including the best-looking models and celebrities. Your lips are works of art." I moved one hand away from my neck and trailed my index finger over his top lip and then his bottom. "So perfect."

He puckered his lips and kissed the tip of my finger.

Then he cupped both my cheeks and brought his lips to mine.

"I love that," I said against his lips.

"What?"

"When you hold my face."

"Oh?"

"It makes me feel so cherished."

"You *are* cherished, baby."

"I know. Even when you're gone all the time, I know that, Brad. I never forget."

I shouldn't have brought up him being gone a lot. He couldn't help it, and he was doing his best for our family. I didn't want him to think about work right now. I wanted him fully in the moment. In *this* moment. With me.

I wanted an amazing night. We hadn't had one in a long time.

One way to make myself stop talking?

I covered his mouth with mine.

How long had it been since I'd kissed my husband like this? How I'd missed his warm mouth, his silky tongue, his full lips. Yeah, this making out on a bench thing had been a great idea.

Too many times in the past few years, our lovemaking had been hurried. He'd overlooked kissing me, holding me.

I'd done the same.

We'd make up for all of that tonight.

His bulge was apparent, and I knew what he wanted. I needed more tonight, though. I needed to be held. To be kissed. To be appreciated.

Our kiss was soft but passionate. Though neither of us held back, we both remained aware of our surroundings. This was a time to enjoy each other. To not rush into the act itself, but to remember all the desire and passion of the time we first met.

I still felt that same passion for Brad. I always would.

A groan hummed from Brad's throat as he deepened the kiss, pulling me closer. Kissing Brad was heaven. Pure heaven.

How long we sat there in each other's arms, our mouths fused together, I couldn't say.

When we finally stopped our make-out session, all the other couples on nearby benches had disappeared.

He trailed his lips over my neck, over the tops of my breasts. "Looks like we outlasted everyone else. They're all in bed now, making furious love to each other."

"Mmm. I'm looking forward to that," I said, "but I wouldn't trade what just happened for anything in the world."

"Truthfully, neither would I. I'm so sorry, baby."

"Why?"

"I've neglected you. I haven't seen to your most basic needs. Can you ever forgive me?"

"Oh, Brad." I touched his cheek, loving his prickly stubble

against my fingertips. "I've neglected you too. I'm always so tired in the evenings."

"Being a mother isn't easy," he said.

"Neither is being a rancher. This isn't all your fault. It's mine, too."

I hadn't been fair to Brad. He worked so hard for us. Yes, the boys and I missed him desperately, but we were always in his thoughts. I knew that without question.

"Baby," he said, "let's stop trying to blame ourselves and go back to the room. I'm dying to make love to you."

I sighed and nodded.

Ten minutes later, we were tearing each other's clothes off in the privacy of our suite.

Brad Steel naked never ceased to amaze me. There couldn't possibly be a more perfect male specimen than my husband. His broad and golden shoulders, his hard chest with the perfect smattering of black hair, his six-pack abs, and that lovely triangle pointing to his perfect cock.

I gripped him, relishing the heat and the hardness.

"Easy, baby, or it'll be over before we begin." He whisked my hand away. "I'm going to make up for some lost time tonight. How long has it been since I've tasted that delicious pussy of yours?"

How long, indeed?

I'd grown used to Brad's graphic language. When we'd first met, it had embarrassed me. I couldn't even think those words, let alone say them. Now? I could be as brash as he was.

"My pussy has missed your tongue," I said in a sultry low tone.

"My tongue has missed your pussy." He led me to the bed and pushed me down onto it. "Spread those long, beautiful legs for me."

I obeyed without question, my heartbeat already racing in time with the throbbing in my core. Brad's tongue. Brad's fingers. Brad's lips. All down there. All where I ached the most.

"Still as beautiful as ever," he said, gazing between my legs. "And still wet. Always wet for me."

Not much had changed over the years. I still craved Brad Steel like I craved air. I always would.

"I'm happy about the new baby, Daphne, but I almost wish we were conceiving her tonight instead. Our last time was so hurried."

Indeed, it had been. He'd just come home from yet another business trip. It was after midnight, and he was horny. I was exhausted, but I hadn't been able to deny him. I could never deny Brad Steel. I loved him too much.

Nearly three months ago. My ultrasound had shown I was about ten weeks pregnant.

How had we let three months pass without making love?

Hard to do when you're not together, but we'd grown neglectful. It wasn't just him. We were both at fault.

"What matters is we made another wonderful child," I said. "Not how we made her."

He kissed the inside of my thigh, making me shiver.

"You're right, baby. You always are." He trailed his tongue up the inside of one thigh and then switched to the other, purposely avoiding that pulsing place in between.

I moaned. "God, Brad. Please."

"We're taking our time tonight, baby. If I end up going crazy and having to pound you, we're going to do it again. Slowly. We'll do it again and again until we get it right."

"It's always right with you, Brad."

"It is," he agreed, nipping again at the tender flesh of my

inner thigh. "Always has been with you."

I lay back and closed my eyes. *Always has been with you.*

I'd been an untried virgin when we first made love. That night that had led to our Jonah. I hadn't had a clue what I was doing, but it had been perfect.

He'd made me feel like I was perfect.

I'd learned a thing or two since then, but I still almost always let him take the lead. Maybe tonight I'd take the reins away from him.

Later, though.

After he'd eaten my pussy. Because God, that was what I wanted more than anything at this moment.

"Baby..." He grazed my wet folds with his lips. "Mmm. So wet. So sweet."

I grasped the comforter with both fists and arched my back. "Please, Brad. Please. Eat me."

I'd never uttered those words before. Never even thought about uttering them even when I'd wanted the outcome more than anything.

"Since you said please." Then he flicked his tongue over my clit.

I gasped, my body turning to flames. I was near climax already. My God, how long had it been?

"Not yet," he said against my wet flesh. "Not fucking yet."

I moved my hips upward, thrusting toward him, trying to get his lips and tongue where I wanted them. He chuckled against my folds, a vibrating hum.

Then he slid his tongue from my clit downward, pushing my thighs forward and licking my asshole.

Something we'd never done. I wasn't sure I'd ever want to. Tonight, though? I wanted everything.

Every. Damned. Thing.

He moved away, though, back to my pussy, shoved his tongue inside. Tingles and sparks shot through me as he moved it in and out, as if it were a mini cock.

I moved my head from side to side, still grasping the covers, until I let go and grabbed at Brad's hair, trying to push his tongue farther into my heat.

I ground my wet pussy against him, searching for that perfect spot for friction, that perfect place where—

"Yes!" The climax hit me with the force of a torpedo. My pussy shattered, making the sparks surge outward to my fingertips and then back into my core.

"You little siren," Brad said between my legs. "I wanted to take it slow."

"Can't help it," I said through clenched teeth. "Need you."

"Then you shall have me." He crawled upward, still pushing my thighs forward so my legs were bent and my thighs hit my chest.

And he thrust his cock inside my still-pulsing pussy.

"Fuck." He pulled out and then thrust back in. "God, you feel good."

"So do you." I grabbed his corded forearms. He was so strong and glorious.

He surged into me again and again, and with each thrust, I became more his than I'd ever been before.

This was life. This was love. This was everything.

This was two people joined not just by children and their love for each other. This was two people joined as souls.

Soul mates. We were soul mates.

I'd always known that, always felt it, but never so profoundly as I did at this moment.

It wasn't just his cock inside me, giving us both pleasure. It was his soul linking with mine. This went beyond the physical, beyond the emotional.

This was spiritual, through and through.

"I'm going to come, Daphne," he said through gritted teeth. "I can't help it. Can't last. But we're going to do this again. And then again. And then a— Fuck!"

He pushed into me hard, staying embedded inside me and releasing. I felt every pulse of his cock, every drip of his sweat as he climaxed, every beat of his heart.

Every cry of his soul.

Every. Last. One.

CHAPTER THIRTY-NINE

B r a d

Elation filled me. Every orgasm with Daphne was amazing, but this one . . .

This one was off the charts.

This one was a fusion of hearts. A joining of two hearts at some kind of molecular level.

Not the stuff romance novels were made of, but that was how it felt to me.

This woman, this amazing woman, was a part of me as no one else ever could be. We'd always be connected in this way. In fact, we always had been. This was just the ultimate exemplification.

"I fucking adore you," I said, pressing my lips to hers.

"I adore you too," she said. "That was . . . amazing."

"Baby, amazing doesn't even begin to describe it."

"I know. I felt . . . I feel . . . " She panted.

"Me too. Me too, baby." I rolled off her and covered my eyes with my arm. "I need a minute, but I promise you, we're not done yet."

She turned and snuggled into my shoulder. "That will last me a good long time, Brad."

"No way," I said. "We're done neglecting each other. We're done putting our lovemaking on the back burner because of work, because of kids, because of all the other crap in the world. From now on, we make time for us."

"I'd love that. I've missed you so much, Brad."

"I've missed you too, baby. And I'm sorry. Sorry for fucking you instead of making love to you like you deserve."

"Don't underestimate the power of a good fucking." She giggled.

"Believe me, I don't. But you deserve so much better than that."

"We both do," she said, "but I have absolutely no regrets, Brad. Not a one."

I smiled and sat up. "Neither do I, baby. And to show you, I'm going to eat that delicious pussy again and finger-fuck you into oblivion."

"I won't say no to that. Let me clean up first." She rose and walked to the bathroom. She returned in less than five minutes.

I moved to the head of the bed and gestured to her. "Come here."

She snuggled into me once more.

"I want to give you everything," I said.

"You already have."

"I mean. I want to experience everything with you."

"O . . . kay."

Was she ready for everything? Licking her ass had turned me on so much. I'd never fucked anyone in the ass. Not even Wendy, and she'd been up for anything. But it was something that, though I wanted, hadn't felt right.

When I met Daphne, she was too young and innocent to even entertain the idea. But now?

"We don't have to do this tonight," I said, "but I was wondering . . . Would you let me fuck you anally?"

She tensed up next to me.

"It's okay," I said soothingly.

"I . . . like it when you lick me there," she said. "I think I might like to . . . "

My heart raced.

" . . . lick *you* there."

"Oh." That didn't sound half bad. "Okay. We can start with that."

"But the other thing, Brad. I don't know."

"It's okay. I love you. I won't ever ask you to do anything you're not ready for."

"I know you won't. But I hate disappointing you."

"Baby, you could never disappoint me."

"But I just did. This is something you want, and I'm not sure I can give it to you."

Daphne didn't know that she actually hadn't been a virgin when we made love for the first time. She'd been viciously violated by three men, which she didn't remember, thank God.

I'd always been curious, but I found I wanted this with Daphne even more because it would be the ultimate in trust and intimacy.

"I'll be happy to wait until you're ready," I said, and I meant it.

"What if I'm never ready?"

"Then we won't do it."

"Brad . . . "

"Daphne, I love you. Your well-being is the most important thing in the world to me. I'll never coerce you into doing something you don't want to do."

"I know that."

"Then we don't have a problem, do we?"

She smiled halfheartedly. "I guess not."

"Good. Now I promised you a good and dirty pussy licking and finger fucking."

She moaned.

"I see you're looking forward to it." I moved toward her midsection. "Oops. I see a problem, though, that needs addressing."

"What's that?"

"I haven't given your beautiful breasts any attention so far tonight."

She sucked in a breath as I thumbed one nipple and then flicked it.

"Your nipples are works of art, Daphne. So beautiful. Of course every part of you is beautiful. I'm going to lick these sweet nipples. Suck them. Pinch them. Drive you absolutely mad with lust before I eat that sweet pussy of yours."

"Oh, God," she groaned.

I pinched one nipple between my thumb and forefinger and then gave the other a suck. Mmm, such a beautiful texture when her dark-pink areolas were wrinkled and taut. The way the smooth-rough surface glided over my tongue.

I kissed between her breasts, massaging both nipples with my fingers and caressing my cheeks with her soft flesh. Her boobs were the perfect size and shape. Enough that I could get lost and smother myself with them, but not so huge that they hung heavily.

So damned perfect.

Too many months—or had it been years?—had passed since I'd paid this much attention to my wife's amazing body. She was as beautiful as the day we'd first met. Oh, her hips were slightly rounder, but for the most part, her body was identical to her eighteen-year-old self.

"Feels so good," she breathed, as I continued to pinch her nipples.

I kissed over the top of one breast and then took a nipple in her mouth and sucked. Mmm, delicious. I kissed it, licked it, sucked it, and bit it.

All while she undulated beneath me, ground against me.

The scent of our lust was thick in the air, and I inhaled, drawing it into me, infusing myself with the aroma of our passion. It gave me strength and drive to want more. So much more.

Her moans fueled me further, and I let one hand drift down to my heart's desire. I groaned as I fingered her slick folds. I found her clit and circled it.

Her rhythm of undulations increased beneath me. I smiled against her rosy flesh, her taut nipple. I could spend hours on her nipples alone.

I dipped a finger into her pussy and then swirled the juices over her clit.

She was grinding furiously now. God, I needed to get to her pussy, get my mouth on her. I replaced my mouth on her nipple with my other hand and slid downward to her perfect cunt.

I spread her legs and then dived in, moving my other hand upward to play with her other nipple.

I pinched her perfect nipples furiously as I sucked at her. She was so juicy and delicious. I loved eating her. Why had I neglected something that gave us both so much joy?

Her pussy was hot and slick, and I shoved my tongue in deeply before heading back to her clit to suck on it.

She moaned and bucked beneath me, and each time I

added pressure to my fingers around her nipples, she moaned and bucked even more.

I didn't want this to end. I could eat her forever, get lost in that tangy paradise between her lovely legs.

My cock throbbed. I'd never been able to get enough of Daphne. I could come, and seemingly within minutes, I was hard again, aching for her.

How had I ignored both our needs for so long?

Had to have her. Had to be inside her tight pussy.

Swiftly I moved upward and shoved my dick into her.

She gasped.

I hadn't given her an orgasm yet. I'd meant to.

No matter. I'd promised we'd do this all night if we had to. All fucking night.

I withdrew.

She whimpered.

"It's okay, baby. I just want to make you come first." In a flash, my face was back between her legs, licking and kissing her most intimate flesh.

This was going to be a hell of a night.

CHAPTER FORTY

Daphne

Was there anything more delicious than having your pussy licked?

Sex wasn't something I ever talked about to anyone. My only close friend was Ennis, and he was a man. Sage and Patty were long gone, and I'd never heard from either of them. Patty had talked about sex to me, but I hadn't to her. It was all so long ago.

Did other women feel this way about having their pussy eaten? Was it this amazing for everyone?

I wriggled against Brad's lips and tongue, helping him find the right spot to trigger those wonderful feelings inside me, that kaleidoscope of emotions and physical sensations that rolled through me like bolts of lightning.

Muffled words of endearment, of satisfaction, rolled off my tongue. I closed my eyes and brought my fingers to my breasts, pinching my own nipples as Brad had.

Each pinch made a spark sizzle through me and land in my pussy, moving me closer and closer to—

"Yes, Brad, yes!" The climax soared through me when he forced two fingers inside me.

I rolled through the waves of passion, coiling like a snake in the grass moving toward prey. The tingles, the sparks, the sheer joy and bliss all surrounded me in a lovely pink haze.

"Again, baby," Brad said against my inner thigh. "Come again for me."

He went back to work on my clit, his fingers still sliding in and out of me. His movements varied. Sometimes his fingers seemed to scissor inside me, sometimes they thrust upward against that spongy spot that made me insane. Sometimes they slid in and out gently as if we were making slow love. Sometimes he forced them far up into me, seeming to touch my heart.

Each movement made me feel something different.

Each movement was amazing in itself, but his discordant rhythm of motion, so I didn't know which would come next, drove me absolutely crazy.

Brad Steel was my only lover, but I was certain I'd missed out on nothing. When he played my body like a fine violin as he was doing now, I knew he was the only lover I was meant to have.

I catapulted into another climax and then another, rolling my head from side to side against my fluffy pillow, screaming Brad's name.

My nipples were stretched tight as I continued pinching them. And my pussy . . . God, my pussy. How much more could I take?

He alternately sucked and licked my clit, keeping me right at the edge of each orgasm and then sending me blasting to the stars again and again. His fingers danced inside me and hit every spot that made me tingle.

One orgasm rolled into another and then another. Thoughts fled from my head until only feeling remained. Pure raw emotion that seemed to encase us in an invisible cloud of desire.

Words formed in my throat, fell off my tongue.

And still he continued to lick me, finger me, grip the globes of my ass as he ate me.

Until finally, a feeling so intense, so pure, rose within me.

It was almost frightening, but oh, it was good. It was new and exciting and bold, and then I shattered into the most intense climax I'd ever experienced, as if diamond dust had encased me and was moving through my veins like molten honey.

I ground against Brad's mouth, lifted my hips in tandem with his motions.

And I came. I fucking came like I'd never come before.

The sensation lasted for moments of pure bliss, and when it finally began to ease off, I found myself panting, sweating, eyes squeezed shut.

I exhaled. I gasped. And then I opened my eyes.

And I realized what had happened, what had spurred me into that glorious heaven.

Brad's fingers were still inside me. Two in my pussy, and . . .

And . . .

I gasped again.

He removed the finger from my ass slowly.

Should he have asked me if it was okay? How could I be upset when his decision had led to the most intense sensation of my life?

He crawled upward and sank his cock deep inside me. He kissed my neck. "You okay?"

"Yeah. I'm good."

"You were so hot, baby." He thrust into me again, a drop of sweat from his brow hitting my forehead. "I licked you there, touched you there, and you responded." He thrust again. "I'm so hard for you right now. I don't think I've ever been this hard in my whole damned life."

I closed my eyes then. Closed my eyes and gave in to the beautiful sensation of Brad inside me, making love to me.

For that was what this was. All of it. Every single part of it.

Even that.

He'd taken me to a new place tonight.

A place I wanted to go again.

And maybe, just maybe, I'd get to that ultimate place he wanted to share with me.

He thrust into me again, and then again.

"So tight," he panted. "So sweet. I love you so much, Daphne. So damned much."

"I love you too." I opened my eyes and met his dark and yearning gaze. "Always, Brad. I love you always."

★ ★ ★

Too soon, our weekend was over and we headed home to the ranch.

I felt exhilarated.

Brad and I had reconnected, and that meant I was now filled with energy to focus on my family. I'd missed my boys something awful. Our Disneyland trip was in two weeks, and they were all excited. Even Jonah, now that Bryce was coming along.

Mazie and Belinda had given them a good report on behavior, which made me happy. My boys were the best.

My morning sickness didn't seem quite as intense as it had been with Jonah and Talon. That was a godsend, since I wouldn't survive Disneyland if I were throwing up all the time, and I wasn't going to disappoint my boys for anything.

Evie had invited me for coffee in town, and though I was nauseated, I went. When I got to the coffee shop, she'd already arrived. She sat at a small round table with another woman I didn't recognize but who looked vaguely familiar.

"Hi, Evie!" I waved and walked over to the table.

"Daphne, you look radiant! You're glowing!" Evie said.

"I do?" I hadn't told her about the pregnancy. The glow she saw was probably sweat from the dry heaves I'd had an hour ago.

"Of course you always look radiant," she said. "This is my sister, Vicki Walker. I hope you don't mind. I asked her to join us."

"Not at all. I'm going to get some tea."

"Tea? You always drink black coffee."

Thank goodness I hadn't said peppermint tea, which was what I meant. It helped settled my stomach. Brad and I hadn't told anyone about the pregnancy yet, and I didn't want to do so without discussing it with him first.

"Just in a tea mood, I guess." I stepped up to the counter, ordered my herbal tea, and then rejoined the women, who were in the middle of a conversation.

"What are we talking about?" I asked.

"Raine Stevenson," Evie said. "She's still missing, and the police don't have any leads."

My heart stopped. How horrible to have your child missing. I couldn't imagine the turmoil her parents were going through.

Wrap. Slice. Hand to customer. "What else can I get for you today?"

I shook my head to clear it.

"I'm so sorry to hear that," I said.

"It's horrible," Vicki agreed. "I know Raine's mother. She's beside herself. I can't say anything to her because I don't know what to say. What on earth can you say to a mother whose child has disappeared?"

Evie shook her head. "I don't know. This is Snow Creek. Bad things aren't supposed to happen here. It's like Justin Valente all over again, except this time no one knows what happened. I feel unsafe. I want to hug Bryce and never let him go. Of course, he wouldn't allow that."

I nodded. I had nothing to add to the conversation, except that I was going to give my boys extra hugs when I got home as well. They were everything to me.

"Daphne," Evie said, "Vicki and I were talking about Luke and what he's going through."

"I'm sorry to hear he's been having trouble at school," I said to Vicki.

"It just started a few months ago," Vicki said. "He's thrilled that school's out for the summer, but in a month, they'll be back."

"Have you considered private school?" I asked.

Vicki reddened. "We can't afford private school."

Now I reddened. Had I lost track of my roots so quickly since becoming a Steel thirteen years ago? My parents hadn't been able to afford private school either. Most parents couldn't.

"I'm so sorry. I didn't mean... That was rude of me. Incredibly rude. I grew up modestly. I should have known better than to make such an unfeeling statement."

"It's okay," Vicki said.

"It's not." I sipped my tea, the nausea not easing a bit. "I feel terrible. Let's come up with another option. Homeschooling?"

"I'd do it in a minute," Vicki said, "but Chase won't hear of it. He says kids need to be around other kids."

I nodded. He was probably right. I'd spent my junior year of high school away from other students, and when I returned, I never fit in again like I had before.

"We'll think of something," Evie said.

"Your son Talon is in Luke's class," Vicki said.

"Would you like to have him come to the ranch sometime?" I asked.

"I'd say yes in a minute," she said, "but Luke is so shy. I'm not sure he and your son are friends."

"Talon's different from most kids his age," I told them. "He's not shy, really, but he doesn't have one best friend, either. Like Jonah and Bryce have each other."

"He's a Steel," Vicki said. "That gives him a protection against the bullies."

What an odd thing for Vicki to say. "It's probably more the fact that he's the biggest kid in his class," I said.

"Probably a little of both," Evie said. "Since when do we have a bully problem?"

"We've always had one." I took another sip of tea. "Jonah and Bryce befriended poor Justin Valente for the same reason."

Vicki shook her head. "You're right, of course. It just hits a little closer to home when it's your kid."

I patted her forearm lightly. I felt for her. I couldn't bear the thought of one of my own children in pain.

"We'll figure this out," I said. "I'll talk to Talon this evening."

CHAPTER FORTY-ONE

Brad

I'd allowed myself to take a breath. To think that maybe my life could move forward with my wife and children. That we could be happy.

Dumbass.

"Start talking," I said. "And don't leave out a single dirty detail."

"You sold a piece of land a while back."

"I buy and sell land every day, Wendy."

"This was a particularly interesting piece."

"For God's sake. Get on with it!"

"An island, Brad. An island in the Caribbean."

An island in the Caribbean... Right. My father had told me about the offer before it came in, and he advised me to take the offer. "I remember. I made a killing."

"I'm sure you did. The buyer had all kinds of cash."

"What's this got to do with anything?"

"Did you check out the buyer?"

"It was a corporation. The documents were all in order and on the up-and-up. Why the hell would I check out the buyer? Like I said, I made a killing."

"Due diligence, Brad."

"I don't need to do due diligence when I'm selling a property to a corporation who's filed all the correct paperwork and is represented by a top New York law firm. Christ, Wendy."

Though maybe I should have. I was young, and I'd relied on my father's advice.

My father who'd disappeared shortly after giving me that advice.

Shit . . .

"Ah, due diligence," she said again. "The only problem is, you could have done all the due diligence in the world and Fleming Corporation would have come up clean."

"How do you know the name of the buyer?"

"Easy enough to find. Title companies have those records."

"But this was an international transaction."

"Still easy enough to find. I'm an investigative journalist, Brad."

"Why are you giving me shit about due diligence if the corporation is clean?"

"I said the corporation would have come up clean if you'd done your due diligence. I didn't say the corporation was clean."

A brick hit my gut. Who had I sold my property to?

She went on, "The Fleming Corporation is a dummy corporation."

"Who's behind it?"

"People you know, actually."

"You?"

"Of course not. I keep my name away from anything dirty."

"Not the others."

"No. Not at first."

"Drugs. Fucking drugs. A private island in the Caribbean is the perfect place."

"Yes, it is. For drugs. And . . . other things."

"What other things?"

"Things. Heinous things, Brad."

Another brick to the gut. Nausea crept up my throat.

"The what *doesn't particularly matter, Brad. Just know that it's heinous. Heinous and very illegal."*

"What does this all have to do with me? You think you have something on me because I sold some property to a dirty corporation that would have come up clean had I done my due diligence? That absolves me of any liability whatsoever."

"On the surface, yes, it does."

"Underneath the surface too, Wendy."

"Except for one tiny little detail."

The nausea grew blacker, like tar oozing up my esophagus. "What detail?"

"I have documentation."

"This is getting tedious. What documentation?"

"Documentation that links you with Fleming Corporation."

"Then it's counterfeit. Completely false."

"Of course it is. But it'll hold up in any court. I've seen to that."

"You little bitch."

"I'd show it to you, but you already know I never lie when it comes to something this important to me. I'm going to have your child, Brad. Because if I don't, your life will be ruined. Not only your life, but your precious Daphne's and those two pretty little boys of yours."

★ ★ ★

My trip to the Broadmoor with Daphne had been an oasis in a hot, raging desert storm.

Now I was back.

It was funny, that feeling of having everything your heart desired but having other things in your life that spoiled it.

That was my life. Had been my life for a while now.

I stared at the file folder lying on my desk in front of me. It had been delivered while Daphne and I were away and was waiting for me at my business office when I got in this afternoon.

Whoever had sent it had known better than to send it to my home.

I laughed aloud.

Whoever had sent it. Right. I knew damned well who had sent it. It had a Washington, DC, postmark. Wendy was currently in DC working on an assignment. Coincidence?

Not likely.

I opened the file.

Only one page of crisp white paper.

Only three lines.

I know.

You betrayed me.

You will pay the ultimate price.

Then my phone rang.

I didn't even have to guess who it was.

"Hello, Wendy," I said into the receiver.

"Five million dollars," she said, her voice icy.

"What?"

"Five million dollars. Transfer it to me immediately."

"Or what?"

"You know what."

Right. Her trump card. Her fail-safe. If anything happened to her, she had documents tying me to the Fleming Corporation. To the heinous things they were involved in.

You will pay the ultimate price.

Did she truly think five million dollars meant anything to me?

"Not until you tell me exactly what it is you think you know."

"Don't be so obtuse, Brad. You've been fucking her all along, haven't you?"

I loved Daphne too much to deny it.

"Yes. She's my wife. Don't you think she'd think it odd if I stopped sleeping with her?"

"You made me a promise years ago, when you gave me your child. I entrusted him to you. Let you give him to her to raise. I made a deal with you, and you welched on your end."

"Wendy, I—"

"Did you think I wouldn't find out?"

"It wasn't planned."

She scoffed. "Of course it wasn't. If she got pregnant, you knew I'd know you were still fucking her."

"Does it even matter? I'm willing to pay your ultimate price. We'll both get what we want."

"I assure you, Brad, you're not getting what you want."

I didn't respond. Fine. Let her think five million dollars was my ultimate price. What did it matter? I'd gladly pay her off.

"Where should I have it wired?"

She gave me an account number.

"Consider it done."

"Good."

"We're even, then? You won't insist that I have Daphne abort the pregnancy?" Not that I had any intention of doing that.

"What good would that do? You already broke your promise to me. You slept with her. The child isn't at fault."

I heaved a sigh of relief. Her statement made it clear she drew the line at hurting one of my children.

Thank God.

If only I could be sure about Daphne.

Wendy loved hurting me. Making me pay. Daphne was my biggest Achilles' heel.

Taking out Murph and Patty had hurt not just me, but Daphne as well. Wendy was capable of anything.

At least my children were safe.

I could sleep a little better knowing that.

CHAPTER FORTY-TWO

Daphne

Luke Walker, a small and awkward boy with an unsightly overbite, sat quietly on the lawn while Talon and Ryan romped with the dogs. Evelyn, Vicki, and I sat on the deck with sparkling water, cheese, and crackers.

I ate only the crackers. Nausea was bad today.

Talon and Ryan were good little hosts and tried to include Luke, but he resisted joining in their fun.

"He's not really my friend, Mom," Talon had said to me when I broached the subject of inviting Luke over to play.

"This is how you make new friends," I'd said.

He'd rolled his eyes and said, "He's kind of weird."

The little boy wasn't weird. He was shy and the victim of bullying. I'd thought my sons could bring him out of his shell, but he wasn't responding.

"Do you think he'd like to ride one of our horses?" I asked Vicki.

"No. Horses scare him," she said. "We have one on our small ranch outside town. Luke won't go near him."

"What about checking out the ranch?" Evie suggested. "He could see the cattle."

"They'd probably scare him too," Vicki said. "He's been so frightened all the time since the bullies started bothering him."

My heart ached for him. I was lucky that my boys were big and strong and made friends easily. Talon was a bit of a loner, but he got plenty of invitations to birthday parties and other events. Ryan had a joviality that Talon and Joe both lacked and had been Mr. Popular since he started school a few years ago.

Everyone loved Ryan.

I smiled. He had a charisma that drew people to him. Odd, really. Neither Brad nor I had that trait.

"We'll find something," I said, standing. "How about a game of Clue? The boys love that one."

"Even Joe and Bryce still play that one sometimes," Evie agreed.

"No," Vicki said. "Just let them be. I don't want to force him on your boys."

"You're not," I said. "They love having friends over."

He's not really my friend, Mom.

What Vicki didn't know wouldn't hurt her.

Talon and Ryan finally traipsed up onto the deck, leaving Luke still sitting by himself on the lawn. Even the dogs didn't go near him.

Strange.

"We're hungry," Talon said.

"Run on in and ask Belinda to make you some snacks. Enough for all three of you."

"Okay."

Talon walked inside, Ryan on his tail. I smiled. Ryan was Talon's little shadow. He followed him everywhere and adored his big brother. Joe had always had Bryce and didn't interact with his brothers that much. It was cute how Ryan followed Talon around, even slid his hand into his brother's sometimes. The day was coming soon, I knew, when Talon would put a stop to it. When he'd be too grown up to be hanging around with his little brother.

Thank goodness that day wasn't today.

I couldn't bear the thought of Ryan's heartbreak.

They returned with smiles on their faces.

"Belinda's making biscuit pizzas for us," Ryan said happily.

"Sounds delicious," I said, rubbing my tummy. In reality, it sounded dreadful. "Run down and tell Luke, okay?"

"I'm sorry, Daphne," Vicki said, "but Luke is allergic to wheat."

"Oh, dear." I stood. "I didn't know that. I'll see what else Belinda can scrounge up."

I hastily walked through the French doors and into our large kitchen. Belinda was at the counter, rolling out the biscuit dough.

"Thanks for doing that for the boys."

"My pleasure. They're always so polite. I could never say no to them. It's a tribute to you, Miss Daphne, what nice little gentlemen they are."

I couldn't hide a smile. I took pride in my boys. In being their mother. Praising my children was the best compliment anyone could give me.

"We have a problem, though. Luke is allergic to wheat. Is there something else we could offer him?"

"Some fresh fruit?"

"If I had it my way, my kids would eat nothing but nutritious food like that, but my guess is he'll want something different."

Belinda laughed. "Potato chips, then? I have a few chocolate chip cookies from the batch I made two days ago, but if he's allergic to wheat . . . "

"I'm sure the chips will be fine. Thank you, Belinda."

She grabbed a bag of chips from the pantry and handed them to me. "You're welcome, Miss Daphne. I'm going to take the fruit punch out to them now."

"I'll take care of that." I grabbed the pitcher of punch and the cups stacked on top of one another.

"Thank you. Tell the boys the pizzas will be ready in fifteen minutes."

"I'm sure they'll help Luke with these chips in the meantime." I headed back out onto the deck.

"Can Luke eat potato chips?" I asked Vicki.

"Yes, he loves them." She motioned to him to come join us on the deck. "Evie was just telling me about how you're taking Bryce to Disneyland with you."

"Yes, Jonah is certainly looking forward to the trip. More now, since he'll have his best friend along and won't have to be saddled with his little brothers." I refilled Evie's sparkling water and then topped off my own. Vicki's was still full.

The boys grabbed the bag of chips and ripped it open.

"Hey, be careful," I admonished.

"I'm always careful, Mom," Talon said.

I rolled my eyes. Out of the mouths of babes. How many times had I seen him rip open a bag of snacks so that they went flying everywhere?

"You guys take your fruit punch and eat out on the lawn," I said.

"Okay." Ryan grabbed Talon's hand, and the two of them ambled off the deck.

Luke stayed put.

"The chips are for you too," I said. "Why don't you go join the boys?"

Luke stayed silent.

"Don't be impolite, Luke," Vicki said. "Answer Mrs. Steel."

"I think I'd rather stay here," he said. "Thank you."

Vicki's face fell. I felt for her. I'd hate to know one of my children was unhappy. As a mother, I felt everything my children felt. It was heart-wrenching sometimes, but I wouldn't have it any other way.

"At least drink your punch," Evie said.

Luke nodded and took a sip. "Thank you. It's good."

It was just Hawaiian Punch out of a can, but I was glad he liked it.

"Bryce is going to Disneyland with the Steels, Luke," Vicki said. "Doesn't that sound like fun?"

He nodded sullenly. "I've always wanted to go there."

Evie shot me an apologetic glance. Really? That was where this was going? Was I supposed to invite this child we hardly knew to go on a trip with us?

We could well afford it, of course, but that wasn't the point.

This was *our* trip. A trip for my boys and me. And Bryce, but he'd always been kind of an honorary Steel brother.

What was I supposed to say?

"Joe is thrilled that Bryce is going along, of course," I said. "This way there will be an even number for rides."

There, that ought to do it.

"What were you going to do before?" Vicki asked. "When it was just you and the three boys?"

"I probably would have gone on the rides with them." I smiled. "I'm so glad I won't have to. Amusement parks and I don't get along very well."

There. If I offered to take her kid along, I'd have to go on the rides again, which I didn't want to do. If she continued to push it, she wasn't paying attention, and I'd tell her flatly that we could not take her son.

"I'm sure you'll get to go to Disneyland soon, Luke," Evie said.

A look passed between the two sisters.

Nothing more was said about Disneyland.

Thank God.

"Tell us about your romantic trip to the Broadmoor," Evie said, in what seemed to me to be a deliberate attempt to change the subject.

Normally I'd be thrilled, but my relationship with Brad was private. I didn't talk to anyone about it. I might have talked to Sage or Patty, but I wasn't that close to Evie, and I wasn't close to Vicki at all.

"It was wonderful. We really reconnected," I said simply.

"I'm envious," Evie said. "Tom and I need some time to do just that. Sometimes I feel like I don't even know him anymore."

"I think all married people feel that way from time to time," Vicki said.

"I can't recall the last time we made love," Evie said.

I hid a gulp. This was getting way too personal.

The silence seemed to linger for hours until Evie finally continued.

"He's so great with Bryce, though. He always has time for his boy. He's the greatest dad ever, and I love that about him."

"Bryce is a wonderful young man," I said. "Always well-behaved when he's here."

"Glad to hear it, since this place is his second home." Evie laughed.

Good. She wasn't talking more about her sex life.

"I wish we could have had more children," she went on. "But then, if we had, he wouldn't be able to give Bryce so much individual attention. Of course, he'd have to actually have sex with me for that to happen too."

God. Back to that again.

"Chase and I do okay in that department," Vicki offered.

They both looked to me.

I cleared my throat. "Yeah. We're fine. You know. There."

This was so none of their business! Brad and I had no problem in bed. Not a one. The only problem I had was that I wanted him around more. Still, when he was around, he always took time with his boys. He taught them everything about the ranch. They all, even little Ryan, knew their way around Steel Acres.

I silently wished for an interruption.

But I wasn't ready for the one that came.

CHAPTER FORTY-THREE

Brad

I opened the French doors to the deck and walked out. Daphne sat with Evelyn Simpson and a woman I didn't recognize.

I cleared my throat.

They all turned.

"Hi, Brad," Daphne said. "Come join us."

"I can't," I said gruffly, sounding a lot like my old man. "I need to speak with you. Alone."

"Oh, of course." Evie stood. "We should be going. Oh... Brad, I haven't had the chance to thank you for including Bryce on your Disneyland trip."

"Of course. Our pleasure." I tapped my foot. The trip to Disneyland probably wouldn't happen at this point. I needed to send my wife and children into seclusion. I just wasn't sure where yet.

I needed to speak to my wife, and I needed these women to get the hell out of here. I wasn't feeling patient at the moment.

The woman I didn't know called for her strange child, a kid I didn't recognize.

"I'll see you out," Daphne said politely.

"Don't be silly. I know the way," Evie said.

The other woman ushered the boy out.

Once we were alone, Daphne whipped her hands to her

hips. "You were pretty rude to my guests, Brad."

I had been, but I wasn't in the mood to offer apologies I wasn't feeling. Wendy was up to something, and I didn't for a minute believe that five million dollars would appease her.

"I need to discuss something with you," I said to Daphne. I eyed Talon and Ryan in the yard. "Where's Joe?"

"Off somewhere with Bryce. I think they took horses out to the north quadrant."

I gestured toward the boys. "I can't have them interrupting us."

"Are you kidding? They're fine. They've been outside playing all day."

"Good. Come with me, please."

"Brad, what is—"

"Just come. Please." I couldn't bear the idea of discussing any of this with my wife. My sweet wife, who I'd tried so hard to protect. How could I tell her I was sending her and the boys away?

She parted her lips and looked up at me with those brown doe eyes. "All right, Brad."

I led her to my office in the ranch house.

"Sit." I gestured to one of the chairs, and I took a seat behind my desk.

"No," she said. "Please. Sit over here with me. Not behind your desk. I feel so . . . far away from you that way. Don't make me feel that way, Brad. Please."

I softened. I couldn't deny her, though I'd have to. Especially when I told her that her trip to Disneyland was off. She'd beg me to reconsider, and I would not. I could not.

I could at least give her this.

I stood to grant her request when the phone rang.

"Ignore it," Daphne said. "Something's bothering you, and I want to know what."

How I wanted to ignore the phone. I wanted to ignore everything except my wife and children. I wanted that life—that life most men had and probably took for granted. The life where you lived with your wife and children, did your work, and provided for them.

And that was it. You had no other worries.

That ultimate life I'd always thought I'd have. The life I'd promised Daphne when I asked her to be my wife.

How naïve I'd been.

"I'm sorry. I have to see who it is." I took the phone off the receiver. "Brad Steel."

"Brad, it's Jonathan."

"Hello, Jonathan"—Daphne's eyes widened at her father's name—"what can I do for you?"

"It's Larry," my father-in-law said. "He's in trouble."

Jonathan had no idea. "I'm sorry to hear that."

"I need your help, Brad. I need you to help me help my son."

"I have my own family to take care of," I said.

"I know that. I appreciate that."

"Then you know my hands are full."

"Larry's your friend," he said.

"Larry and I haven't been friends for a long time. He went his way, and I went mine."

"Please. For Daphne's sake. He's her brother."

"She doesn't even know him."

"I know. I know. Believe me, I know." His voice got progressively softer and slower. "I made some bad decisions."

"What bad decisions?"

He cleared his throat. "None of it matters now. I love both of my children, Brad."

"I know that."

"I need to get my son some help, and I don't know where to turn."

"Jonathan, I can't—"

"Please, Brad. I know you have the resources."

"You're going to have to give me some more information, then. I can't just open up my coffers on nothing specific."

"He's gotten in with a bad crowd."

"He's thirty-five years old. You sound like he's gotten in with the bad crowd in high school."

"That's kind of what I mean. I know he's an adult, but he's kind of a sheep. He always has been, and he should be thinking about Greta and the kids."

"At some point, he has to take responsibility for his own decisions."

"He's . . . had some mental health issues in the past."

"Oh?"

"Yes. Daphne knows about it."

"She does?" I raised my eyebrows at my wife, who was still sitting patiently.

"Well . . . she knows he had a few issues. She doesn't know the details."

"You want to give *me* the details, then?"

"Larry is very suggestible. He doesn't have a good sense of self."

"The man got through law school and appears to be happily married. I'd say his sense of self is fine."

"It's not. He hides it well on his face, but he's a follower, Brad. And he's following some bad people."

"Are Theo Mathias and Tom Simpson by any chance involved in this?"

"I believe so."

I cleared my throat. "So you know about their business."

"Brad, I know a lot more than I've ever told you."

"I see." A black shadow cloaked me, as if a dark phantom was digging in its claws.

Jonathan Wade isn't who you think he is, son. Be careful.

My father's ominous words.

I had a really bad feeling.

"Sounds like you and I need to meet."

"I'm ready for that anytime. Lucy and I are at a hotel in Grand Junction."

"Oh? You're already here? Why didn't you let us know you were coming?"

"I couldn't risk you telling us not to come."

"Does Lucy know why you're here?"

"No. She thinks we're here on a visit."

"And she didn't think it was odd that you're not staying here at the house?"

"I told her I had a gift certificate to the Carlton."

"I see." I cleared my throat once more. "Come to the house, then."

"I'd rather you come here, if possible. I don't want Lucy involved. I'll send her out shopping or something."

"No. Come to the house. You and I can meet in my office building."

"All right. That will work. We'll come first thing in the morning."

"Good. See you then." I hung up.

"What did my father want?" Daphne asked.

"He and your mother are in the city, staying at the Carlton. He had a gift certificate."

"Oh, how lovely. Mom will love that. But what's up with Larry?"

"He didn't elaborate. Just wants my help, I guess. They're coming to visit in the morning." I sat back down next to Daphne and took her hand in mine. "Daphne, you and I need to talk."

CHAPTER FORTY-FOUR

Daphne

Brad's tone of voice made me shiver.

Something was coming.

Something I wouldn't like.

"My first duty is to our family, Daphne."

"I know that. Mine is too."

"Then I hope you'll understand why I need to do what—"

The phone rang again.

"Damn it!" Brad's fist went down on his desk.

"Ignore it."

"I can't. I fucking can't."

"But you just said yourself that your first duty is to our family."

"Believe me, I never forget that." He picked up the phone. "Steel!"

Pause.

"Fine. We'll see you in an hour." Brad hung up the phone and turned back to me. "That was your father again. He and your mother are coming tonight."

Elation filled me. "Will they be here for dinner?"

"I suppose so."

I stood. "I'll go tell Belinda. The boys will be thrilled!"

"Daphne," he said, "we still need to talk."

"Of course. And we will. But right now I need to let Belinda know we'll have two more for dinner." I scurried out of the office.

★ ★ ★

The deli owner's daughter walked, her pace measured, to the kitchen. The housekeeper stood at the sink, peeling potatoes.

"Belinda."

The housekeeper turned. "Yes, Miss Daphne?"

The housekeeper always called the deli owner's daughter Miss Daphne. It made a certain sense, and the deli owner's daughter never questioned it. She never questioned a lot of things. Instead, she remembered her mantra.

Pull. Slice. Wrap. Hand to customer and smile. "What else can I get for you today?"

"We're going to have guests for dinner. My parents."

Whose parents? Didn't matter. The deli owner's daughter had a job to do.

"How nice. Thank you for letting me know."

The deli owner's daughter nodded and left the kitchen.

She knew Daphne's parents. She came out a lot when they were around, and something about this impromptu visit raised her hackles.

She'd be here for Daphne. To protect her. That was her job. She'd come out during the time three men raped Daphne. She'd taken the violence and dealt with it logically.

She'd taken over during the nine months that the other woman carried Brad's child.

She gladly protected Daphne.

Someone had to.

CHAPTER FORTY-FIVE

Brad

I sat at the desk in my business office, Jonathan Wade facing me.

"Who paid for Daphne's treatment, Jonathan?"

"That's not what I came here to discuss."

"I realize that, but if you want my help, you're going to have to explain to me where that money came from."

"What does it matter, as long as she got the treatment?"

"What matters is you've hidden this from me for over a decade now. You've hidden it from your wife. You've hidden it from Daphne. There's absolutely no trail as to where the money came from, which means you paid cash. Over a hundred thousand dollars in cash that appears to have no source."

His facial muscles tensed.

"Now, Jonathan. It's time to pay the piper. If you want any help from me regarding Larry, you need to spill your guts about this."

"You won't believe me if I tell you."

I heaved a sigh. "Jonathan, you have no idea the things I've seen in my short life. The things I've had to deal with. At this point, I'll believe just about anything."

"I can't."

"You can, and you will, if you want my help with Larry or anything else."

He shook his head and ran his fingers through his brown hair. "All right. It came in cash. To my office."

"What's that supposed to mean?"

"It means exactly what I said. A hundred grand in cash was delivered to my office. Via the US Postal Service. In a plain brown box. No return address."

I nodded. Then, "You're right. I don't believe it."

"I told you so."

"Uh-huh. How about the truth now, Jonathan?"

"That is the truth! Why do you think I've kept it from you? I knew you wouldn't believe it. You'd think I was hiding something or protecting someone, but the truth is, I'm not."

"Okay, for the sake of argument, I'll assume you're telling me the truth. Was there anything inside the package to indicate who had sent it?"

"Nope. Nothing. And you can bet I searched through every single bill to see if anyone had left a note on one of them."

"What investigation did you do after you received it?"

"What do you mean?"

"To try to figure out who sent it?"

"I didn't."

"Right. Someone sends you a hundred grand in the mail, and you don't even question it?"

"Brad, it was an answer to a prayer. It was the money to pay for Daphne's treatment. I was looking at a second mortgage on my house, maybe selling my car. So no, I didn't question it. I just thanked God."

I didn't believe him. Not even for a second. But what could I say? I couldn't fault his story. I'd looked high and low, and the money had no trail.

Which meant his story could actually be true.

But it didn't ring true to me.

I'd point-blank asked Larry if he'd paid for Daphne's treatment, and he'd point-blank told me he hadn't.

But I didn't trust Larry, either.

It could have come from Larry. He'd had that kind of money at the time, but why would he hide the fact that he was paying for it?

Something didn't add up.

Tom and Theo and Wendy all had that kind of money as well, but they wouldn't pay for Daphne's treatment. Why should they? Because they were Larry's friends? Business partners?

If Larry hadn't paid, why would they?

"Who do you know who might have had that kind of money and would want to help you and your daughter?" I asked.

"No one."

"Think harder."

"I'm not lying to you. Do you think I haven't wondered myself? Who would do this for my family? I racked my brain and came up with nothing."

I sighed. What could I say? I couldn't prove otherwise because there was no trail. None at all.

"Did you think about seeing if there were any fingerprints on the box?"

"I considered it, but then decided not to."

"Why?"

"Why? Because I needed the money. I wanted the money. For Daphne. For Lucy. Fuck. Even for myself. I didn't want to mortgage the house. I needed the house for my wife and daughter."

"And you were afraid the money might be dirty and might get confiscated."

"The thought crossed my mind. Tell me, Brad. What would you have done in my shoes?"

It was an interesting question, and one that in all honesty hadn't occurred to me. I had my own problems, but money had never been one of them.

"Probably the same thing. I would have put Daphne's well-being first. I do that every day."

"Then you understand."

"I do. Now tell me about Larry."

CHAPTER FORTY-SIX

Daphne

"How far along are you, honey?"

My neck nearly snapped at my mother's questions. Was it that obvious?

"About three months. How could you tell?"

"Your body changes. Your hips are a little curvier, your cheeks a little rosier."

"Really? Because I feel like crap."

"Yes, the morning sickness. It should subside soon. You look beautiful. You looked exactly the same when you were pregnant with Jonah and Talon."

"And Ryan?"

"We didn't see you when you were pregnant with Ryan. Brad said you were on bedrest and couldn't have visitors."

I nodded. "Right." No use telling her I didn't remember that pregnancy. That would only worry her. I hadn't experienced any significant time loss since then. Only a blip here and there. Nothing to worry about. If it didn't affect my family, I had no reason to worry.

"Have you told the boys?" she asked.

"Not yet. Brad and I haven't talked about when we should do that."

"I'm sure they'll be thrilled."

"Yes, I hope so. I really hope this morning sickness calms down before our trip to Disneyland next week. Thank goodness Joe's best friend is coming along. That way there's an even number and I don't have to go on any rides."

"The boys will have a blast," Mom said.

I smiled. I could get through morning sickness at Disneyland for my boys.

I'd do anything for my boys.

★ ★ ★

Dinner was weird.

My father and Brad were off again—that strange energy between them that I couldn't put into words.

My mother talked animatedly with the boys, so at least we didn't have that awkward silence. We ate on the deck, and Brad took over grilling from Belinda. I ate a potato and a cob of corn. I couldn't do red meat when I was pregnant, but the rest of them seemed to enjoy the sirloin steaks.

What seemed like hours later, dinner was over, and my mom and dad got ready to drive back to their hotel.

"Why don't you stay here?" I said.

"Oh, no," Mom said. "I'm getting pampered at the Carlton. But we'll come back for a longer visit soon."

I kissed her cheek. "I'd like that."

She pulled me into a hug and whispered, "Take care of yourself and the little one."

I nodded.

My dad hoisted Talon and then Ryan up. Joe, of course, was too big for that now. He got a handshake instead.

Once they were gone and the boys had resumed their

evening activities, Brad took my hand.

"We need to finish our talk, Daphne."

His eyes were heavy-lidded. He looked troubled. Maybe he'd level with me about what was going on between him and my father.

He led me to the home office and sat with me again in the chairs across from his desk. He took my hand.

"Baby, I love you."

"I love you too, Brad."

"This isn't going to be easy to say."

"Oh my God. What's wrong? Is it one of the kids?"

"No. The kids are fine. I'm going to make sure everything *stays* fine."

"Okay."

"Which is why I need you to—"

The phone rang.

"Damn!" he yelled.

I grabbed both of his hands in mine. "Please. Ignore it." But he didn't.

He stood and went to the damned phone. "Steel."

Pause.

"Yes."

Pause.

"That's not surprising."

Pause.

"I can't discuss this right now."

Pause.

"Fine. Goodbye." He hung up.

"Who was it?" I asked.

"Just business stuff. Now"—he sat back down next to me and took my hand again—"where were we?"

"I don't know."

He shook his head. "I love you so much."

"I love you too."

"You and the kids are everything to me, baby."

"I know that."

"Which makes this difficult. I'm sending you away."

My eyes popped into circles. "What?"

"Not just you. You and the boys. Some things are happening, Daphne. Things I might not be able to control. I need you and the kids out of harm's way."

My blood boiled. "Where do you think you're going to send us?"

"I have a little island in the Caribbean."

"What?"

"It's a safe place."

"Wait. Are you telling me we're in danger?"

"No, no. You don't need to worry. I'm just erring on the side of caution. I can't take any chances with you or the kids."

"But . . . the Disneyland trip."

"They'll go another time. Once you have the baby. It will be better then."

"No, Brad. I won't leave my home. I won't disappoint my children."

"Daphne, I'm not doing this to upset you. I'm doing this to keep you safe."

"Keep us safe? We live in a fortress! Cliff hovers over me daily to the point that I don't even notice him anymore. The boys are on summer break."

"Only for another month."

"But they're safe here, Brad. They aren't going into town to school. They—"

He gently pressed two fingers to my lips. "Baby, I will not take any chances where you and the boys are concerned."

"Then level with me. Why? Why now of all times do you think we're in danger?"

He didn't respond.

"Does this have something to do with the tension between you and my father?"

Again, no response.

"I see." I stood. "Let me make this clear, then. The boys and I aren't going anywhere, and we *are* going to Disneyland next week. We're taking Bryce with us. We're going to stay in the Disneyland Hotel and we're going to meet Mickey Mouse and we're going to ride Space Mountain. All things I wanted to do when I was a kid but never got to because my parents couldn't afford it. Well, *we* can, and I am *not* disappointing my babies."

"Daphne, be reasonable."

A green vase sat on Brad's credenza. A green vase filled with Mazie's stupid-ass pale-green tulips.

"I'm not a colorless flower!" I screamed.

Brad stood and reached for me. I backed away toward the credenza and picked up the transparent green vase.

"I hate these tulips! I fucking hate these tulips!"

★ ★ ★

The scary guy raised his tattooed arms over his head and threw the vase onto the hardwood floor.

Green shards of glass shattered and flew everywhere.

The scary guy walked out and slammed the door.

★ ★ ★

Bullshit.

Brad wasn't going to get his way this time. The kids and I were going to Disneyland, and when we returned, we were staying right here.

We weren't going anywhere.

Something edged into my consciousness. Something dark, as if someone was trying to hide something from me.

Pull. Slice. Wrap. Hand to customer and smile. "What else can I get for you today?"

I tamped it down, determination overwhelming me.

I was *not* a colorless flower.

I was done hiding.

I was *done*.

CHAPTER FORTY-SEVEN

Brad

"Steel."

"It's me," Wendy said.

"Yes."

"The money hasn't come through yet."

"That's not surprising."

"What good is wiring me money if it doesn't come through right away?"

"I can't discuss this right now."

"Fine. I'd better have it in twenty-four hours, or no deal. Everything will be made public."

"Fine. Goodbye." I hung up.

Why was I replaying the phone call with Wendy in my mind when my wife had . . .

What had she done? Yelling at me and breaking a vase was out of character for her, but was it out of character for this situation? Anyone would be angry at what I'd told her. I was forcing her to leave her home and go to a safe house. At least she could take the boys with her.

Her reaction had flummoxed me. She was her own person, but in the past, she'd always gone along with what I'd asked, even if it didn't make any sense to her. She was pregnant, and her hormones were probably out of whack, but still . . .

For God's sake, she'd gone along with the fake pregnancy when Wendy was carrying Ryan.

But *this* was too much?

I hastily dialed Dr. Pelletier's home number.

"Hello," a woman's voice said.

"Good evening. I'm calling for Dr. Pelletier."

"Of course. Could I tell him who's calling?"

"Brad Steel."

"Just a minute, please."

A few seconds later, "Mr. Steel."

"Doctor, I'm sorry to bother you at home—"

"Then why are you?"

"I need your help. I mean, I need your help with Daphne."

"I haven't seen her in a while."

"I know that. Can you see her tomorrow?"

"I won't be at my Snow Creek office until next week."

"All right. I want to get her on your schedule then."

He sighed. "I'll fit her in, but only because I'm fond of her and I want to help her."

"Great. Thank you. In the meantime, I need to ask you something."

"What's that?"

"She broke a vase."

"And ... ?"

"Sorry. I mean she got angry with me and broke a vase with water and flowers in it. She threw it down on the floor in my office."

"What was her motivation?"

"I told her I wanted her to take the boys and ... Let's just say she was angry with me, and that's what was odd. It was totally out of character for her."

"To be angry with you?"

"Yes. I asked her to do something, and let's just say I've asked her to do other things—more difficult things—that didn't seem to bother her this much."

"Sometimes people snap. It's not uncommon."

"That's my point. It's uncommon for Daphne. She's never snapped. She's always been a dutiful wife and mother."

"Hmm..."

"What?"

"I won't know until I speak to her, but if it's truly out of character for her, she may be dissociating."

"You told me over a decade ago that she was likely to dissociate, but it never happened."

"It never happened during a session with me. It might have happened some other time."

"But it didn't. I would have noticed. Or my mother. Or one of the kids."

"Don't be so sure. She would have still been herself, just a little out of character, as you described today."

No.

No, no, no.

"Are you saying someone other than Daphne threw that vase and broke it?"

"Not exactly. That wouldn't hold up in a court of law. But I'm saying the person you know as Daphne may not have been the one who broke the vase."

All this time...

All this time, I'd been protecting my wife and children as best I knew how, all while descending to a place that had become more and more comfortable over the years, only to find my wife was dealing with her own descent?

No.

No. Just no.

"You have to help her, Doc."

"I'll do what I can. This is all just theory until I can speak to her and examine her."

"Right. Right. She'll be there next week." I hastily scribbled the appointment time on a piece of paper.

I ended the call and plunked down at my desk, my head in my hands.

What had I expected?

Daphne was already fragile. She always had been. I knew her history, knew what she'd been through in her young life.

Yet still I pushed her.

I hid things from her. I abandoned her and the kids to go off on "business" trips that more often had to do with Wendy and the Future Lawmakers.

And then the final straw.

I'd asked her to accept that I'd been unfaithful with Wendy. Right here on this very desk. I'd tied Wendy up and fucked her.

Sure, my motives might have been pure—

Bull.

My motives had *not* been pure.

Wendy had the ammunition to ruin me, to ruin my family. Most of it was fabricated, but I knew this woman. Anything she had would have been backed up to the hilt.

Damn, I'd gotten good at lying to everyone over the years. I even lied to myself.

No, my motives had *not* been pure.

Losing me would have hurt Daphne, Jonah, and Talon.

But they would have survived. They'd have had all the Steel money. They'd have had my mother.

Daphne found strength in her children, and she would have persevered.

No, I didn't fuck Wendy to protect my wife and sons.

I fucked her to save my own sorry ass.

It was me. All me. I didn't want my life upended, so I told myself I was protecting my family.

In truth, my family would have been just fine.

Fuck.

The truth fucking hurt. Hurt like someone slicing into my gut and pulling out my entrails.

Hurt like being drawn and quartered.

This was all on me.

And I hadn't done it for anyone else but *me*.

CHAPTER FORTY-EIGHT

Daphne

Four months later . . .

My baby girl kicked.

I smiled and touched my growing belly. She was strong, this one. Her kicks were just as powerful as her brothers' had been.

The boys were due home from school soon, and Belinda was in the kitchen fixing their snack. Jonah was thirteen now, and boy, did he have an appetite. His little brothers nearly kept up with him as well.

The phone rang. "I'll get it, Belinda!" I grabbed the extension in the family room.

"Hello, Steel residence."

"Daphne?" Evie's voice was breathy.

"Yeah, hi, Evie."

"Daphne, are the boys home yet?"

"Not yet. I haven't seen the bus come by. Soon, though."

"Call me when they get home."

"Sure. Why?"

"The most terrible thing, Daphne. Luke has disappeared."

"Luke Walker? Your nephew?"

"Yeah. He never came in from recess after lunch. Vicki

and Chase have been with the police all afternoon."

My stomach lurched, and I felt my uterus contract. I breathed in and exhaled. Braxton-Hicks contractions. That was all it was. Just Braxton-Hicks. I'd had them before. Nothing to worry about.

"Maybe he cut school."

"Luke wouldn't cut school."

"He might if the bullies—" I stopped. Evie was worried about her nephew. She didn't need to be reminded of his problems with bullies.

I wished, at that moment, that I'd taken him to Disneyland with my sons and Bryce.

I wished it hard.

Evie went on, "We've been through all that. The bullies are all accounted for, and they all swear they had nothing to do with Luke's disappearance. I haven't been able to get hold of Tom to tell him, either. He loves that boy."

"Where's Tom?"

"Out of town again."

"That law firm keeps him busy."

"I know. I miss him."

"I understand." More than she knew. "I'm so sorry, Evie. Is there anything I can do?"

"That's why I'm calling. When the boys get home, can you ask them if they saw anything? The police haven't questioned any of the kids yet."

"Of course. I'll call you after I talk to them."

★ ★ ★

The boys weren't close to Luke, but finding out he'd

disappeared haunted them. They decided to be junior detectives, which gave them something to focus on but scared the hell out of me. I didn't want them going anywhere near what might have happened.

I finally calmed down, though, until one day, about a week later, when my Braxton-Hicks contractions started up again.

The school bus picked the boys up and dropped them off at the edge of our long driveway. The rural kids had a forty-minute drive to and from Snow Creek School each day. If Brad or I were going into town, we drove them, but most days they rode the bus.

I hastily checked my watch. Hmm. They should be home by now. I walked out the front door and down to the end of the driveway, rubbing my arms. The October day had turned a little brisk. I should have grabbed a jacket.

Where was the bus?

I heaved a sigh of relief when I finally saw the orange bus coming toward our driveway.

"Thank God," I said aloud.

The bus meandered down the country road, seeming to go in slow motion, but when it finally halted in front of me, it seemed giant.

The door opened, and Jonah walked off.

I waited for Talon and Ryan.

"Where are your brothers?" I asked.

"They stayed in town. Tal wanted to look for Luke Walker."

"What?" My eyes nearly popped out of my head, and my heart began to thunder.

"Mom, they've stayed in town before. I figured—"

"Why in hell didn't you go with them?"

"I didn't want to."

"Damn it, Joe. They're your brothers! Luke is missing! And they went looking. Did you really think for a minute your two little brothers would be safe out there?"

"It's Snow Creek, Mom. Luke hasn't been gone for that long—"

"Damn it!" My oldest son was as tall as I was now, and no doubt twice as strong. Still, I grabbed his shoulders and shook him, my adrenaline going crazy inside me. "A week is a long time for any child to be missing. If anything happens to your brothers, it's on you, Joe. On you!"

My uterus clenched then, and I doubled over.

"Mom!" Jonah grabbed me and walked me into the living room. "Here. Lie down on the couch."

I stretched out supine. "Talon, Ryan. I just want them home."

"They'll be fine," Jonah soothed. "Is Dad home?"

"Of course not," I said, not in a nice tone.

"All right. Just relax. I'm going to get Grandma, and we're going to call your doctor, okay?"

"It's fine. I'm fine. Just get my boys— Aaauuugh!" My uterus cramped up.

This one I felt. It didn't hurt so much as scared me.

My adrenaline. Needed to control my adrenaline.

"Mom!"

"Don't leave me, Joe. Please."

"I've got to get Grandma. She'll know what to do."

Yes, Mazie knew who my doctor in the city was. She'd take care of it. But I couldn't bear the thought of being left alone here on the couch.

"Don't leave me, baby," I said. "Please. I'm sorry for what I said. Nothing's your fault. I'm just . . ."

"Pregnant," he finished for me. "I get it."

I smiled and closed my eyes, willing my uterus to relax. The baby gave me a swift kick. Thank God. She was okay.

Mazie ran in then. "What's going on? Daphne, I heard you cry out!"

"It's a contraction or something," Joe said. "Can you call her doctor?"

"Mazie, it's just a Braxton-Hicks. She kicked. Everything's okay."

"I'm calling him anyway, honey." Mazie hurried out of the room.

I regarded my oldest son and cupped his cheek. "You look so much like your father."

He didn't say anything. I could tell my motherly touch made him a little uncomfortable. He was a teenager now, after all.

But I couldn't drag my hand away. Soon this smooth face would be covered in dark stubble.

Soon.

So very soon.

Where had all the time gone?

"How are you feeling?" he finally asked after five minutes.

"Okay. It was just a Braxton-Hicks contraction. I'm all right. Here." I grabbed his hand and put it on my swollen belly. "Your sister is kicking the daylights out of me."

Joe smiled. "She is. You've got a soccer player in there."

"Maybe. More likely just another Steel sibling who will kick butt like her big brothers. If you don't spoil her rotten."

"She'll probably be a pain in the ass," Joe said jovially.

"But you'll adore her. All three of you will."

Mazie hurried back in. "Daphne, I've got the doctor on

the line. Can you get up to talk to him?"

"Why don't we have an extension in here?" I grumbled.

"Because we never use this room," Mazie said. "I'll call and have one installed as soon as you're off the phone."

"When Brad had security installed over ten years ago, he put phones in every room but this one and the formal dining room." I sat up, holding on to Jonah for support. I inhaled and exhaled. Once, twice, one more time. "I feel better now." I rose and followed Mazie into the kitchen and picked up the telephone. "Doctor, this is Daphne Steel."

"Mrs. Steel, it sounds like you're having more Braxton-Hicks contractions. How is the baby's movement?"

"She's kicking all over the place."

"Good. Very good. Any more contractions?"

"Not since the big one that made me double over. That was about fifteen minutes ago."

"All right. I'm sure there's nothing to worry about, but let's get you in tomorrow just in case."

"Yes, of course. What time?"

"My only opening is at eight a.m."

"I'll be there, Doctor."

"I'd like to do an ultrasound, so your husband should come along."

"Sure. Of course." *If he's in town.*

"Good. See you tomorrow, Mrs. Steel."

I hung up the phone, feeling a little more relaxed. Marjorie was kicking up a storm.

Yes, Marjorie. I'd always liked the name, and I'd been considering it seriously since I'd learned from my baby name book that it meant pearl. A little research from the local library informed me that pearls are supposed to offer protection.

Now? After that little kicking storm, I wasn't sure my Marjorie needed protection, but just in case...

Marjorie was her name.

I'd named all our children. Jonah was my little dove. Talon meant claw, but I liked the name anyway. Brad had wanted to name him John, but that seemed too common to me. I agreed to it for Talon's middle name.

Then Ryan...

Had I named him? Strange. I didn't remember.

So much I didn't remember about his pregnancy.

I walked to the family and grabbed my baby name book off the coffee table. Hastily I flipped to Ryan.

Ryan. Irish origin. Most sources said it meant "little king," but the original meaning had never been confirmed.

Odd.

I didn't remember the pregnancy, and the meaning of his name was unconfirmed.

I always checked out the meaning of my children's names, and I doubted I'd choose anything that might not have a meaning.

Strange that I hadn't checked that time.

Very, *very* strange.

CHAPTER FORTY-NINE

Brad

You don't shit where you eat.

Philosophy from George Steel.

The disappearance of Raine Stevenson months ago, and now Luke Walker ...

It was horrendous and gut-wrenching. Who would harm an innocent child?

Problem was?

I knew.

I didn't have proof, mind you, but I knew. Wendy had already told me about Fleming Corporation and how they were into some bad shit. Heinous had been the word she'd used. I also knew Theo, Tom, and Larry had hooked up with gangsters.

It didn't take a genius to put it all together.

Wendy knew that.

That was why Wendy had told me.

Damn! She was a mother herself. A mother to my child, even though my child would never know that. How could she condone such horror? How could anyone?

Wendy had a place in Grand Junction. She was there now. I knew because I had her watched twenty-four seven.

She knew I had her watched.

I made sure of it.

It was all part of my master plan.

Wendy was brilliant, but she could be manipulated by one person, and that person was me. As long as I let her figure out everything I was doing—but didn't let her know I knew she knew—I could keep one step ahead of her.

I had to.

Because in the end, I knew I'd have to move my wife someplace secure.

Ironically, she'd be in hiding, close to the island owned by Fleming Corporation. The perfect plan. Hide in plain sight.

Plain sight beyond a twenty-five-foot stone wall and security guards, actually, but still in plain sight considering the close proximity to the den of horrors.

I parked my truck and walked to her door.

It was a modest suburban house, one of several she owned throughout Colorado. Her mother and father still lived in Snow Creek, but her father wasn't in good health. Wendy planned to move her mother in with her once her father passed away.

That would be interesting, but I had no doubt Wendy could continue to pull off her double life while living with her mother.

The woman could pull off anything.

Which was why I had to tread very carefully.

I walked to the front door and knocked.

She opened the door.

I half expected her to be naked. During our college years, she almost always answered her door naked.

Thank God she was fully clothed.

"I've been expecting you," she said.

I nodded. She had . . . because I'd made sure she was.

Staying one step ahead of Wendy Madigan was hard work, but it was work I had to do.

For Daphne.

For my children.

"I need answers," I said.

She lifted her eyebrows so her blue eyes looked wide and innocent.

Innocent. I held back a scoff. She was anything but.

I walked into her house.

"I was just going to pour myself a glass of your lovely Steel Vineyards wine," she said. "Would you like a glass?"

"No, thank you."

"Your winemaker is a genius. So sad about what happened to his girlfriend back in college."

Hold it together, Brad.

Wendy didn't know I'd found out she'd been the mastermind behind the murders of Murph and Patty. Nothing I could do about it, anyway. Much better for me to play dumb.

"Ennis moved on with his life long ago."

"Still, such a pretty little redhead. And then Sean, too. So sad."

"You remember Sean well, don't you? You held him at gunpoint, as I recall."

She laughed it off. "That was so long ago. I was just a kid."

Right. Holding someone at gunpoint was small potatoes for today's Wendy. How well I knew.

"I trust the money made it into your account?" I said.

"Yes, thank you."

"What else do you want?"

Again with the fake innocent look. "Why would I want anything else?"

"Because you already *have* five million dollars, Wendy. You have twenty times that amount."

"Let's just say I needed it."

"For what?"

"You'll find out."

"For God's sake. Tell me what my *real* punishment is, and let's get it over with. I'm really tired of your cat-and-mouse routine."

"How's my son?"

The old sidestep. Damn, I was sick of her.

"Ryan's fine."

I refused to refer to him as her son. He was Daphne's son, and she loved him as much as she loved her other two.

"I'd like to see him."

"No. We made a deal."

"I don't care. I miss him."

"Sorry. I will not waver on that. My son is my responsibility. You agreed to the terms."

"You know ... I'm still a young woman."

"You're thirty-three."

"I want another child."

"Then go fuck someone. Or go to a sperm bank. I don't give a shit."

Except that I did. God help the innocent kid that got saddled with Wendy Madigan for a mother. That was why I'd made the deal with her to keep Ryan with me. She would have fucked him up good.

"I only want *your* child, Brad."

"He exists. He's just not yours."

"I want one of my own."

"I will not go there again. It nearly destroyed Daphne."

"Too bad it didn't."

Anger surged through me like red fire. I held myself in check. I wouldn't get what I'd come for if I played into her games.

She walked forward then and grabbed at my crotch. "No one ever turned you on like I did."

I slapped her hand away. "Don't touch me."

"That night in your office, when we made our son. You didn't want to make love to me, but you got hard. So hard. You can't resist me, Brad. You never could." She glanced down. "You're erect already. I can tell."

I wasn't, but why not let her think I was? Maybe I could get the truth out of her.

"My body responds like any other man's."

She shook her head, a sly smile on her lips. "Your body has always responded to me, and mine to you. We were always meant to be, Brad. We *will* be together one day."

"Maybe one day"—*when pigs fly*—"but not today."

"I suppose that's something."

"You can keep up hope," I said, "but I guarantee you we'll never be together if you don't level with me."

"Ah, yes," she said, the sly smile still snaking across her face. "Your punishment. You did break a promise to me."

I said nothing. I wasn't going to apologize for making love to my wife. I wasn't going to apologize for getting her pregnant. I was thrilled about the baby.

"The five mil. What's it for?"

"I could tell you, but then I'd have to kill you."

"Funny." I let out a fake laugh.

"I have people who owe me," she said. "They owe me big. But even they won't do what I ask for nothing. So I need the money."

"I'm getting sick of your riddles, Wendy."

"Did you ever find out who raped your wife?"

. My eyebrows nearly flew off my forehead. Where the hell had that come from?

"No one was ever caught."

"I know that. But *I* know who did it."

It took all my strength not to wrap my fingers around her neck and strangle the life out of her right in her foyer. No one knew. It was long ago—years before I even met Daphne—and there were no clues left.

She was manipulating me. Trying to anger me. She knew as well as anyone that the thought of three masked strangers violating my innocent wife made me insane.

I would *not* play this game.

"You don't know shit."

"Maybe not. But someone knows."

"Only the rapists themselves."

"They do. But they're not the only ones."

"I'm out of here." I turned.

She gripped my shoulder, but I shook myself free.

"This is over," I said.

"Only I decide when it's over, Brad."

I walked out without meeting her gaze.

As I got into my truck and drove back to the ranch, a black cloud seemed to hover over me.

Wendy had something in the works.

Something that was going to hit me hard.

I had to be ready with everything.

This time, my family was disappearing.

Daphne could break all the vases in the house if she wanted to.

I would *not* take no for an answer.

CHAPTER FIFTY

Daphne

Nerves.

All my nerves skittered across my flesh.

"You need to relax, honey." Mazie held a cool washcloth to my forehead. "It's not good for the baby."

"It's been two hours, and the boys haven't called to get picked up. Why did I let this go? As soon as Joe came home without them, I should have driven into town. I need to go now. Right now."

"Stop it. The boys are fine. You're going to start having those contractions again if you don't settle down."

Settle down?

My boys were gone.

Two other children were missing from our small town.

How was I supposed to settle down?

I jumped when the phone rang.

"Easy. I'll get it." Mazie rose and grabbed the phone. "Steel residence." Mazie's face went pale. "Yes, yes. She's here." She brought the phone to me. "It's the . . . police."

"The police!" I sat up and grabbed the receiver. "Hello, this is Daphne Steel. What's going on?"

"Mrs. Steel, we have your son at the station."

"Son? You mean *sons*?"

"No." A pause that seemed like an eternity. "Your son Ryan. He's . . . I'm so sorry to have to tell you this, Mrs. Steel. Ryan and Talon were attacked. Ryan got away, but Talon is . . . missing."

★ ★ ★

Pull. Slice. Wrap. Hand to customer and smile. "What else can I get for you today?"

The deli owner's daughter listened intently as the police officer continued to speak. Ryan was upset, but he was okay.

Talon was missing.

Grabbed by two men.

He protected his little brother.

Ryan got away.

But Talon . . .

Two men had Talon . . .

Pull. Slice. Wrap. Hand to customer and smile. "What else can I get for you today?"

"You need to come to the station," the officer said. "Your little boy needs you."

Except Ryan wasn't the deli owner's daughter's little boy. He wasn't Daphne's little boy.

He'd grown in some other woman's body.

But that didn't matter. She had a job to do—to protect those whom Daphne cared about.

"Yes, of course. I'll be right there. Have you contacted Mr. Steel?"

"He's not answering his office line."

"Try his car phone." The deli owner's daughter recited the number.

"*We will. And ma'am? We're so very sorry. We'll do everything we can to find your son.*"

The deli owner's daughter turned to Daphne's mother-in-law. "*I need to go into town. Talon is missing.*"

Daphne's mother-in-law clasped her hands to her mouth. "*No! They're wrong. They're wrong.*"

"*They're not wrong, Mazie. They're the police. Call Brad on his car phone. Tell him to meet me at the police station. Please.*"

"*Yes, yes. Of course. I'll go with you.*"

"*No. Stay here with Jonah. I don't want him out of your sight.*"

"*Okay. If that's what you want.*"

"*Yes. Protect him, Mazie. Please.*"

★ ★ ★

Brad.

My rock.

My world.

He beat me to the police station, and I crumbled when I saw him.

Crumbled into his arms.

Tears didn't come. When you're numb, you can't cry.

Brad spoke to the police, gathering all the information, and my Ryan... My baby... He was so strong. Like his father. He told the story again and again.

He was frantic and tear-stained, but not a cut or bruise anywhere on him, thank God. Brad's and my presence seemed to calm him.

"It was an old cabin. Somewhere on Luke's ranch," Ryan said, sniffling. "Two men came out. They wore masks. They grabbed us. Talon kicked the one who had me and I got away. He yelled at me to run. So I ran. I ran until I couldn't run anymore. When I got to Luke's house, Mrs. Walker brought me here."

Vicki Walker sat silently.

"Thank you," I whispered to her.

Now we had something in common. Both of us had a son missing.

I should have taken Luke to Disneyland.

How selfish I'd been!

How fucking selfish.

At least Talon had gotten to go.

My Talon . . .

But Talon was fine. Talon had to be fine.

Raine Stevenson, Luke Walker, a few other children as well, I found out.

And now Talon.

My Talon.

But we had a witness this time.

We had Ryan.

Only seven years old, and witness to a terrible crime.

My poor sweet boy.

But at least he was here. Unharmed.

Where was my Talon?

"We've got our best men on it," a detective was telling Brad. "We'll find your son."

"Just like you found the others?" Brad said snidely.

"We're doing the best we can."

"Your best isn't good enough. I'm going to have my men on this."

"Please do," the detective said. "We appreciate all the help we can get. Unfortunately, our resources are limited."

"Mine aren't," Brad said. "I need to get my wife and son home. They've been through enough today."

"Understood." The detective nodded. "We'll be in touch."

I still clutched Brad.

"You and Ryan come with me," he said, kissing the top of my head. "Cliff will drive your car home."

I nodded into his shoulder. I couldn't make my voice work. Not yet.

Two men had my little boy.

Two men in masks.

Two men in masks had my little boy.

Two men in masks were . . .

Couldn't.

Couldn't let my head go there. Couldn't—

Pull. Slice. Wrap. Hand to customer and smile. "What else can I get for you today?"

The deli owner's daughter would get through this. This was her job. Keep things logical. Always a certain rhythm to life.

A logical rhythm.

She stared straight ahead at the road.

In the back seat, the other woman's child lay down, his arms wrapped around himself, his cheeks streaked with tears. Such a young thing. Poor little young thing.

No. Don't get emotional.

Stay logical.

The child will survive.

But the other child? Daphne's child?

Daphne needed protection. Her children needed protection. Especially the one living inside her now.

The deli owner's daughter patted Daphne's pregnant belly. It felt hard. Yes, another Braxton-Hicks contraction.

The doctor wasn't worried, so why should the deli owner's daughter worry?

Worry wasn't logical.

Mr. Steel drove up the driveway to the ranch house and parked the truck.

The deli owner's daughter settled in.

Pull. Slice. Wrap. Hand to customer and smile. "What else can I get for you today?"

She had work to do.

CHAPTER FIFTY-ONE

Brad

Daphne stared into space as I parked the car.

She stared into space as I opened the back and gathered Ryan into my arms. He made no sound, but silent tears still streamed from his eyes. He sniffled into my shoulder.

She stared into space as I opened the passenger door for her.

She stared into space as she exited the truck and took my hand.

She stared into space as we walked into the house.

Jonah was waiting just inside the door, his cheeks also streaked with tears.

Crying is for girls.

Words from my father.

Words I'd said to my sons.

Words Joe and Ryan weren't heeding.

Words I was having trouble heeding myself.

"I'm so sorry, Dad," Joe sobbed. "I should have gone with them. I should have—"

"Stop," I told him. "Please. Your mother and brother don't need this right now."

He gulped down his sob and nodded.

Yes, we were all hurting.

I didn't want to abandon my oldest, but he was the least of my concerns now.

His brother. His mother.

And God...

Talon.

My innocent second born.

Thank God Ryan got away—

My stomach dropped.

Ryan got away.

Ryan, who was smaller and weaker than Talon.

Ryan.

Wendy's son.

Wendy was behind this. She had to be.

I knew that five million wouldn't satisfy her need for vengeance, but I never thought—

Never imagined she was so full of hatred that she would see a child harmed. See *my* child harmed.

I'd underestimated her, and now I was paying the ultimate price.

I'd make her suffer if it was the last thing I did.

And knowing Wendy, it just might be.

Ryan clung to me as I carried him into the house, my other arm around my wife, who was clutching her belly.

"Baby? You okay?"

God. Stupid fucking question! Of course she was not okay. None of us were okay.

Talon had been taken by masked men.

And I was pretty fucking sure I knew who'd paid them to do it.

I had.

The money I'd given Wendy.

My stomach churned, acid burning me and crawling up my throat.

Fucking bitch. Fucking whore. Paid off derelicts with *my* money!

He's a child! A damned child!

I had to get on the phone. Had to get out and find Wendy. I'd fucking kill her. With my bare hands. Oh, yes. I could do it right now. Right fucking now.

"Mom," I said, "could you please get Daphne to our bedroom? She needs to rest."

"No. I don't need to rest. How can I rest when my baby is—" Her eyes widened.

"What, baby? What is it?"

"Brad. I think my water just broke."

★ ★ ★

I was a father for the fourth time.

Except my daughter wasn't going to live.

I sat with my sweet wife in recovery after her C-section. Daphne had been right all along. This was our girl. Daphne was awake but staring into space.

I caressed her hand. "We have to name her," I said softly. "Have you decided? You were talking about Marjorie."

"What does it matter? My son is gone. My daughter is going to die."

"We don't know that. Babies born earlier have survived."

"And a lot of them haven't."

What could I say? She was right.

"She still needs a name. I like Marjorie."

"No."

"You like it because it means pearl, and pearls offer protection."

"Naming her Marjorie won't protect her. She's so small. Brad, did you see how small she is?"

I nodded. Indeed, her size scared me. But she was beautiful. She had translucent skin and a head of black hair. And she was fucking beautiful.

My daughter.

"Maybe it *will* protect her," I said. "There's a chance she'll survive, and you know I'll see that she gets the best medical attention in the NICU. Nothing's too good for my little girl."

"She's not Marjorie," Daphne said. "She's Angela. I want to name her Angela."

"Angela's pretty, but why?"

"Because she's going to be an angel soon. She's going to . . . " Daphne shook her head. "I can't lose two children in one day. I can't!"

I smoothed her hair, wet from perspiration, back from her forehead. Even here, my Daphne was beautiful.

"How about Angela Marjorie?" I said.

"Fine." She nodded and then closed her eyes.

Anger.

Rage.

Wrath.

Please don't make Daphne pay for my sins. Please. She needs her son. She needs her daughter. Please.

I squeezed my eyes shut, repeating the prayers over and over in my mind.

I don't deserve your grace, but Daphne does. Daphne does.

Daphne was asleep, so I headed to the NICU to see Angela Marjorie. An oxygen tube was inserted in her tiny nose, and she lay inside a transparent incubator.

So small.

So fucking small.

But her little chest rose and fell, rose and fell. She was breathing.

"Mr. Steel?" A nurse touched my shoulder.

"Yes?"

"She's a strong baby. The doctor says her lungs are working extraordinarily well for twenty-six weeks. You have reason to be optimistic."

I nodded.

But I wanted to scoff. I wanted to yell and curl my hands into fists and punch her. Break into that stupid glass crib and hold my daughter.

And my son! I wanted to hold my son!

How many times had I told him to man up? Taught him how to do a good day's work on a ranch? Made him figure out his own mistakes?

My God, he was ten fucking years old!

I should have played with him. I should have taught him how to throw a football. I should have read him bedtime stories. I should have taken him to Disneyland with Daphne. I should have . . .

Could have . . .

But hadn't.

And now I might never get the chance.

"How is your wife?" the nurse asked.

How do you think my wife is? What a fucking stupid question.

I said only, "My daughter's name is Angela Marjorie Steel."

Then I walked out of the NICU.

CHAPTER FIFTY-TWO

Daphne

Panic.

Sheer panic as I ran through a dense forest. Someone chased me. An animal? A person? I had no idea, but if I didn't run faster, I'd—

I jerked my eyes open.

Where am I?

My breasts were heavy and tender. I moved my hand to—

Beep! Beep! Beep!

A woman wearing green scrubs rushed in. "Mrs. Steel. Remember? You can't bend your elbow. It sets off the alarm."

"I want to see my baby," I said.

"She's in the NICU. But she's doing very well."

"I want to see my baby," I said again.

"Your husband told us you chose the name Angela. That's very pretty."

Did this woman have a hearing problem? "I want to see my baby."

"I'm sorry, Mrs. Steel. You can't get out of bed yet. Your epidural hasn't worn off. I can't bring her in here because she can't leave the NICU. But your husband was just in to see her. She's doing just fine."

"If she's doing just fine, I should be able to see her."

The nurse smiled. "Let me see what I can do."

★ ★ ★

The deli owner's daughter waited for the nurse to leave.

"This is ridiculous," she said aloud. "If Daphne wants to see her baby, Daphne will see her baby."

She moved, careful not to bend her elbow. That beeping had been horrendous. She moved first one leg and then the other over the side of the bed.

Now, to stand. How to stand with this stupid IV? Well, she'd just have to make it work.

She carefully moved the thin tubes to the side, braced her arms on the side of the bed, and rose.

★ ★ ★

Beep! Beep! Beep!

How had I gotten on the floor?

"Mrs. Steel!" Someone in green scrubs rushed to my side. "What happened?"

"I'm not sure."

"I told you not to get up. Your epidural hasn't worn off yet." She pulled me up and back into bed. "I'm going to have to check your incision." She moved my gown and removed the bandage. "Thank goodness. You didn't rip out any stitches. You need to be more careful, Mrs. Steel."

"I want to see my baby."

"I talked to a doctor. We're in the process of getting a wheelchair for you."

"I want to see her now!"

"You're not the only patient here," the nurse said.

"I'm Mrs. Bradford Steel. My son is missing, and I want to see my daughter. Right. Fucking. Now!"

Brad rushed in then. "What happened?"

"She tried to get out of bed, and she fell. Her legs gave out because of the epidural."

"My legs feel fine," I said. "I can feel them fine."

"You can feel them, yes, but they're not quite ready to walk, as you found out. You need to listen to—"

"That's enough," Brad said. "You don't know what my wife has been through today. Get a wheelchair in here now, and I'll take her to see our daughter myself."

★ ★ ★

"She's so tiny, Brad."

"Yes, but her lungs are working well, baby. She has a fighting chance."

I didn't buy it. I'd named her Angela for a reason. I was going to lose her. My only hope was that I wouldn't lose Talon as well.

But I had to brace for that.

I had to brace for a lot of things.

"I wish I could hold her," I said.

"I know. I do too. But she's safer in that incubator for now. We'll be able to hold her soon."

I shook my head. He didn't understand. I wanted to hold her while she was alive. I wanted her to feel her mother's love.

I wanted so much for this beautiful little girl—so much that she'd never have.

She'd never get to watch a gorgeous Colorado sunrise.

She'd never smell the sweetness of a bright yellow tulip.

She'd never taste a juicy Steel Ranch steak.

My sweet little Angela would miss so much.

"She's beautiful, isn't she?" Brad said.

I didn't reply.

Yes, she was beautiful. She'd been given that gift. But what good would it ultimately do her?

A nurse approached us. "Excuse me, Mr. Steel."

"Yes?" Brad said.

"There's a phone call for you. You can take it at the nurse's station, or we can transfer it to Mrs. Steel's room."

I allowed myself a glimmer of hope. Just a glimmer.

"Talon?" I said anxiously.

"I don't know, baby," he said. "I hope so."

He kissed my lips chastely and then turned to the nurse. "I'll take it at the nurse's station."

CHAPTER FIFTY-THREE

Brad

"Brad Steel," I said into the phone at the nurse's station.

"It's me, son."

George Steel's voice—I hadn't heard it in over a decade. Nurses milled around me. No one was listening to my call. They all had more important things to do.

"How did you know I was here?"

"I called your home office. Your mother answered. I disguised my voice and said I had to speak to you on an urgent business matter. I'm so sorry, son."

I cleared my throat. "How much do you know?"

A slight pause. Then, "Everything. I know everything, Brad."

"Talon..."

"Yes, I know."

"The baby..."

"I know. I'm so sorry, son."

"I don't know what you want," I said, "but you already know my hands are full. I have to find my son. I can't let anything—" The words stopped coming. I couldn't let my mind go to that dark place. That place where my son might be—

No. Just no.

"I understand. But I have information for you. Information

I can only give you in person."

"This is a hospital line, Dad. It's got to be secure."

"It probably is. I can't be sure that mine is, though."

"I can't leave Daphne right now. This is destroying her."

"I know that, and I wouldn't ask you to if I had any other choice, but my time is limited."

"How the hell is your time limited? You're dead, for God's sake."

"Not yet," he said. "But it won't be long."

★ ★ ★

I agreed to meet my father during the night. Daphne had been sedated because she needed her sleep, and the hospital was on their honor to call my car phone if anything changed with Daphne or the baby.

Any other time, I wouldn't have left, but if my father had information on Talon, I had to get it.

"I tried to stop it, Brad. Please believe me. I tried."

My father lay in a hospital bed in a makeshift MASH unit on the corner of our property. That lifetime of smoking had finally gotten him. He was dying of lung cancer. Only yards away from the barn where I'd found Patty Watson's dead body.

"What are you talking about?"

"Your son. Wendy. Everything."

"I know Wendy's behind it. Who else could be?"

"He's alive."

His statement gave me a glimmer of hope. "How do you know?"

"They won't kill him. They can't."

"Who *are* they, Dad? Help me. I need to find them. I need to find my son!"

"I don't know. I only know the corporation behind the veil."

"Fleming Corporation," I said.

"Yes. If I'd known..."

"I know. I already know about them."

"I'm so sorry."

"Please, Dad. Just tell me what you know about Talon."

"I only know this. They won't kill him."

I tried to take solace in his words. But not killing him left a lot of things they *could* do to him.

"Is he...?"

"He'll be put to the test," my father said. "But if he's your son, he's strong. I know you raised him right."

"Will we ever get him back?"

"I wish I knew."

"I have to find him, Dad. Daphne won't survive this. Especially if we lose the baby too. Please."

"I've told you all I know."

"How can you be sure they won't kill him?"

He stayed silent for a moment. Then, "Because... Wendy wants you punished. The death of a child is something no parent should have to experience, but grief does subside in time."

I gulped. I knew where this was headed.

He continued, "They want to break him. They want to break something that's valuable to you. Something you'll never get over, so that every time you look at your son, or think about your son, you'll remember what they did to him and how he'll never be the same."

"Damn it!" I balled my hands into fists. "Damn it, Dad! Where is he?"

"If I knew, I'd tell you."

"You do know. Don't keep anything from me."

"I don't, son. Do you think I care about what happens to me at this point? I'm a dead man anyway. I'd tell you if I knew."

"I'll find him. I'll find my son."

"Take solace in the fact that he's not dead. That he won't die."

"What about the others? Luke Walker? Raine?"

"The girl is alive. The boy is not."

"Fuck." Tom's nephew. This would kill Evie.

"I tried," he said, his breath short. "I tried to find out where they took him. I tried to . . . " He puffed out a gasp of air.

"Easy," I said.

"I tried. I tried."

"I know, Dad."

"Can you ever forgive me? For everything?"

Everything? That was a tall order—one I wasn't sure I could fulfill.

But my father lay dying. My father, who'd left his life thirteen years previously to help me deal with mine.

And the fallout from Wendy, from the rest of the Future Lawmakers, was mine and mine alone. My father hadn't made that mess.

I had.

I'd spent the better part of my life cleaning up after myself.

I couldn't clean up this mess. I couldn't undo what was being done to my son.

My precious, innocent son.

What my past sins had cost him, had cost his mother, his brothers, and his new baby sister.

How much longer would Daphne hold out?

Not long, I feared, which was why I'd made plans to relocate her to a facility in Florida, and eventually to my Caribbean island. She'd be safe there, and well looked after. I'd finally found a way to keep Wendy at bay. Once my baby girl reached adulthood—and she *would* reach adulthood—I'd pull a George Steel.

I'd fake my own death and go take care of my wife.

Never fake your own death. It's not worth it.

My father had no doubt been right, as he spoke from experience. I had a deeper understanding now, though—a deeper understanding of why he'd done it.

And why I'd have to as well.

All those years ago, Jonathan Wade had said to me, "Daphne's your responsibility now, just as Lucy is mine."

I had no love for my father-in-law. He'd made a mess of his daughter's life long before I got involved with her.

But instead of making her life better, I'd made it worse. So much worse.

I'd never forgive myself.

But could I give my old man what he was asking for? Could I forgive *him*?

No.

I could not.

But I could say the words and let him go in peace.

I was a fucking good liar.

When had lying become so easy?

A long, long time ago.

"Please, son," he said again. "I wish I could change so much. I'd do a lot of things differently if I had the chance."

Wouldn't we all?

"I forgive you, Dad."

"Thank you, Brad." He closed his eyes. "You were a good son. The best. I've always been proud of you."

He drew in a deep breath and then another.

One more—a deep gasp.

Then he was gone.

I felt nothing. Not a loss. Not a gain. No guilt at never letting him meet his grandchildren.

No guilt about anything.

No resentment, which surprised me more than a little.

Nothing.

Simply nothing.

"Rest in peace, Dad," I said softly.

Maybe he'd find a sliver of peace in hell.

One day, I hoped I would as well.

For I was hell bound.

I knew that now.

The end to my story had already been written.

EPILOGUE

Brad

My daughter survived.

Against all odds, my baby girl thrived.

While her big brother was held captive, was violated in heinous ways, she grew like a beautiful rose. When we left the hospital, Daphne asked me to call her Marjorie instead of Angela.

"She's not an angel, after all. She's a pearl. She protected herself."

"Of course. She's our Marjorie." I'd have given Daphne anything she wanted.

Two months later, Talon returned to us, a shadow of his former self.

And I found out who'd been his abusers all along.

In the back of my mind, I'd always known. I just didn't want to think those three men—men I'd once considered friends—could be capable of such horrific acts.

Wendy had numerous fail-safes in place so I couldn't touch her or any of the Future Lawmakers without sacrificing everything.

Which meant we couldn't tell anyone what happened. Talon couldn't get the help he needed.

For a while, I allowed myself to think we'd be okay. Talon

didn't want to talk about what happened, and he seemed to be himself. A little quieter, but still Talon. He loved his little sister and spent a lot of time with her. She seemed to be healing him, at least a little bit.

I wanted to get him help. Wanted to so badly, but I couldn't.

For reasons I now realize were complete bullshit.

But you make the decisions you have to at the time, because you don't know what else to do.

And in the end, I made the right one.

Less than two years later, Daphne completely broke from reality. I staged her suicide and whisked her to the safe house in Florida.

I was all my children had at that point. I had to be there for them, and I was, until Marjorie turned eighteen.

Then I gave my life to Daphne once more. I moved her to the island where I'd had a replica of our ranch house built. I'd planned for the two of us to live there for the rest of our lives.

I sighed, as I often did when running through the events of my life. Would I do anything differently?

How could I? I wouldn't have my four children if I had. And despite my many mistakes, they all ended up healthy and happy.

No thanks to me, of course, but for that I'm truly grateful.

★ ★ ★

Jonah came once more.

Alone.

I'd been certain I'd never see his face again.

Indeed, he wouldn't have come unless he had something big to tell me.

I cleared my throat as I picked up the phone. "Son."

"Dad."

"To what do I owe the pleasure of another visit?"

"I'm here on behalf of the four of us. We talked about all coming, but the other three weren't sure they could hold it together."

"And you could?"

"I *will*. I'm the oldest, and I have to."

His words could have come out of my own mouth. He was so like me. So strong. So eager to protect those he loved. So willing to hold everything together in the face of horror.

"What is it, then?"

He shook his head slowly. "You kept so much from us."

"I know. I've said I'm sorry, but I can't do anything other than that. I'm paying for my sins. I'll never make peace with my children or myself."

"Did you ever make peace with Mom?"

How I wanted to say yes. I still loved Daphne more than anything, but the last time I'd seen her, she didn't even know me.

I shook my head. "No, Jonah. I did not."

"I can see why."

I scoffed. "You *think* you can see why. There are things you don't know. Things you'll never know. Things I'll take to my grave."

He stared at me for a moment.

Then the stare turned into a dark glare.

"Now's the time for confession," my son said.

"I have nothing more to confess."

He sneered at me. "How about the names of the three men who raped Mom?"

A dagger struck my heart. Nausea clawed up my throat. I opened my mouth to speak, but no words emerged. The acid had lodged in my larynx, or so it felt.

"Did you think we wouldn't find out?"

"I don't— No— They were never caught."

"No thanks to you."

"But I never knew— How did you—"

"It took me a long time to deal with this. Finding out my mother had been viciously raped by three men when she was sixteen made me want to go out and shoot someone. So I did. I shot a target. Used over a hundred rounds. But you didn't teach me to shoot, did you, Dad?"

"You know my reasons for that."

"But you know who *did* teach me, and you knew. All that time. Before Tal. Before Luke Walker. Before Justin Valente."

Thoughts whirred in my head like a buzz saw. What? My son was talking nonsense. No one knew who'd raped Daphne. No one.

No one.

"Your mother didn't remember. We kept it from her. Her parents, her doctors, and me. It was better that way."

"Better? You let her live with that horrendous memory trapped in her subconscious? Damn it! You did the same thing to her that you did to Talon."

"No. Daphne didn't remember. It was different."

"It wasn't any fucking different, and you know it. But that's not even the worst thing you did."

He wasn't wrong. It was far from the worst thing I'd done.

"The worst thing is that you kept the names of the men who raped her secret."

I jerked in surprise. "I didn't! They were never caught. I

never knew who they were!"

"Stop lying, Dad. It's over."

"I'm not lying!"

A guard cocked his head at my outburst, so I lowered my voice.

"I'm not. I swear on your mother's life."

"Sell it to someone who believes you. Remember how I told you Mom was asking for her puppy? We found it. It was tucked away in the crawl space, like you said."

"Did it bring her comfort?"

"No, it did not."

"I'm sorry, son. You've lost me. What the hell are you trying to say?"

He regarded me a moment, one eyebrow raised. Then, "Are you saying you truly don't *know*?"

"Who raped your mother? No, I don't! Do you think if I did, I'd have let them *live*?"

He stayed silent for another moment, never dropping his gaze from mine.

Then, "You always loved her."

I nodded. "I always loved *all* of you."

"If you'd known, you'd have killed them."

"Of course!"

Another moment. Then, "I don't believe you."

"Why?"

"Because you didn't kill them when they did the same thing to Talon."

Reality suspended itself for a moment. My son's image blurred, and white noise invaded my head. White buzzing.

The chickens have come home to roost.

A voice.

So like my own.

Words. Couldn't make them out. Just buzzing, but in my own voice.

Until something gripped my shoulder.

The guard stood above me. "You all right here?"

I nodded.

Because you didn't kill them when they did the same thing to Talon.

"Joe," I said.

"What?"

"Are you telling me that Tom Simpson, Theo Mathias, and Larry Wade are the three men who raped your mother over forty years ago?"

"Yes."

"How? How do you know?"

"Mom. That's the secret. Mom intercepted a delivery for you when I was a baby. She made a call, and the person gave her the three names. Mom wrote them down. Then she hid the small piece of paper inside her stuffed puppy."

My son's words buzzed in my head, and my body felt trampled, as if I'd been hit by a semi. "Then she . . . what?"

"She didn't remember, or something. She buried the information inside her mind."

God, her dissociative identity disorder. It had protected her all those years. Dr. Pelletier had been right.

"She didn't remember," I said, "but another identity did."

"What?"

"Daphne has dissociative identity disorder. The trauma of the rape caused her to split off. She eventually broke completely from reality after Talon's abduction and Marjorie's premature birth. God, if only I'd known."

"She's been carrying this secret a long time."

"Why? Why didn't she tell me?"

His eyes turned even colder. "What would you have done?"

Because you didn't kill them when they did the same thing to Talon.

What *would* I have done?

I'd let the bastards live to save my own hide. Wendy would have had me jailed for things I didn't do. I thought I could save Daphne. I thought I could save Talon.

All the while, I let those demons live and violate countless others.

None of it mattered now.

Tom, Theo, and Larry were all dead.

All dead, thanks to my sons.

My sons, who were better men than I could ever hope to have been.

Jonathan Wade isn't who you think he is, son. Be careful.

Everything fell into place. Jonathan Wade. He knew. *He fucking knew.* And he lied. To save his son.

I stared at my firstborn, and I oddly understood Jonathan's dilemma.

How do you choose between your children? How do you make Sophie's choice?

Answer?

You don't.

Not when you can save them both.

The descent to evil for Theo, Tom, and Larry had begun far sooner than I ever suspected.

Larry Wade had raped his own sister. Raped his own nephew.

But in the end, he'd freed Talon.

In the end, he'd led Jade to the information that would help my sons and their wives figure everything out.

In a way, he'd done more for my children than I had.

I'd let the bastards go.

While Jonathan Wade lied to save his son, I hadn't been able to tell the truth to save my own. Who was the weaker father?

Though I knew the answer, I couldn't bring myself to think the actual words.

What would you have done?

I hadn't answered Jonah's question, and after all this time, my son deserved the truth.

"I don't know what I would have done."

"You let them go after you found out about Talon."

"I did. To save my own ass. But if I'd known who they were before—"

"You'd have done the same thing. Wendy would have held something over your head, and you'd have done the same thing."

I had no lies left in me. "I would have."

He said nothing. Just stared at me, the phone glued to his ear. But he didn't stand and leave, and for that I was grateful.

"Jonah."

Silence, but he was listening. The phone stayed at his ear.

"You're a good man. You, your brothers, your sister. All great people."

"No thanks to you."

I deserved that. I wouldn't fight it. "No thanks to me."

"There were other notes inside the stuffed animal," Joe said. "Mom knew a lot more than she ever let on."

"One of her alter egos knew," I said.

Jonah nodded. "That makes an eerie sort of sense."

"What else did you find in the toy?" I asked.

"She knew about the rape at the time it happened. She knew about someone named Sage, who killed herself. She knew about a journal she kept long ago. She destroyed it."

So that was why her journal had disappeared all those years ago.

I shook my head, my eyes tearing up. "I kept all of that from her. Or I thought I did."

"Apparently she overheard you talking to her father once. That's what the notes seem to indicate. There was even a note inside that mentioned Ryan being Wendy's child."

Had Daphne dissociated during Wendy's pregnancy? How had I not known? "God. My poor sweet Daphne."

"She loves you," Joe said. "In spite of all this shit, she still fucking loves you."

"I love her." I closed my eyes, picturing sweet Daphne Wade on the afternoon I first met her so long ago at a campus keg party. "I have *always* loved her."

Jonah didn't speak for another moment. Then, "She doesn't have a lot of time."

"What do you mean?"

"After she opened the stuffed animal and pulled out all the old notes, she lost consciousness."

I rubbed my forehead. "God. What happened?"

"She suffered a massive stroke, and now she's in a coma. The doctors have asked if we're willing to withdraw life support."

My heart thudded almost painfully in my chest. Was this what a heart felt like when it broke? "No. I have her durable power of attorney. Absolutely not."

"Dad, what kind of life does she have? She was keeping a secret, and now it's out. She knew. She always knew, somewhere inside her mind, and now she's let it out. Please. Let her be at peace."

"Fuck," I said.

"I have the paperwork with me. Our attorneys drew it up. You can transfer the durable power of attorney to me."

I said nothing.

"Marj, Tal, and I have all agreed. This is what's best for Mom."

"Ryan?"

"He didn't feel he had the right to an opinion. We told him he did, but he was adamant."

I disagreed. Ryan *did* have the right to an opinion.

Sadly, the one who did not was *me*.

I signed the paper.

★ ★ ★

A few days later, when Daphne drifted into peace, I felt her leave. My bright yellow flower had dimmed, leaving me in darkness. She took my heart with her. My soul.

That was how connected we always were. I actually felt her spirit leave the earth.

I was now nothing but an empty shell, almost as if I'd been given a chance to begin again.

Except that I couldn't.

That night, lying on my cot, as I fell into sleep, she came to me.

A vision in light—that beautiful eighteen-year-old girl I

fell in love with. That woman I loved with my whole heart. The woman I'd tried to protect.

The woman I'd failed in so many ways.

Yet in her ultimate goodness, she'd continued to love me.

My children were whole. My children were happy.

Despite my mistakes, they'd learned to survive. To thrive.

They didn't need me.

Not anymore.

So when my beautiful Daphne held out her hand—offered me her love, her forgiveness, and the salvation I craved—the decision was an easy one.

I floated with her into the light.

CONTINUE THE STEEL BROTHERS SAGA
WITH BOOK SIXTEEN

MESSAGE FROM HELEN HARDT

Dear Reader,

Thank you for reading *Descent*. If you want to find out about my current backlist and future releases, please like my Facebook page and join my mailing list. I often do giveaways. If you're a fan and would like to join my street team to help spread the word about my books, please see the web addresses below. I regularly do awesome giveaways for my street team members.

If you enjoyed the story, please take the time to leave a review on a site like Amazon or Goodreads. I welcome all feedback. I wish you all the best!

Helen

Facebook
Facebook.com/HelenHardt

Newsletter
HelenHardt.com/SignUp

Street Team
Facebook.com/Groups/HardtAndSoul

ALSO BY HELEN HARDT

The Steel Brothers Saga:
Craving
Obsession
Possession
Melt
Burn
Surrender
Shattered
Twisted
Unraveled
Breathless
Ravenous
Insatiable
Fate
Legacy
Descent
Awakened
Cherished
Freed

Blood Bond Saga:
Unchained
Unhinged
Undaunted
Unmasked
Undefeated

Misadventures Series:
Misadventures with a Rock Star
Misadventures of a Good Wife (with Meredith Wild)

ACKNOWLEDGMENTS

Man...

This one was a bitch.

There's a thin line between love and hate, and writing an anti-hero like Bradford Steel forced me to truly examine this concept. So much to love about him...and so much not to love. I have new respect for the writers of the television series *Breaking Bad*. They created one of the best anti-heroes to ever grace pages or screen. I hope I've done half as well with Brad Steel.

Huge thanks to the following individuals whose effort and belief helped make this book shine: Jennifer Becker, Audrey Bobak, Haley Boudreaux, Keli Jo Chen, Yvonne Ellis, Jesse Kench, Robyn Lee, Jon Mac, Amber Maxwell, Dave McInerney, Michele Hamner Moore, Chrissie Saunders, Scott Saunders, Celina Summers, Kurt Vachon, and Meredith Wild.

Thanks also to the women and men of Hardt and Soul. Your endless and unwavering support keeps me going.

To my family and friends, thank you for your encouragement.

Thank you most of all to my readers. Without you, none of this would be possible.

Once again, the Steel Brothers Saga has come to an end...

...or has it?

ABOUT THE AUTHOR

#1 *New York Times*, #1 *USA Today*, and #1 *Wall Street Journal* bestselling author Helen Hardt's passion for the written word began with the books her mother read to her at bedtime. She wrote her first story at age six and hasn't stopped since. In addition to being an award-winning author of romantic fiction, she's a mother, an attorney, a black belt in Taekwondo, a grammar geek, an appreciator of fine red wine, and a lover of Ben and Jerry's ice cream. She writes from her home in Colorado, where she lives with her family. Helen loves to hear from readers.

Visit her at HelenHardt.com

ALSO AVAILABLE FROM

HELEN HARDT

THE BLOOD BOND SAGA

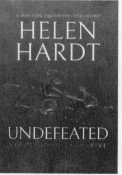

ALSO AVAILABLE FROM

HELEN HARDT

SEX AND THE SEASON SERIES

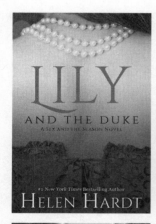

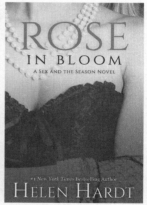

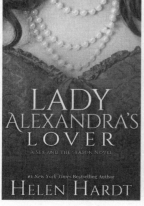

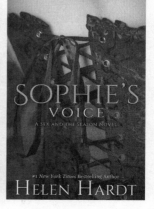